OLIVES FOR THE STRANGER

HAVE BODY, WILL GUARD ADVENTURE ROMANCE

BY NEIL S. PLAKCY

Copyright 2010, 2021 Neil S. Plakcy. All rights reserved, including the right of reproduction in whole or in part in any form.

This book is a work of fiction. Names, characters, places, and incidents either are products of the author's imagination or are used fictitiously. Any resemblance to actual events or locales or persons, living or dead, is entirely coincidental. This book was originally published by Loose Id and is the fourth in the Have Body, Will Guard series. Maryam Salim did an awesome job of editing this book, and the rest in the series.

When thou beatest thine olive tree, thou shalt not go over the boughs again: it shall be for the stranger, for the fatherless, and for the widow.
—Deuteronomy 24:20

Reviews for Neil Plakcy and the Have Body series:

"Never slows down" – Literary Nymphs Reviews on *Three Wrong Turns in the Desert*

"Plakcy's characters... charm" – Kirkus Reviews

"An engrossing writer" - Publisher's Weekly.

"Plakcy's Tunisia is the perfect exotic locale for your fantasy summer vacation, if you don't mind dodging an assassin or two along the way." – Dick Smart, reviewing for the Lambda Literary Review

1 — Little Monsters

There were two of them, and they came at Liam McCullough fast and low, both screaming as they did.

The one on the right went for his leg, while the other tried to climb up his chair and get to his head.

"Children! Please!" their mother called. "Leave the nice bodyguard alone." Her English was heavily accented, and she switched into her native Brazilian Portuguese, following with a string of speech that did nothing to pull the boy or the girl off him.

He smiled grimly and grabbed them both under his arms and stood up. The little girl kicked at the back of a gilt chair, which fell to the plush carpet with a *thud*. "Why don't I take the kids outside so they can run around?"

The middle-aged saleswoman who had been showing Zoraida Figueroa hand-embroidered shawls looked relieved. She had been twisting the pearls around her neck with long, elegant fingers as the children rampaged through the narrow store.

Liam and Aidan, his partner in love and business, had been watching Zoraida and her two children for three days by then, while her husband concluded a deal to sell Brazilian rubber to the Tunisian government. Zoraida, twenty-eight, had bonded immediately with Aidan, the two of them chattering away and shopping like best girlfriends.

That left Liam to watch the kids. João was four and Morena three. They were like wild animals, spoiled beyond reason. Their mother could not discipline them, and their father was caught up in business so often that he didn't either.

Liam carried them, kicking and squirming, across the hot, sun-drenched street, dodging the onrush of taxis, buses, and luxury SUVs that ignored the traffic signals with impunity. The girl pressed her hand against his chest, and when she grasped the gold ring in his right nipple, he quickly shifted her away.

The air was redolent with sweat and automobile exhaust, and stepping into the cool greenery of the Parc Habib Thameur was like entering another world. The date palms and cork oaks created a leafy bower above, and tiny green geckos and furry, inquisitive gerbils darted through the lush undergrowth. Though it was in the low sixties in the sun, under the trees it was at least ten degrees cooler, and Liam could feel the heat generated by the two squirming bodies in his arms.

Liam set the two kids down on the gravel path and stood up to stretch his back. They immediately ran toward a group of children playing on swings, screaming like banshees.

Liam liked being a bodyguard, but he hated this job. Zoraida's husband, Gilberto, was insanely jealous—with good reason, Liam thought. Zoraida was a dark-haired beauty who oozed sexuality, and she dressed to accentuate her massive breasts and her long, tanned legs. The dress she wore today was cut so low that you could almost see her nipples, and it was so short that when she sat down, Liam had realized she wasn't wearing panties.

Liam was astonished when Gilberto first called to hire them and asked if he and Aidan were gay. Years of "Don't Ask, Don't Tell" in the military had made Liam wary of such questions, but he had stopped lying when he resigned his commission. It turned out that there had been an unfortunate incident with a bodyguard in Canada, and Gilberto would only hire men who couldn't be a threat to his marriage.

The whole deal made Liam uncomfortable. Kids were too unpredictable; they didn't understand about threat factors or appropriate behavior. Hell, since they only spoke Portuguese, he couldn't even talk to them. He couldn't wait for this assignment to finish.

A half hour passed, the two Brazilians tormenting every child they met, before Zoraida and Aidan left the boutique, burdened with shopping bags. Liam called the children, but they ignored him.

They were experts at avoiding capture. When Liam strode toward them, they split up, going in separate directions. He feinted toward Morena, then caught João off guard. He grabbed the boy, who kicked him in the shins.

"Ow! That hurt. Stop that."

He was sorely tempted to immobilize the little brat, but that wouldn't go over well with the client. "You want to give him to me, or you want me to go for the girl?" Aidan said, coming up to him.

"Take him. But watch out. He kicks and he bites."

Amazingly, the little boy nestled into Aidan's arms as Aidan cooed to him in some broken combination of English and Portuguese. He looked like the sweetest little angel—until Liam caught him smirking as Aidan turned away.

Morena was darting among the palm trees, using her small size as an advantage to crawl through the underbrush. Liam grew increasingly frustrated as aloes stung his arms and palm trunks bruised his shins.

"Come on, Liam," Aidan called from the limo. "Get a move on."

"I'm going to kill someone here," Liam muttered. "Maybe Aidan. Maybe one spoiled little girl." He swooped on Morena, and she squirmed away from him. He narrowly missed falling on his face.

Her long hair proved her undoing. As she scooted past Liam, he grabbed a handful and used it to pull her toward him. Not the best tactic in child care, but it was effective. He got her under one arm, careful of her flailing arms and legs, and walked back to the limo.

By the time they returned to the Hotel Africa, Liam was fed up. The children had screamed and cried the whole way in the limo, their mother and Aidan ignoring them for chitchat and giggles. Liam had a pounding headache, and he was delighted that the Figueroa family was leaving Tunis that afternoon.

Zoraida set the children up in the living room of the suite with snacks and juice boxes, and Liam stood against the wall, watching them. The food kept the children occupied as Aidan helped Zoraida finish packing, and by the time the bellman had taken all the suitcases downstairs, Gilberto Figueroa had returned.

They all piled into a small airport bus. The kids ran back and forth while their father spoke on his cell phone and their mother gossiped with Aidan. At the airport, Zoraida kissed Aidan and Liam on both cheeks and thanked them effusively.

Gilberto stopped speaking on the phone long enough to pull a wad of bills out of his pocket, held together by a gold money clip. He handed a stack to Liam. "Hazard pay," he said in English only slightly less accented than his wife's. "Thank you."

Aidan and Liam watched as Gilberto led his family and a skycap loaded with bags into the terminal. "Thank God," Liam said as the doors closed behind them. "Never again."

"What?" Aidan said. "That was a pretty easy gig. Just wandering around from store to store with Zoraida."

"For you, maybe. For me it was hell. What a pair of little monsters," Liam said as they walked down the sidewalk to the taxi rank.

"They're good kids. You just have to know how to handle them."

"Morena bit me," Liam said. "If I get tetanus, I'm suing."

Aidan laughed. "Don't be a wimp."

As they prepared to get into a cab, Liam leaned down to Aidan's ear. "When we get home, I'll have to show you who's a wimp."

Aidan laughed, but he shivered a bit. Good, he thought.

There was a demonstration ahead, and the cab slowed. Liam saw a cluster of young men with placards clogging the narrow street and hear the low rumble of their chants. "What's going on?" he asked the driver in Arabic, leaning forward.

"They are calling it the Jasmine Revolution," the driver said. "Now it comes to Tunis."

Liam had read news reports of uprisings in small towns all over the country since mid-December. A vegetable seller in the small town of Sidi Bouzid, south of Tunis, had been arrested for peddling without a license, and his cart and goods had been confiscated. After enduring insults and a fine at the hands of a policewoman, the young man, Mohammed Bouazizi, had gone home and set himself on fire.

His story had galvanized hundreds of desperate, downtrodden young men and women in Tunisia. Many of them were university educated but couldn't find work, and they felt that the unwritten compact their parents' generation had made with President Ben Ali—trading political freedom in exchange for economic opportunity—had come undone. They had begun protests against the government in Sidi Bouzid, and the fever had caught.

"The president says he will fire the Interior Minister and free people arrested during the demonstrations." The cab driver shook his head. "No good will come of this, I tell you."

By riding on the sidewalk for a few hundred feet—dangerously close to a storefront selling hammered brass tea urns and an elderly man in a shabby housecoat—the cabbie made his way to a side street and bypassed the demonstration. As they drove, Liam checked the Facebook and Twitter feeds on his cell phone. They were full of reports of protests in and around Tunis.

Liam had no idea what was going to happen. Would the

president crack down? Would there be widespread riots in Tunis? He called his police contact, Faisal Qasim, but the call went right to voice mail. Not surprising if Faisal was out handling demonstrations.

It was close to five o'clock by the time he and Aidan got back to the small house they shared behind the Bar Mamounia, just off the Boulevard Habib Bourguiba. Their little mixed-breed dog, Hayam, jumped and yipped joyfully as they walked inside, then darted past them to pee on the date palm out front.

"Remember, we're meeting Louis and Hassan for dinner at seven," Aidan said, as he closed the front door.

Louis Fleck's official title at the US Embassy in Tunis was cultural attaché, though Liam had known for years that Louis worked for the CIA. Until recently, though, he hadn't known that Fleck was gay or that he had a Tunisian partner. A few months before, Aidan had met Louis and twigged immediately. Bold as brass, Aidan had asked if Louis was seeing anyone, and just like that, they'd become a pair of gay couples who got together once or twice a month for dinner and conversation.

Once they were inside, Liam grabbed Aidan's waistband and pulled him close. He leaned down and kissed Aidan hard on the lips. He cupped his broad hand around Aidan's smooth, pert ass. Whatever was going on in the city could wait.

Aidan kissed him back, opening his mouth to accept Liam's tongue. With his other hand, Liam reached under Aidan's shirt and found his right nipple. He pinched it, and Aidan shivered. He leaned his head back, and Liam nipped at his throat like a horny vampire.

"We'll see who's a wimp now." In a swift motion, Liam pulled Aidan's polo shirt over his head and tossed it to the couch. Then he unbuckled Aidan's belt and unhooked his pants. They dropped to the floor.

Aidan was already hard, his dick straining against his cotton boxers. They were decorated with tropical fish in neon colors. Liam thought they were silly—he preferred simple white cotton jockstraps himself. But they were all part of the charm that was Aidan.

Aidan kicked off his deck shoes and stepped out of his pants. He lifted his right leg to wrap around Liam's as Liam licked his throat and rubbed his five o'clock shadow across the tender skin. Aidan groaned with pleasure.

Liam jerked Aidan's boxers down, catching his dick in them, and Aidan said, "Ouch! Watch it."

"Watch this." Liam sat down on the sofa, still fully clothed, and pulled Aidan down on top of him sideways, so that Aidan's ass was in Liam's lap. He raised his right hand and slapped Aidan's butt.

"Who's a wimp?" Liam said.

"You are," Aidan said, his voice muffled by the sofa cushions.

"Wrong answer." Liam spanked him again. He could feel Aidan's stiff dick pressing against his thigh. He began playing Aidan's butt like a pair of bongo drums, slapping one, then the other, then both in sync.

"Sometimes you need to be reminded who's the boss around here," Liam said.

"You are," Aidan said, turning his head.

Liam sucked on his index finger, then slid it into Aidan's butt crack and stroked it. His partner squirmed beneath him.

"Oh God," Aidan said.

"That's right. I am a god to you, aren't I? You worship me, don't you?"

"I worship your dick," Aidan said. There were tears at the corners of his eyes, but he was smirking.

Liam removed his finger from Aidan's ass. "Put it back, Liam, please."

"Nah. I'm done here." He squirmed out from under Aidan and stood up. "I'm going to take a nap. Wake me in time for dinner."

"Liam!" Aidan turned over, wincing as his tender ass hit the textured sofa cushions. "You aren't going to leave me like this, are you?" He cupped his dick in his right hand.

Liam laughed. "Who's the wimp now?"

"I am. I'm a big pussy wimp. You're the macho man. You're the boss in this relationship."

Liam looked down at him. Aidan was so cute, so charming, so sexy. Who was he kidding? He was dick-whipped. He dropped to his knees and took Aidan's dick in his mouth. It felt so good, so right. He swallowed the whole thing, felt the dick head tickling the back of his throat, and began sucking.

He hadn't been a virgin when he'd met Aidan, a year and a half before. He'd had sex with men, furtive encounters in hotel rooms and bars. But he'd never been in love, and he'd never had sex with a man he loved before. Sucking Aidan, fucking his sweet ass, getting sucked and fucked himself—it all felt so much better because of Aidan.

He sucked his partner's dick furiously, bobbing his head up and down, suctioning, licking. His own dick, trapped in his jockstrap and his pants, was so stiff it hurt. He reached one hand down and stroked himself, rubbed the palm of his hand over the bulge in his pants. He felt like a crazy teenager, hepped up on lust.

Aidan was bouncing his ass up and down on the sofa, wincing when his reddened cheeks touched down but not letting up the pace. Liam felt his blood race and the amazing, beautiful pain of orgasm as he spurted off in his pants, the come soaking his jockstrap. As he did, Aidan bucked one last time and came in Liam's mouth. He swallowed it all, then licked his lips and sat back against the chair across from the sofa.

Aidan turned to look at him. "There's a wet spot in your pants. Did you come?"

Liam nodded.

"You didn't save it for me? You bastard."

"You want your ass spanked again?" Liam said, a smile dancing on his lips.

"Maybe later." Aidan turned on his side, and Liam could see the redness on Aidan's cheeks, rising beneath the fine layer of dark hair on his ass. Liam loved the way Aidan's hairy body slid beneath his smooth one.

The gloppy come was cold against his dick, still trapped in the jockstrap. But Liam could feel his dick rising again, despite the workout. "I need a shower before dinner," he said, standing up. "Care to join me?"

"I'll never turn down an offer like that." Aidan turned on his back again to get up and winced from the pressure of the sofa against his tender ass.

Liam leaned down and pulled him up, then nestled against his partner's naked body. "After we shower, I'll rub some ointment on your butt."

Aidan's cell phone rang as Liam was pulling off his polo shirt. "Leave it," he growled to Aidan, who was already reaching for the phone.

"You know I can't do that." He looked at the display. "It's Madame Abboud."

"That witch?"

Mme. Habiba Abboud owned an employment agency for teachers and translators called the École Internationale de Tunis. As an accredited instructor of English as a Second Language, Aidan worked for her on occasion. Liam didn't like her and didn't trust her.

While Aidan spoke, Liam dropped his pants. The jockstrap was wet and sticky with come, and he pulled it off.

"Tomorrow?" Aidan said into the phone. "Sure. I'm free. Give me the address."

"What's up?" Liam asked when Aidan hung up the phone.

"Quick job. Businessman needs help with a translation. I'm meeting him at the Hotel Africa tomorrow morning."

"Not a good idea," Liam said. "Not with these demonstrations going on."

"I'll be fine. You forget I'm a bodyguard too."

Aidan got down on his knees and began licking Liam's sensitive dick, and the touch of Aidan's tongue made him shiver.

Liam heard the evening call to prayer begin at the Zitouna mosque nearby and realized they were running late. "We've got to shower and get ready for dinner," he said. He reached down and pulled Aidan up by his underarms. Aidan nestled against him, rested his head on Liam's shoulder, then followed him outside to the courtyard shower, grabbing towels as they went.

By the time they were finished, the redness on Aidan's butt had subsided for the most part. Aidan bent over the sofa, and Liam rubbed his cheeks with analgesic cream. "You going to be okay?" he asked.

Aidan stood up. "Yup. Let's just hope they have padded chairs at this restaurant."

2 – Dinner

Aidan noticed the feeling of unrest in the air as they walked to the Italian restaurant near the Tunis waterfront, just a few blocks from their house. The night crackled with static electricity, and he heard the low, distant rumble of a crowd cheering. Maybe Liam was right, and he shouldn't go to that client the next day.

But then he caught his reflection in the plate-glass window of a store selling unlocked GSM phones. His chest filled out the polo shirt in a way he wasn't used to. His skin, always a medium olive, was tanned, and the hint of five o'clock shadow made his chin seem stronger. He was in better physical condition than he'd ever been, and more confident as well. As long as he steered clear of any demonstrations, he'd be fine.

Louis Fleck was waiting at the hostess stand as Aidan and Liam walked into the restaurant. "Hassan's in the men's room making himself pretty," he said, shaking hands with both of them.

Louis was about forty, a guy who in the States would have been called a bear. He had a bulky build and was hairier than Aidan. His head was shaved, but he had a dark mustache and goatee. He wore a short-sleeved, button-down shirt that hung loose over the waistband of his khaki slacks. Aidan had long since figured out that meant Louis was packing a gun.

"I invited another couple to join us," Louis said. "Potential client for you."

Liam groaned. "No more kids, I hope."

Louis shook his head. "Just the two of them. James Gardiner's from Silicon Valley. Made a mint off some software company, then took off to travel the world and find himself."

"Did he?" Aidan asked.

"Well, he found a boyfriend here in Tunis, from a family that owned a few hundred hectares of olive groves in the Medjerda Valley. A couple of years ago, Farid's father died, and he and James moved out there and started making their own oil."

Hassan returned from the men's room then. He was about Louis's age, with a buzz cut and dark-framed glasses. Everything about him was precise, from the starch in his shirt to his amber cufflinks to his spit-shined black loafers. He was an architect with a designer's attitude toward everything in his life. Aidan had been to their apartment, which was spare and immaculate, a dramatic contrast to the sloppy, crowded house he shared with Liam.

"We're expecting two more," Louis told the hostess in Arabic. "But we'll sit now."

She led them to a large round table in a corner of the restaurant. "Why does this couple need a bodyguard?" Liam asked as they sat.

"I'll let James give you the details," Louis said. "But the bottom line is that they're preparing to debut a super-premium olive oil at a trade show in LA, and they've had a couple of incidents that might be sabotage. They want someone to keep an eye out until they get the oil shipped."

They ordered a bottle of Vieux Magon, and the waiter was just pouring when Louis said, "There they are." He stood up and waved, and the two men approached.

James Gardiner was older than Aidan expected, at least sixty, with wavy salt-and-pepper hair and a deep tan. His partner, Farid Mansoor, was twenty years younger. Both were slim and fit and oozed money, from their expensive gold watches to their designer clothes.

Louis made the introductions, and they all sat down as the waiter brought a platter of sliced bread with olive oil for dipping. "Cheap stuff," James said, looking at the bottle.

"Louis says you make your own?" Aidan asked.

"It's all down to Farid," James said, nodding toward his partner. "He's the one who knows the olives. I just pay the bills."

"We have about two hundred hectares outside Tebourba," Farid said. "It has been in my family for many generations, but my father did not have the money to invest in new production techniques. We have modernized and experimented with different olive blends. We've been shipping for two years now, but we have finally found the right mix."

"Mix?" Aidan asked.

"There are many different kinds of olives, as I'm sure you know," Farid said. "Just like grapes, olives vary based on breed and *terroir*—the characteristics of land, sun, water, and so on."

"Like cocoa beans and coffee beans," Aidan said.

"Exactly. But there is further variety with olives. Table olives have fleshy fruit but yield little oil. Some varieties need better soil than we can offer here in Tunisia, while others require colder temperatures to bear fruit. And each has its own taste profile to offer. We have tried many different combinations, searching for the best."

The waiter took their orders. Liam drank some wine, then said, "This is all very interesting. But Louis said you might need bodyguards. That's the part I'd like to hear about."

James said, "We've had a number of incidents lately. It could just be bad karma, but it's enough to worry us. We're struggling to bottle our new oil in time for this big trade fair in LA, and every little problem slows us down."

"What kind of incidents?" Liam asked.

"The olives are very fragile," Farid said. "We pick by hand to make sure that they are perfectly ripe and there is no damage. And yet, when we sort, we find unripe fruits in the mix, and skins are bruised."

"That's all?"

Farid shook his head. "We have a traditional mill on the property, and we grind the olives ourselves into a fine paste. There have been many problems with the machinery—many more than we might expect."

"Is there anyone who might have a grudge against you?" Aidan asked.

"There are those who do not like us because we are gay," Farid said. "And those who distrust James because he is American. We have competitors who would like to see us fail." He smiled. "My father was not a kind or gentle man, and there are many in the area who hold grudges against him. The Arab memory is a very long one."

"Have you reported these incidents to the police?" Liam asked.

"Yes, but each one is so small," Farid said. "Our local police, they are not very sophisticated. And because of everything I have said, they perhaps help us a little less."

"I spoke to Louis about the problems," James said. "And he recommended you."

The waiter brought their appetizers—thinly sliced beef carpaccio, a platter of fried artichoke hearts, cherry tomatoes stuffed with goat cheese, and gleaming spears of asparagus drizzled with olive oil and lemon.

They shifted conversation as they ate. Louis was concerned about the increasing scale of the protests against the government, but Hassan stopped him. "No politics tonight," he said. Instead, he spoke about a building he was designing, and then Liam complained about the Figueroa kids. They laughed and told stories and enjoyed their dinners.

When they finished, James asked, "Are you available to work for us? We'd need you to come out to Tebourba and keep an eye on things for a couple of weeks, until we're ready to head to LA."

"We have a guest cottage where you can stay," Farid said. "You'll take your meals with us—we have a wonderful cook."

"I'm not sure what you want from us," Liam said. "Our business is what we call personal protection. We safeguard human targets from potential dangers. It sounds like you need private security guards stationed at your mill. That's not what we do."

"They need someone with brains and brawn to track down who's responsible for these problems," Louis said. "That sounds like you guys."

Liam shook his head. "We're not private investigators either."

Aidan pushed his chair back and stood up. "If you'll excuse me, I'm going to the men's room. Liam? You want to come with me?"

"You need me to hold your hand?"

"Or his dick," Louis said, laughing.

"We do enough of that at home," Aidan said. "Liam?"

"Yes, dear," Liam said, standing up.

In the men's room, Aidan went to the sink. "Is there some reason why you're not interested in this job?" he asked as he began washing his hands.

Liam shrugged. "We just finished one. I was hoping we could have a few days off."

"A guest cottage out in the country, with gourmet meals? Sounds like a vacation to me."

Liam went up to the sink next to Aidan's and began washing his hands too. "Weren't you paying attention? Someone may be sabotaging their operation. That sounds like a job, not a vacation."

"And isn't that what we do? Accept jobs? They seem like a nice couple. If we can help them out and make some money and get out of the city for a while, why not?"

Liam shook his head. "It's not what we do. And I'm not comfortable leaving Tunis while there's so much uncertainty over the government."

"Fine," Aidan said. "I have that translation job tomorrow anyway."

Liam dried his hands on a paper towel. "We'll see. If there are still protests going on, I don't want you out wandering the city."

"You're my partner, remember? Not my boss." Aidan dried his hands. It was love, he thought, as he walked back to the table, Liam behind him. Sometimes Liam was just too bossy, but Aidan had to remind himself it came from a good place. And there were times when he had to go along with Liam, despite what he wanted. This was one of them.

When they were seated at the table again, Aidan said, "I think we're going to have to pass on the job. But I'm sure Louis knows other people who could help you out."

James Gardiner insisted on paying for dinner, and they all walked out of the restaurant together. The night was quiet, the only lights coming from the port where freighters were constantly being loaded and unloaded.

"Are you going back to Tebourba tonight?" Liam asked James and Farid.

James nodded. "We had a couple of business meetings here, and we tried to see Farid's niece, but her mother's being a bitch. Doesn't like the fact that Farid is gay, so she's keeping him from seeing Leila."

"Families," Louis said.

"Especially Arab families," Hassan said. "I am lucky to be an only child. This girl is your brother's daughter?"

Farid nodded. "He was a high-ranking officer with the Muslim

Leadership, and he went into exile in France two years ago. As his brother, I should have taken on responsibility for his wife and daughter, but they refused. Instead, Khadija took Leila to live with her brother, who is also involved with the group and, I am afraid, with these protests."

"What's the Muslim Leadership?" Aidan asked.

"A very Islamist political group," Farid said. "They wish to make Tunisia a Muslim society like Saudi Arabia."

"That won't happen," Liam said. "The educated middle class in Tunisia won't stand for it."

Louis shook his head. "You forget who is protesting, Liam. The men and women in these demonstrations are not the poor and uneducated. They're people much like us who have been denied opportunities. If the Muslim Leadership provides a viable option to Ben Ali's government, who's to say they won't succeed?"

The three couples parted, and Liam and Aidan walked back to their house. "What do you think would happen to us if Tunisia became an Islamist country?" Aidan asked. "Could we even stay here?"

"Not going to happen. Louis has his head up his ass. The Agency always does."

Aidan wished he could believe his partner, but he had a feeling that in this case, Liam might just be wrong.

3 – Leila

Aidan straightened his shirt collar in the mirror. Behind him, Liam said, "This is a bad idea. You don't know what's going to happen out there today."

"Liam. I'll be fine. If there are any problems, I'll stay at the hotel until the police have everything under control."

"Call me if you run into anything. Wherever you are."

"Yes, Dad."

Liam smacked Aidan on the butt, and Aidan said, "Ow! That hurts."

"Good. Maybe you'll learn something." He went out into the courtyard to exercise, and Aidan walked down the Avenue Habib Bourguiba to the Hotel Africa. Cabs, buses, and luxury cars jockeyed for position along the broad avenue. A teacher led a group of uniform-clad schoolchildren, holding hands in pairs, into a gleaming office building. It was a bright, sunny day, and Aidan had trouble imagining that the city would be in real danger from any demonstrations.

His client was an elderly Scot who spoke only a few words of Arabic but had a complicated business proposal he needed to understand before he could sign. Aidan sat at the small table with his laptop and worked on a basic translation. His Arabic wasn't perfect, but with the help of an online translation tool, he was able to make sense of the document and explain it to the client.

Mr. MacDonald ordered them room service, and they worked through lunch. By four o'clock, Aidan had completed the translation and printed it out in the hotel's business center. "This is excellent, laddie," Mr. MacDonald said. "Thank you so much."

"My pleasure. I'll let Madame Abboud know how many hours I put in, and she'll invoice you."

Though it was barely sixty degrees, the afternoon sun struck Aidan like a laser beam as he left the dimness and air-conditioning of the hotel. As he walked down the street, he heard men and women yelling in the distance, glass breaking. Someone was blasting the elephant-trumpet sound of a *vuvuzela*, made popular at the World Cup in South Africa. Aidan hurried ahead, but as he approached the cathedral at the intersection of the Avenue Habib Thameur, the demonstrators swarmed around him, young men in tracksuits or jeans and T-shirts, carrying Tunisian flags and protest signs. There were a few young women among them, and all were chanting in Arabic.

The crowd was suddenly so dense he could hardly move. The smell of sweat and garlic was almost overwhelming. Then he heard sirens and saw flashing red and blue lights in the distance. Riot police in camouflage uniforms and metal helmets appeared from the side streets, holding clubs and teargas guns. Sweat began dripping down his forehead and pooling under his arms.

Aidan was momentarily paralyzed with fear. How had he gotten himself in the middle of this? He had to get out. But which way to go? There were people all around him, and he had no idea which way the police were coming from.

A man next to him was knocked to the ground. Aidan tried to reach down to help him up, but the crowd pushed him forward. Ahead of him, he saw the Cathedral of St. Vincent de Paul. As a Jew, he'd never had a reason to visit the cathedral before, but now it seemed like his best chance to get out of the way of the crowd.

He pushed his way down the street, working toward the edge of the crowd, as the men and women surged around him, yelling and shaking their fists. He kept his head down, hopeful no one would recognize him as an American and turn the crowd's frenzy his way.

His blood pressure and heart rate accelerated as he struggled to find a way out. A vendor's stall next to the cathedral fell to the ground as the crowd reached it. Aidan saw his chance and darted through an opening. He hurried up the half-dozen steps and under the triple arches that led into the cathedral.

A smaller, nervous crowd huddled inside, others who had sought refuge from the demonstration, including elderly men and women and young mothers with babies in their arms. The inside of the building was shivery cool, and the sounds of the crowd outside echoed under the high arches. People milled under the stained-glass windows or sat on the hard wooden chairs facing the altar. An elderly woman with a white shawl draped over her shoulders knelt under a crucifix mounted on a side wall and prayed.

Aidan stepped to a quiet corner and pulled out his cell phone. "Aidan? Where are you?" Liam demanded before Aidan could even say hello.

"At the cathedral. I'm fine." His voice quavered.

"You don't sound fine. Stay right there. I'm coming."

"No, Liam. Stay where you are. The demonstration is going to pass in a few minutes, and then I'll be able to come home."

"I told you not to go out today, but you wouldn't listen."

Aidan took a deep breath. Sounding more determined than he felt, he said, "We'll talk about it when I get home. Just stay there."

"I'm not stupid enough to go out," Liam said. Then Aidan heard him take a deep breath. "Just be careful, all right?"

"I will be."

Aidan ended the call and looked around. Had anyone heard him speaking English? It looked like everyone around him was focused on the demonstrations outside.

He walked around the cathedral for a few minutes, calming himself down and waiting for the crowds to pass. As the noise outside faded, people inside the cathedral began moving toward the doors. Aidan lagged behind until he could move freely.

When he stepped outside, the square in front of the cathedral was a mess. The grass and flowers in front had been trampled underfoot, and the poor vendor's stall had been scattered in pieces over the pavement. Empty water bottles and shredded signs littered the square, making it look like a hurricane had swept through.

In the corner, a man lay on the ground, bleeding from the head and moaning, and two EMTs tended to him. Aidan hurried back toward home, sticking to the side streets until he saw Liam standing in the doorway of their house.

Liam ran toward him and wrapped his arms around him. "I was so worried about you! Why don't you listen?"

"I was fine, Liam," Aidan said with more certainty than he felt.

"Whatever. Neither of us is going out until this is all over." He took Aidan by the arm, and they walked back to the house.

"Did you at least make dinner?" Aidan asked as they walked inside.

"Are you kidding? I couldn't concentrate on anything while I was worrying about you."

"Or you just figured you'd wait for me to get home."

Fortunately, there was plenty of food in the refrigerator and freezer, and Aidan threw together a chicken-and-vegetable stir-fry as they watched TV coverage of the demonstrations. "That's where I was," Aidan said as the camera panned past the cathedral.

"I don't want to talk about it anymore," Liam said.

Typical, Aidan thought. Whenever something important happened, Liam shut down, despite Aidan's desire to talk things out.

They ate in silence, watching the TV until there was nothing new to see. Liam stayed in the living room when Aidan rose to go to the bedroom. He wanted Liam to recognize that he was upset and still a bit frightened, and comfort him. But that wasn't Liam's way. After nearly two years together, Aidan should have accepted that, but he couldn't help wanting things to be different. He sat up in bed, unable to concentrate on his book, replaying what had happened earlier that day and what he might have done differently.

Just before ten o'clock, Liam's cell phone rang. "Who the hell is calling this late?" he grumbled. Aidan came out of the bedroom to see him answer the phone.

"Who's this?" he demanded without preamble. "Oh, James. Sorry. What's up?"

Aidan watched Liam as he listened. "How did you hear?"

"Hear what?" Aidan asked.

Liam held up his hand. "I need a pencil and paper." Then he spoke into the phone. "Give me the address. You want us to bring her to you tonight? It's going to be dangerous. Why don't we camp out at your sister-in-law's apartment, then drive out tomorrow?"

He listened some more. "Yes, I know it's not the Muslim way, James. But we don't have much choice."

He listened some more, then hung up.

"What?" Aidan asked.

"Remember Farid talking about his niece last night? Well, her mother and her uncle were arrested during the demonstration today, and she's all alone. James wants us to pick her up and bring her out to Tebourba. He agreed we could go to the girl and stay with her, then drive her out tomorrow."

"I'd better pack." Aidan put aside his irritation and unhappiness and focused on the task at hand. It was what Liam did.

While Aidan put together their clothes and toiletries, Liam checked their guns and ammunition. It was too late to make arrangements for Fadi, the bartender at the Bar Mamounia, to keep an eye on Hayam, so she would have to go with them.

They finished at about the same time. "Where are we going?"

Aidan asked.

Liam opened a program on his phone and punched in the address. "Apartment building off the Rue Mongi Slim," he said.

After a particularly lucrative assignment, Aidan and Liam had bought a used Jeep, which they kept parked at a lot a few blocks from their house. They walked to it and loaded it up with clothes and gear. The streets were quiet and eerily deserted as they drove inland. Stores had turned off their neon signs and display lighting, and there were few street lamps. "Everyone with sense is indoors," Liam grumbled.

"What do you know about this girl?" Aidan asked. "How old is she?"

"Thirteen. Her name is Leila. Farid doesn't know much more because the mother has kept him away for the last few years, since his brother, the girl's father, went into exile."

"Thirteen, and her family is into radical Islam," Aidan said. "She's probably old enough to wear a hijab."

"Women don't wear the hijab in the city," Liam said. "Even the most religious ones."

It took them twenty minutes to find the Rue Mongi Slim and locate the apartment building, then to park nearby. Liam drew his gun from its holster before he stepped out of the Jeep. Aidan did the same, though there was no one around to threaten them. Hayam refused to stay in the Jeep, jumping out behind Aidan and quickly peeing against a curb.

They walked quickly to the building, hyperalert to any sound or movement. The lock on the front door was broken, so they walked inside and climbed to apartment 3G, Hayam trotting with them on her short legs.

Liam knocked on the door and spoke in Arabic. "Leila? My name is Liam, and your Uncle Farid has sent me and my partner to look after you while your mother can't be here."

There was silence on the other side of the door. Liam knocked again. "Leila? Are you there?"

The door opened just an inch, and Aidan could see a dark-haired girl peeking through. "My mother does not like my Uncle Farid," she said in Arabic.

"That's true," Liam replied. "But you know a young woman needs a male relative to look after her. Your mother was arrested today at a demonstration, and she called your uncle. He could not get into the city from Tebourba this late at night, so he asked us to come to you and then bring you to his house tomorrow."

She opened the door a bit wider. Aidan could see that she was wearing jeans and a long-sleeved top despite the warm temperature. "My mother was arrested?"

Liam nodded. "May we come inside?"

She stepped back and opened the door, and Liam and Aidan walked inside. "You have a dog!" Leila got down to the floor and petted Hayam, who rolled on her back and waved her little legs in the air.

The living room was simple, with a low sofa along two walls, a couple of chairs, and a television set on a wooden table. There were frayed carpets on the floor, and the only art on the walls were a series of verses from the Koran written in a flowing Arabic script.

"You are American?" Leila said in English as she stood up from petting the dog and backed away.

"You speak English?" Aidan asked.

She nodded. "But I must not speak to men outside of my family, except when my uncle is present."

"Well, that's going to be a problem," Liam said. "Since one of your uncles is in jail with your mother, and the other is in Tebourba. We're going to have to bend the rules a little."

"I do not have to listen to you," Leila said, crossing her arms. "You are infidels."

Liam shook his head. "Ah, Leila, you don't know your Islamic law, do you? I'm a Christian, and Aidan is a Jew, and that makes us both People of the Book. The Koran says it's a punishable offense to call any member of the People of the Book an infidel."

Aidan would have snickered if he hadn't been so irritated by the girl. "Let's not argue tonight," he said. "It's late, and we're all tired. Liam and I will sleep out here in the living room. You sleep in your room. Then in the morning, we'll discuss where we go and what we do." He crossed his arms in a mimicry of her own actions. "And besides, according to the Koran, men are the maintainers and protectors of women. You are required by your faith to obey what we say."

"I want to talk to my mother."

"She's being held at the Mornaguia Prison," Liam said. "You can call there, but I don't know if they'll let you talk to her."

"We have no telephone," Leila said.

Liam pulled his phone out of his pocket. He looked up the phone number for the prison and dialed it, then handed the phone to Leila. She took it reluctantly.

Aidan could only follow Leila's side of the conversation, but he understood that whoever Leila was speaking to could not confirm that her mother was being held there, and even if she was, Leila could not speak to her.

As she argued with the prison official, Aidan looked at her more closely. She was not a pretty girl; her face was round and already pockmarked with acne, and the perpetual frown she wore didn't help.

Whoever she was speaking with must have hung up on her, because Leila cursed and looked like she was ready to spit.

"Would you like to talk to your Uncle Farid?" Liam asked gently.

She frowned, but she nodded slightly. She handed the phone back to Liam, who dialed the number in Tebourba. "James? Liam McCullough. I'm here with Farid's niece. She'd like to speak with him."

He waited until Farid was on the line and then handed the phone to Leila. She spoke in a rush of Arabic that Aidan couldn't follow at all. All he could do was watch her body language move from anger to resignation. She handed the phone back to Liam, looking down at the ground.

"We'll bring her out to you tomorrow," Liam said into the phone. He listened. "Good. We'll call again in the morning."

He shut the phone off. "You have a bathroom here?"

Leila went into her bedroom and locked the door. Aidan and Liam both used the bathroom, then rolled sleeping bags out on the carpeted floor.

* * *

When Aidan woke the next morning, filtered golden light streamed in through the living room windows, and dust motes danced in the air. The sounds of morning traffic rolled in through the open window. He shifted and realized that Liam's arm was sprawled over him. Hayam was curled up at their feet. It was a lot like being back home, only surrounded by other people's furniture and without a bed beneath them.

He looked up to see Leila standing over them. She was wearing a black-and-silver scarf over her head and wrapped around her neck, a long-sleeved shirt, and jeans.

"You are homosexuals," she said, spitting the words out. "In the Hadith, Mohammed says that homosexuality is an abomination and a grave sin. If a man comes upon a man, then they are both adulterers."

Aidan groaned and pushed Liam's arm off him. "Good morning to you too, Miss Sunshine." He sat up. His back was out of kilter from sleeping on the floor, and he shifted and twisted to stretch.

"When a man mounts another man, the throne of God shakes," Leila said. "The Hadith says that we should kill the one that is doing it and also kill the one that it is being done to."

Liam was still asleep. "Okay," Aidan said to Leila. "Go for it. Kill us. But I'm warning you, we're both trained bodyguards. We know hand-to-hand combat, and we have guns." He pulled his out from under his pillow, where it had rested while he slept. He left it in his hand as he looked up at her and smiled.

"I want to talk to my uncle!" Leila crossed her arms over her chest and pouted in the universal gesture of teenaged defiance.

Liam yawned and looked up. "What's going on?"

"Leila announced that you and I should both be killed," Aidan said. "We're just discussing how she's planning to do it."

"Aidan, behave. Good morning, Leila. Would you like me to call your uncle for you?"

Aidan understood how Liam had felt with João and Morena. He sat up. "Call her uncle and tell him we're getting on the road as soon as possible. This is one job I'll be happy to finish."

4 – Tebourba

Liam was glad when they finally got Leila packed up and into their Jeep. Clouds had swept in from the Mediterranean, and the day had turned gray and somber. The streets had a jittery quality, as if every child, shopper, or businessman was looking over his or her shoulder. He turned on the radio and listened carefully to an Arabic news broadcast that recapped the growing unrest throughout the country. There was no mention of Tebourba or any of the towns along their route, which was a good thing.

He threaded the Jeep through the usual scrum of traffic until they got onto the Route Nationale 7 out of Tunis, heading east. Only when they were on the highway and had picked up speed did he feel he could relax, as low fields spangled in green and brown slipped past.

The clouds cooled the air, but there was little humidity, and the breeze wicked away any moisture that rose from their skin. It had been a warm, dry winter, and the forecasts Liam had seen indicated the spring was going to be a hot one. He glanced in the rearview mirror, where Leila pouted in the backseat, her arms once more crossed over her chest.

"Have you been up this way before?" Aidan asked, leaning back in his seat, his arm on the open windowsill. He looked to Liam like he was going on vacation instead of being in the middle of an assignment, and that was mildly irritating.

"No," Liam said. "Do you have the directions?"

"Yup. We take the C32 to Al Battan, where we cross an arched stone dam from the sixteenth century. It's hard to believe people have lived here that long. And without air-conditioning."

Liam said, "Water has been strategically important throughout history. People need water to drink, to raise livestock, and to irrigate crops. It's logical that the earliest civilization grew up around sources of water."

"Listen to you, Mr. Historian," Aidan said.

"There was a big battle around Tebourba in World War II," Liam continued, ignoring the jibe. "The US and the British held the town for four days before finally giving in to the Germans."

"All infidels," Leila grumbled from the backseat.

"Get it right, Leila," Liam said. "We talked about this last night."

"Horrible People of the Book. Invading my country. You wait, when my father returns to Tunisia and takes control, things will be different. You will all have to leave."

Liam and Aidan shared a look. Liam would be glad to be able to drop Leila with her uncle and then return to Tunis, no matter what kind of demonstrations were going on.

When they reached the bridge, they stopped to stretch their legs and let Hayam empty her bladder. The Medjerda River, the longest one in Tunisia, flowed under the bridge. It wasn't very large or deep, but since most of Tunisia was desert, beyond its Mediterranean coast, it was a welcome sight. The oppressive dryness of the morning dissipated as they stood by the water's edge, and Liam felt he could breathe more easily.

Back in the Jeep, they passed through the town, a few wide streets lined with bright orange and red flowering plants, surrounded by the gray rock face of mountains. A white stucco building with the bright blue ironwork common to Tunisia displayed a sign that read USINE DES CHECHIAS.

"So that's where all those little hats come from," Aidan said.

Liam had several of the round red hats that Tunisian men wore; he often used one to help him blend into a crowd.

From Al Battan, they drove to Tebourba. With its palm trees and ornate iron lampposts, the stucco town had the feel of a seaside resort, though it was miles inland. Following a narrow local road, they found their way to Ferme Deux Hommes, or Two-Man Farm, where Farid's family's groves hugged a bend in the river.

Aidan twisted around to speak to Leila as they drove up a broad driveway lined with spiky aloes. Down the slope toward the river, a small group of men worked in the grove. "Have you been here before?" he asked her.

"A long time ago," she said. "When my grandfather was alive. Not since my uncle moved here."

Liam parked in front of the main house, a low-slung stucco building surrounded by squat date palms and wiry gray-trunked olive trees. It looked very Mediterranean, with its orange barrel-tile roof and glossy green vines that snaked up the front walls.

Farid came out the front door as they were getting out of the Jeep. "Leila! You look just like your mother when she was your age."

Hayam jumped out of the Jeep and immediately peed at the base of a date palm.

Farid tried to hug Leila, but she squirmed away.

James followed Farid out the door. "I'm so glad you're here," he said. "There's been another incident."

"Welcome to your vacation," Liam muttered to Aidan.

Farid stepped back from Leila. "Come with me. I'll show you your room."

"I want to talk to my mother," she demanded once again. "I tried to call the prison last night, but they wouldn't even tell me she was there. Where is she?"

"Why don't we call your father and see what he knows?" Farid said.

"My father? You know where he is?"

"He's my twin brother. Of course I know where he is." She trailed along behind him, and they disappeared into a wing of the house.

"What happened?" Liam asked as James led them in the other direction. It was cool inside, decorated like a luxury resort, with overstuffed cane furniture, overhead fans that swirled the air, and oil paintings of olive trees and the tawny hills that surrounded the area. Aidan picked up Hayam and carried her with them.

"Someone sabotaged our irrigation pump." James led them down a hall to a large room that had been outfitted as an office. "Let me show you the layout of the property."

He opened a large, flat book of maps and laid it out on a

wooden table. "Here's where we are," he said, pointing. "Our property follows a curve of the Medjerda River. The original groves were along the river because the soil there is damper. We've expanded significantly, and that meant installing drip-line irrigation."

He traced a line along the map. "The main pump is here, and the lines run from there throughout the grove."

"Any security?" Liam asked.

James shook his head. "Never had a need for it before."

"So anybody could just walk up to the pump and take it out?"

"You'd have to know where it was."

"That implies someone who knows your property." Aidan set Hayam down on the floor, and after a brief sniff, she sprawled out, resting her belly on the cool tile.

"Anyone locally have a grudge against you?" Liam asked.

James shrugged. "There are always people who grumble. The local imam doesn't like the fact that we're gay. A couple of the other olive farmers are worried that we'll knock them out of the market. But there are just as many who welcome us and hope we'll bring the rest of them along with us as we grow and improve."

They sat down in armchairs, and James said, "Let me give you a little background before we go outside. Olives have been cultivated here for centuries, and about seventy percent of the oil is exported. But Tunisian olive oil has a reputation for poor quality, in part because of the technology, in part because of drought. Some presses still use a donkey that walks in a circle dragging a stone or wooden mortar, the way the Phoenicians did."

"Do you press your own oil?" Aidan asked.

"We have to, to control quality."

"Just your own olives?"

"I see where you're going," James said. "We buy high quality olives from some of our neighbors. And we do some contract work as well, grinding for some other farms. But the people we're putting out of business? They don't have the skill level to come after us. And we're hiring local people, paying good wages, trying to bring up the whole town. The women sing their traditional songs and tell jokes as they pick up the olives shaken to the ground by the men. And we always leave something behind on the trees for the poor. The people here call that 'olives for the stranger,' and Farid's family has been doing it for generations."

There was a knock on the door to the study, and Farid and Leila walked in. Hayam hopped up and walked over to Leila, sniffing around her feet.

"Leila spoke to her father," Farid said. "He's going to investigate what happened to her mother and her uncle. Until then, she's going to stay with us."

"Well, then, we'll be heading back to Tunis," Liam said. "Good luck with everything."

"Wait," James said. "Won't you at least stay for a day or two? We could really use your help figuring out what's going on."

Liam looked at Aidan. They had nothing urgent to return to in Tunis, and it would be safer for them to stay out here in this isolated spot until the unrest in the city had calmed down. Knowing Aidan, he would refuse to stay put in their little house behind the Bar Mamounia—he'd always be going out to the market, to a client, and so on.

James saw his indecision. "Let me show you the guesthouse," he said.

"Come on, Hayam, let's see the guesthouse," Aidan said, and she came over to his side.

They walked back down the dim hallway and out to the backyard, where there was a lushly landscaped pool and a small cottage just beyond. It was made of white stucco, with big windows that looked out at the pool. Inside there was a living room and a large bedroom with a king-size bed. Hayam immediately sprawled out on the floor again.

"Hayam likes it," Aidan said.

It was obvious Aidan wanted to stay, and Liam knew when to give in. "I guess we should unload the Jeep," he said. "Then I'd like to look at the pump you say was sabotaged."

James, Farid, and Leila went back to the house, and Aidan and Liam walked out to the Jeep. "You don't mind staying here for a few days, do you?" Aidan asked. "It's beautiful, and there's a pool."

"And someone causing trouble. Not exactly a vacation. I still think James and Farid would be better off calling the police."

"The police have more to worry about right now than a sabotaged irrigation pump," Aidan said, pulling duffle bags out of the back of the Jeep.

"I suppose. We are safer out here than in Tunis right now.

Though it's not exactly the kind of romantic getaway I know you'd prefer."

"We can make it as romantic as we want. We'll put up a sign that reads 'If the guesthouse is rocking, don't bother knocking.'"

Liam laughed. They carried everything in and set Hayam up with a bowl of water and a biscuit. As they walked out to the pool deck, they saw Farid arguing with Leila.

"I can't," she said, crossing her arms in a gesture that Liam had already come to recognize. "There are strange men here. It's not right."

"Leila refuses to swim," Farid said.

"We're going out with James," Aidan said. "And you're her blood relative. If we're gone, Leila, will you go in the pool?"

She looked at the blue water shimmering in the sunlight. "I don't have a bathing suit," she said.

"Not a problem," Farid said. "Your mother left one here the last time she came to visit, when you were just a baby. I'll bet it would fit you. And it's very modest."

They went into the house, and James stepped out, wearing a broad-brimmed straw hat. "I'll take you down to the groves." He picked up two more of the hats from a table by the pool. "You'd better wear these, though. Despite the cool temperature, the sun is very strong out there."

The three of them walked around behind the guesthouse and down a gentle slope toward the groves. The sun was high and bright, the air cool, reminding Liam of springtime back home in New Jersey.

"Whoever planted these groves a hundred years ago knew what he was doing," James said as they walked. "Light and air will increase a tree's health and yield, and even back then they knew that the trees should be planted in north-south rows. That lets sunlight penetrate the trees as the sun moves across the sky."

"Farid's family has been here that long?"

"Longer, probably," James said. "We lost a tree to lightning last year, and we checked its age; near as we can figure, it was close to two hundred." He stopped a few hundred feet from the edge of the grove. "Though we have a mechanical harvester, we've found that by hand-picking, we get a better quality of fruit, and we provide employment for a lot of the locals."

"You're harvesting now?" Liam asked.

James nodded. "We harvest between November and February, so we're coming to the end of this year's cycle. So far our production has been excellent—twenty percent more than last year. But if these incidents keep up, we'll be in real trouble."

They walked up to the edge of the new grove, and James stopped again. The gnarled trunks marched like sentinels through the sandy soil, holding their branches up in supplication to the sun, rain, and wind. James leaned down to point out the drip irrigation system. "We have a series of cisterns that capture rainfall—most of it comes from September to April, with December and January our biggest months. Whatever else we need comes from the river."

He led them uphill through the grove to what looked to Liam like a wild tangle of hoses, connectors, and valves in a multitude of colors—red, blue, orange, and purple. The valve that controlled the pump had been sawed off and lay on the ground.

Liam knelt down to examine the damage. "Looks like a hacksaw," he said. "Pretty common tool, so that doesn't tell us much."

"Can you dust for fingerprints?" James asked.

Liam looked up at him. "And compare them to what? You want to take prints of everyone in town?"

"There has to be something we can do," James said.

Liam stood up. "Let's take an overall approach to this problem. We'll need to walk around the whole property and identify the security risks, then figure out what we can install to protect you. That's going to take some time."

5 – Grove Security

Aidan was happy to leave Liam and James to walk the grove and look for places they could enhance security. He walked back up to the guesthouse, listening to be sure he wasn't interrupting Leila at her swim. The pool was quiet, so he crossed the deck to the guesthouse and unpacked their gear. As he put their clothes away, he noticed that the closet had been stocked with bathing trunks, terrycloth robes, and plush towels.

Late in the afternoon, Farid came out in a pair of swim trunks and dove into the pool. Aidan chose a pair that fit him from the selection and walked outside. "Come on in; the water's cold at first but refreshing," Farid said. His smooth skin was a golden brown, though Aidan wasn't sure if it was from tanning or genetics.

Aidan walked in from the shallow end, feeling the cool water engulf him. "This is wonderful," he said.

"Couldn't convince Leila to swim, though," Farid said. "Her mother has her so brainwashed about Muslim standards of decency. I tried to explain that she could do what she wanted around me because I'm family. But my brother cut me off when I came out of the closet, and so Leila hardly knows me."

"He's your twin?"

"Fraternal. I am, of course, much handsomer." His short, dark hair was so well cut it looked perfect even wet, and everything about him oozed careful grooming.

Aidan laughed.

"Omar is ten minutes older than I am, a fact he has never let me forget. By birthright, these groves should belong to him, but he preferred politics to olive-growing. And then, of course, his activism caused him to have to leave the country."

"What did he do?" Aidan leaned back against the pool's rim and let his legs float out in front of him.

Farid ducked below the water, then rose and shook his head, sending shimmering droplets around him. "As the head of the Muslim Leadership, he led many protests against Ben Ali and his government. He was arrested several times. Finally, he decided to leave the country. Things are changing now, and if Ben Ali falls, then there may be a power vacuum and a place for my brother."

James and Liam approached from the groves. While James looked cool under his straw hat, Liam was sweating, rivulets dripping down his impressively muscled arms and water staining his tank top under the neckline and over his nipples, the rings forming a circular imprint on the fabric. "Enjoying yourselves?" he asked.

"Dinner is in the oven," Farid said. "We are taking a break before the cocktail hour."

"And in a swimsuit," James said. "We don't see that around here that often."

"A gesture toward my niece's modesty. Will you join us?"

"There's a suit in the bathroom closet that would fit you, Liam," Aidan said.

James said, "Suppose we combine swim time with cocktail hour.

I'll change and have Hakim bring some beverages. Sangria for everyone?"

There was general agreement, and a few minutes later, they were all in the pool, sipping from tall plastic glasses brought by a dark-skinned manservant.

"So, Liam, you can protect us?" Farid asked.

"I still have more to see," he said. "But I have some ideas."

"I have a man coming from Tunis to repair the pump tomorrow," James said. "He's going to bring a metal cage with a lock to put over it. But Liam has already helped me identify several other places where we are vulnerable."

Aidan couldn't help noticing the admiring glances both Farid and James cast at Liam. With his brownish-blond hair plastered down, an almost too-tight pair of body-hugging trunks, water dripping from his impressive musculature, and his gold nipple rings glistening in the sunshine, his partner looked like a porn star. He tamped down his jealousy by reminding himself that he would be the one in Liam's bed that night.

They talked about Tunis and their mutual friendship with Louis and Hassan, and then the servant, Hakim, announced that dinner would be ready in fifteen minutes.

Aidan and Liam showered quickly and dressed, then met James, Farid, and Leila in the cool, dim dining room, lit by flickering candles in hammered brass wall sconces, protected by glass hurricane globes.

"Very atmospheric," Aidan said as they sat down at the elegant teak dining table. There were six matching high-backed teak chairs with plush cushions covered in a nubby eggshell fabric. An impressionistic painting of olive trees against a turbulent sky hung in the center of the far wall.

"Energy efficient as well," James said. "We installed solar panels on the roof when we modernized the property, and now we generate our own electricity. But we're still careful. It takes a lot of power to keep this place going."

Hakim brought a large porcelain platter of chicken roasted with olives and artichokes to the table. The smell of sage and onions rose as Farid sliced into the succulent chicken. Aidan's mouth watered.

The chicken was moist and tender, the olives redolent and tangy, the acidity of the artichokes enhanced by capers and parchment-thin slices of fresh lemon. Aidan savored several mouthfuls, then asked Farid, "How long has your family been here?"

"Many generations. My father and his brother were born right here in this house. They were twins, just like Omar and I."

"Does your uncle's family still live here in Tebourba?" Liam asked.

Farid shook his head. "Like Omar, my uncle Esam was not happy in the country. He left and moved to Tunis. We have not heard from him or any of his family for many years." He looked to Leila. "Unless you have seen him?"

"No. The only family we see in Tunis is my mother's. She and my Uncle Burhan are very close."

"Burhan is an ally of Omar's," Farid explained. "With Omar in exile, he is the party leader, though he keeps a very low profile and defers everything to Omar."

"My father is a very important man," Leila said.

"Yes, he is," Farid said. "But if he were here, he would tell you to eat your chicken so you become a strong fighter for the Islamist cause."

"It tastes funny," Leila said.

"I think it's delicious," Aidan said. "If you don't want yours, Leila, I'll eat it."

She glared at him and picked up her fork. Aidan caught Liam's eye and winked, but Liam just shook his head.

James and Farid had a satellite dish and a big-screen television, and after dinner they sat on the plush couches and chairs of the living room and tuned into the news. The lead story was an announcement by President Ben Ali promising cuts in the skyrocketing prices of milk, bread, and sugar. He also said that he would not run for reelection.

"Do you think that will make the protests stop?" Farid asked Liam.

He shrugged. "It's your country. I just live here."

"The people will not stop protesting until the corrupt leaders have been toppled and replaced with a government that rules by the Koran," Leila said.

"So your father says," Farid said. "I am not so sure."

The news carried reports of ongoing demonstrations, in Tunis and around the country, and Aidan was glad that they were secure out there in Tebourba. The government had announced that they were no longer going to use live ammunition to stop the demonstrations, which seemed to encourage the protesters.

After the news, they watched a movie together in the living room, an innocuous comedy Farid thought Leila might like. What she seemed to enjoy most, though, was criticizing the teenage girls in the film—for their clothing, the way they wore their hair, and their general lack of modesty. Aidan found it a downer, but he was determined not to let one bratty little girl ruin his country idyll.

When the movie was over, Aidan and Liam walked back to the guesthouse. The sky was dark, and they heard distant rumbles of thunder. "This is the rainy season," Liam said. "Reasonable to assume there'll be some rain."

"As long as it doesn't interfere with my pool time," Aidan said.

"This isn't a vacation. We're here to do a job."

"Yes, Liam. And whenever you need me to do anything, you let me know. But if you don't need me, you'll find me in the pool or sunbathing."

While Liam used the bathroom, Aidan stripped down and lay naked on the bedspread. He was sitting up against the pillows with a photo book of the Tunisian countryside when Liam returned. "Any idea who's causing the trouble?" Aidan asked.

Liam pulled off his polo shirt, and Aidan marveled again at how handsome he was. His body was sculpted by his workouts—broad shoulders and massive pecs that tapered down to a narrow waist. His skin was smooth, with a few tufts of dark blond hair under his arms and at his groin, unlike Aidan's body, which was covered with a fine layer of dark hair.

"No clue." Liam shucked his khaki shorts and jockstrap. His uncut dick hung half-hard, the foreskin nearly stretched to its limit, and he scratched behind his balls. "No obvious suspects and too many vague possibilities."

He climbed onto the bed next to Aidan, who put the book on the bedside table and turned toward him. "Enjoying yourself here?" Liam traced his index finger between Aidan's pecs and down his chest.

"Could be more fun, if I had a handsome guy to make love to me. You up for the assignment?"

Liam looked at his groin, where his dick had unfurled to full stiffness. "Guess I am."

He leaned over and kissed Aidan, his lips feathering against Aidan's at first, and Aidan groaned with pleasure and need. He put his hand behind Liam's head and pulled him closer. They kissed deeply, Aidan opening his mouth to accept Liam's tongue, which pressed against his lips, his teeth, and his tongue.

Liam climbed on top of Aidan, resting his long, tanned body over Aidan's. It was Aidan's favorite sex position ever, having Liam's body touching his in a hundred different places, feeling the pressure of his lover over him. He reached up and took one nipple ring in each hand. He tugged them gently, and Liam's fleshy nubs plumped. Slowly, Liam began sliding up and down on Aidan, their dicks pressing against each other.

Aidan groaned with pleasure as Liam nipped at his neck. Then he arched his body as if he was in some erotic yoga position and began the frottage in earnest, his dick against Aidan's leg, Aidan's dick against Liam's flat stomach. Their precome lubricated the movement, and Aidan felt his body swell with the pressure of his coming orgasm. He moaned and banged his head against the pillow as he pushed up against Liam, rubbing and pressing and then— release. Liam kept pressing and rubbing until he grunted, and Aidan felt his warm semen spurt against cool skin.

Liam slid down over Aidan again, their fluids merging as they kissed once more. Then Liam turned onto his back and said, "Big mess."

"I'll get a washcloth." Aidan stood up, the come already drying against his skin in the arid air. He cleaned up in the bathroom, then returned with a wet cloth to wipe down Liam. By the time he took the dirty cloth back to the bathroom and came back to bed, Liam had burrowed beneath the covers and was already out cold.

As a US Navy SEAL, Liam had mastered the ability to fall asleep at a moment's notice, and wake refreshed, no matter how long or how little he slept. It was a technique Aidan envied. He got into bed next to Liam and adjusted the pillows behind his head.

A moment later, Hayam jumped up onto the foot of the bed and nestled between them. She too fell asleep almost immediately, her tiny belly rising and falling with the rhythm of her breathing.

It wasn't so easy for Aidan. He worried about the rioting in Tunis and what it might mean for his future with Liam. What if Ben Ali's government fell and was replaced by a more Islamist one—one that might be less tolerant of Americans, Jews, or homosexuals. He couldn't help his fears; he had grown up on stories of his grandparents' flight from Eastern Europe and on Sunday-school tales of the Jewish diaspora. His people had a history of being chased from place to place, a heritage Liam didn't understand.

Religion had never come between them before. But as an assimilated Jew in the United States, Aidan had taken acceptance for granted. It was only when he came to live in the Arab world that he understood that religious differences were still so strong. Suppose he just couldn't stay in Tunisia anymore—what would happen? Would Liam leave with him? Or would the world come crashing in on their relationship?

The first roll of thunder was soft, but the storm grew quickly in intensity. Flashes of lightning threw scary patterns on the rough ceiling, and the rolling booms of thunder shook the house. When the rain finally came, in a pounding on the roof that reminded Aidan of Noah's flood, he turned on his side. The rainfall lulled him to sleep, and when he woke the next morning, Liam was already awake, out on the pool deck, doing his exercises.

Hayam was outside too, lying in the shade watching Liam do sit-ups. Aidan knew Liam would do a hundred of those, then switch to push-ups, clap push-ups, and who knew what other exercises he would improvise out there.

He got up, yawned, and put on his bathing suit. It was only seven-thirty, and the pool water was cooler than he preferred, but he dived in anyway and began swimming laps. When he had done twenty, he surfaced and shook the water from his head. Liam was doing jumping jacks, and Hayam was still watching him intently.

Aidan showered and dressed and went into the kitchen, where Hakim brought him a plate of sweet rolls and a glass of orange juice. Aidan sat by himself, watching Liam work out. He couldn't imagine a life without Liam—no matter where that would be. If Liam was determined to stay in Tunisia, then Aidan would have no choice but to stay with him, no matter what the consequences.

Then he remembered his great-grandfather. Zalman Kushner was a prosperous farmer in a rural area of Poland. His oldest son, Aidan's grandfather, had moved to the United States in the late 1930s. He wasn't rich, but he made a good living distributing baked goods in Trenton. He had tried many times to convince his father to leave Poland, but Zalman refused. He was Polish, he said, and his roots were in the land. He could not see himself living anywhere else.

Zalman and his wife, Aidan's great-grandmother, were among the Jews rounded up when the Germans took over their village. No one knew what had happened to them, but it was assumed they had died in a concentration camp, if they'd even made it that far. Aidan doubted that things would get that bad in Tunisia, but he felt he had to remain alert to avoid his great-grandfather's fate.

After breakfast, Aidan began researching land ownership in the area online so that he could list neighbors who might have a grudge against the two gay men. Liam walked the rest of the groves with James and then drove into Tebourba to buy materials. James supervised the installation of the new pump, then stayed among the olives to make sure it was working properly.

Aidan ate lunch with Farid and Leila, who was fussy and worried about her mother and her uncle.

"I don't understand why we can't just drive up to the prison and ask about them," she said. Hakim had made them wraps—chicken salad and hummus in pita, with a green salad and fresh lemonade. Leila picked at hers.

"You cannot just drive up to a prison," Farid said. "I know a man in the United States embassy. I have asked him to make inquiries about Khadija and Burhan. He will call soon, I am sure."

"Why are you involving the United States? My father has many allies right here in Tunisia who could help."

"Yes, but your father has been very careful not to introduce them to me," Farid said. "He is embarrassed by me, when all I want to do is love him and be part of his life."

"If you were not a homosexual, he would not be embarrassed by you," Leila said. "You should stop."

Farid's laugh was more like a short bark. "That is like asking you to stop being a girl. It is who I am. If my brother cannot accept me, I cannot force him to."

There was still half her pita on her plate when she stood up abruptly and walked out of the dining room. "This is why the world can't get along," Aidan said when she had gone. "Because people raise their children to be intolerant."

"She is still a girl," Farid said. "I hope that staying with us for a few days will bring her to a new understanding."

"Good luck with that," Aidan said.

When Liam returned, Aidan helped him inspect the cage around the new pump. Liam didn't believe it was strong enough, so he got to work on it himself, with Aidan to hand him materials and fetch tools. Inland, in the sun, the temperature rose to the mid-sixties, and though they were shaded by the shapely branches and glossy, narrow leaves of an olive tree, they were hot and sweaty by the time they were finished, late in afternoon. Liam snicked the padlock shut, and they walked back up to the guesthouse.

"I wish we didn't have to bother with bathing suits," Liam grumbled as they approached the pool. "I'd strip down and jump in right now."

"We'd horrify poor Leila," Aidan said. "I'm sure a proper girl like her has never seen a man's penis."

There was no sign of James, Farid, or Leila, so Aidan and Liam hastily pulled on their suits and jumped into the pool. The water was cold and made Aidan's skin tingle, but after his afternoon sweat, it was a delight.

Liam swam a dozen laps, while Aidan relaxed and closed his eyes. He was startled by an eruption of water a foot away as Liam surfaced, then shook the droplets from his short hair. "Did you find anything online this morning?" he asked.

"I made a list of everyone who owns property in the area as well as all the other olive-oil producers. But nothing jumped out at me."

Liam submerged, then reappeared right next to Aidan, swooping up out of the pool in a cascade of water. "You mean like this?" he asked, and Aidan laughed. They were fooling around in the water, dunking and splashing, when James came out of the house.

"We just heard from Louis Fleck," he said. "Something happened while she was in custody at the prison, and Khadija is dead."

6 – Lighter than Water

"What happened?" Liam asked.

James adjusted the striped cushion on a wooden lounge chair next to the pool, then sat down. Liam could see the distress in his face; for the first time, he looked his age. "Louis couldn't provide any details. Apparently, there are even more demonstrations going on in Tunis, and things are crazy. Farid is with Leila now, calling Omar to tell him the news."

"It must have been political," Aidan said, stepping out of the pool and wrapping himself in a towel. "Someone who disapproves of the Muslim Leadership and saw this as a chance to strike a blow."

Liam followed him out. He picked up his towel, then began drying off.

"It's a bad business," James said. "I only met Omar once, before he left the country. He's as far from Farid as two brothers can be—he's full of fire and anger, while Farid is kind and gentle. He's an intellectual who spouts political theory and quotes from the Koran, while Farid is happiest when he has his hands in the earth or working around the olives."

"What do you think will happen to Leila?" Aidan asked. "Will she stay here with you?"

"Honestly, I hope not," James said. "I know how important family is to Farid—but she's a sour little pickle."

The door from the house opened, and Farid stepped out,

holding Leila's hand. She was dressed as usual, in jeans and a long-sleeved T-shirt. She had changed her black-and-silver hijab for another in plain navy blue. Liam wasn't normally fashion-conscious, leaving that to Aidan, but he thought the hijab was a bad look for her; it accentuated the roundness of her face, and by hiding her hair, it made people notice her pockmarked skin.

"We're so sorry about your mother," he said to her. A brief breeze swept through, chilling the water droplets on his skin, and he shivered.

"My mother was a martyr to the cause of Islamist unity," she said, though without much conviction.

As Farid led Leila to a table shaded by an umbrella whose stripes matched those on the chair cushions, Hakim appeared behind them with a pitcher of lemonade and a stack of plastic glasses on a broad tray. He poured a glass for Leila and hovered over her until she had begun to drink. Then he bowed slightly and returned to the house.

Liam and Aidan pulled up chairs next to James. "Have you heard anything about Burhan?" Liam asked.

"Still in custody," Farid said. "Louis is making inquiries about him. And Omar has his own network. His people will try to discover what has happened."

Leila stood up. "I want to go inside."

"Of course, my dear," Farid said, standing with her.

"By myself." She turned and walked back into the house, leaving Farid standing by the table.

"She's upset." James reached a hand out to Farid, who took it.

James stood up then and nodded toward Aidan and Liam. "We'll see you at dinner." Then they went inside.

Aidan turned to Liam. "Is there anything we can do?"

Liam picked up his cell phone from the table. "I'll see if Faisal knows anything." He dialed, and the call went immediately to voice mail once again. "Faisal. It's Liam. I'm trying to find out what happened to a woman in police custody named Khadija Mansoor. Can you call me as soon as possible?"

They went into the guesthouse. Liam went into the bedroom and made a few more calls while Aidan booted up the laptop and searched the online news services for information about Khadija. "There's nothing online," Aidan said when Liam finished his last call and returned to the living room.

"I'm sorry this hasn't turned out to be the vacation you wanted," he said, putting the phone down on the table.

"Oh, sweetheart." Aidan stood up, put his hand on Liam's arm, and leaned up to kiss him. "I don't care where we are or what we're doing, as long as we're together."

"Even if that means staying in Tunisia under a new regime?"

Aidan nodded. "All this uproar is scary. And sometimes I wonder if we can stay here if the Islamists come into power. But then I look at you, and I know that whatever happens, we'll make things work."

"We will." Liam leaned down and kissed Aidan again, and once more he marveled at how lucky he was to have found the perfect partner. Aidan just needed a little reassurance now and then.

They went into the main house and turned on the TV, watching live coverage of the demonstrations in Tunis and around the country. Police officers holding body shields kept back surging crowds. The mostly male group yelled and shook their fists while the TV commentators spoke about Ben Ali and his policies.

"It's scary," Aidan said. "I've never been in the middle of something like this before."

"It is a big change for my country," Farid said. "In the past, we have simply accepted what the politicians did. But now things will change, I am sure."

"When my father returns, you will see many changes," Leila said.

The announcer broke into the coverage with a news bulletin. President Ben Ali was gone, leaving behind a handpicked government to succeed him. Leila jumped up and down and cheered.

"Don't get so excited, Leila," James said. "This is just another government. I'm sure it will be no different from the rest."

Even as the word spread through the crowds of Ben Ali's departure, there was no easing of the tension in the streets of Tunis or other cities, and Liam and Aidan went back to the guesthouse unsure of what would happen next.

"How rigid do you think this new government will be?" Aidan asked as they got ready for bed.

"What do you mean?"

"Suppose the Islamists take over and they start cracking down. Rules against foreigners. Homosexuals. Tunisia could turn into another Saudi Arabia."

"That won't happen," Liam said, though he wasn't completely sure. He had spent many years in the Arab world, and he had seen leaders come and go. But there was a new sense of conservatism and xenophobia in the air, and he was worried about the future. There was always work for bodyguards in turbulent times—but was that the life he wanted to lead?

More important, was it the right life for Aidan? He had such a gentle, caring heart. He wouldn't be able to survive if Tunis became a dangerous place. But where else could they go? Liam had tried living back in the States, after he left the SEALs. He hadn't been able to adjust to the complacency and consumerism, the downright utter boredom of ordinary life.

His own father had longed for some other life, and Liam was sure that dissatisfaction with his life was partly the cause of his dad's alcoholism and rampant anger. If he gave up living a rough-and-tumble life to provide safety and security for Aidan, would he fall prey to the same problems?

Usually, he had no trouble falling asleep—but that night, he shifted restlessly in bed, trying not to wake Aidan but unable to drift off until the evening rain swept in, and Hayam squirmed up between them and buried her head under the covers.

* * *

When they woke the next morning, the news buzzed with the story of a young police officer who had been ordered to fire on civilians protesting in the beachside town of Ez Zahra, just outside

Tunis. He refused, crossed the street to join them, and then pointed his gun back at his fellow officers. The police backed away, and he was hailed as a hero. But the government was shaky, and protesters filled the streets.

James had hired a security company from Tunis, but they were unwilling to leave the city when there was so much unrest. Liam had done all he could do on his own, so he spent the early morning hours after breakfast restlessly walking the groves, looking for vulnerability, wearing a pair of khaki shorts and his favorite leather vest, cinched loosely over his chest. The air was crisp and dry, and the occasional breezes stung his cheeks.

He couldn't help thinking about Aidan as he walked. They had thought this place would be an oasis of peace amid the country's uproar, but instead it was beset with danger. If they weren't safe a few hours outside the city, where could they go? The news reports showed that unrest was growing all over the Arab world. What country would fall next?

The irregular ground was scattered with rocks and clumps of dry grass. He stopped in a patch of sun beside an ancient olive tree, its trunk twisting around on itself before branching out. He wondered how long that tree had stood there and who had planted it.

Generations of Farid's family had lived there, men struggling to make lives for their families. Aidan was his family, more than his mother, his sisters, his nieces and nephews. It was his responsibility to make sure Aidan could live safely and be happy. He just didn't know how to do that, and that failure frustrated him.

To avoid that problem, he focused on the groves. If he wanted to sabotage James and Farid's operation, what would he do? The pump had been the obvious target, and that was secure. The next was the cold-press operation.

He climbed back up to the house, dodging tree roots and the bones of a dead rodent. He found James up at the house, and the two of them walked down toward the river.

"Eventually, I want to build a modern facility down here," James said as they approached a square building made of the native stone, the irregularly sized blocks carefully mortared together. It was about the size of the small house he and Aidan shared back in Tunis, less than a thousand square feet.

The building was surrounded on three sides by ancient olive trees, their branches forming a shaded canopy. The narrow door was heavy oak, but there was no lock, only an iron ring. "We're going to have to find a way to secure this building," Liam said. "I can buy a lock in Tebourba and install it this afternoon."

James nodded and pushed the door open. Two older men were at work, one at an ancient-looking machine, the other working with a ladle at a barrel.

"We handpick the olives when they are at their best maturity, when the olive is half-green, half-dark. Then we crush them at a slow speed. The olive is a fruit, after all, and you get the best juice and the best flavor if you handle it gently," James said.

The room was dim and almost chilly, the only light coming from narrow slits in the stone. "It's very cool in here," Liam said. "Is the temperature important?"

"Absolutely. Keeping the olives cold preserves their antioxidant qualities. As I'm sure you know, that's something consumers are looking for these days."

Liam looked up at the rough-hewn wooden beams that framed the ceiling, about eight feet high. He could tell from the deep striations that they had come from the same kind of olive trees that populated the grove. He was struck by the need, out there far from the city, to make do with what you had—rock from the earth, lumber from the trees, mortar made of sand and water. Life was simpler out there, yet still as dangerous as any city.

"Someone could sabotage you by changing the temperature in here or in the machine." Liam walked over to a side wall and found a toehold in one of the irregular blocks. He kicked off his sandals and stepped onto the wall, using hand and toeholds to clamber up to where he could reach above the beams.

The roof was tin; between it and the beams were layers of dried grasses in bundles that served as insulation. Good tinder for a fire, he thought. He dropped back to the ground and wiped his hands on his cargo shorts. "We'll have to get you a fire extinguisher," he said to James.

James led Liam over to where the man was working slowly to remove the oil from the barrel. The aroma was pungent and reminded Liam of dipping bread in olive oil at an Italian restaurant. Then they walked back up to the house, carrying a cruet of fresh-pressed oil, which they used at lunch. He smiled at the way Aidan enjoyed the meal. Aidan's exuberance reminded him to stop and enjoy life, even when things weren't going perfectly. To appreciate the little things like fresh olive oil.

After they finished eating, he drove into Tebourba and bought a fire extinguisher and a heavy-duty lock. It was difficult to get it installed, between the heavy oak door and the stone wall, but he managed with a combination of drills supplied by James. By the time he finished, he was hot and tired, and he walked back up to the guesthouse, where he found Aidan once again in the pool.

"You know, there is work to be done around here," Liam grumbled.

"Tell me what to do. Right now, I'm keeping an eye on the house and on James, Farid, and Leila."

"From the pool?"

"Where else do you want me? Sitting in the house watching everything they do? You know as well as I do that we shouldn't interfere with the normal lives of the people we're guarding."

"You have an answer for everything, don't you?"

"Come on, Liam. Get in the pool. Relax."

Liam stood there uncertainly. His instincts told him there was more work to do—but Aidan had a point. He couldn't turn the Ferme Deux Hommes into an armed camp, especially when the only real threats so far could have been mischief. And this was supposed to be their vacation, after all. "I'll get a suit."

He returned to the pool a few minutes later and dove into the cool water. "Where's everyone else?" he asked when he surfaced.

"James is working in his office. Farid is down at the groves, watching the harvest. And Leila is holed up in her room, pouting."

"At least you're enjoying yourself." Liam went under the water again and then began swimming laps, using the combat sidestroke he had learned as a SEAL.

After he finished, he and Aidan relaxed on the lounge chairs around the pool, waiting for James or Farid to appear. "Did you ever hear back from Faisal?" Aidan asked.

Liam shook his head. "He must be up to his ass in alligators."

"Do they have alligators in Tunisia?"

"You know what I mean."

"I know." Aidan looked at him and grinned, and just like that, Liam felt that bubble of uncertainty brewing inside him pop open, and he took a deep breath and smiled. "You never know about alligators." He opened his hand wide and then snapped it closed around a chunk of Aidan's thigh, making a growling sound as he did.

As the sun dropped behind the house's roofline, the air cooled. The pale blue sky began to darken, and an owl hooted in the distance. The olive trees rustled their leaves in a smooth susurrus, and though the area around them appeared calm and pastoral, Liam knew it was full of dangers and predators.

"I'm ready to go in," Aidan said. He stood up, and Liam followed him into the guesthouse, where they showered and dressed. At six, Hakim knocked on the door and announced that dinner was ready.

As they crossed the pool deck toward the main house, Liam

noticed that the sun had set and stars had begun to appear in the night sky. With so little ground light out there in the country, the Milky Way glowed like an invitation to distant worlds.

As he'd been trained in the SEALs, he first sighted alpha Centauri and beta Centauri, two bright stars just above the horizon. They pointed toward the kite-shaped Crux, the Southern Cross, and from there he could make out Centaurus. He marveled at the inventiveness of ancient man and the way he had attempted to understand and tame the world around him.

They passed Leila, sitting on the living room sofa, reading. "Coming to dinner?" Aidan asked her.

"I'm reading the Koran," she said.

"Even Mohammed had to eat," Aidan said.

She looked up at him and scowled. "I will come when I finish this Hadith."

They walked into the dining room, where James and Farid were already sitting at the table. "Leila is charming as ever," Aidan said.

Farid shook his head. "I try to talk to her, and she refuses. All she wants to do is read the Koran. I tell you, I have wanted to spend more time with my niece since she was born. Now I will be glad when I can return her to her father."

Leila missed the salad course, not joining until Hakim served a casserole of lamb and root vegetables. The adults drank a French red wine with their meal; Leila refused soda, settling for sparkling water. She was antsy to return to her book, but Farid insisted that she join them in the living room after dinner to watch the TV news.

The reports focused on the continuing protests around the country. The government Ben Ali had left in place had collapsed, and a new one was forming, but there was little optimism in the streets of Tunis.

"I'm worried, Liam," Aidan said when they were back in the guesthouse. "We're safe out here for now—but what happens when we go back to Tunis? Getting caught in that demonstration freaked me out. What if Tunisia is torn up for months? Or years?"

"I don't know what to say, Aidan." Liam pulled his shirt over his head and tossed it on the chair in the corner. "As long as we keep our heads down, we should be fine no matter what goes on around us."

"Easy for you to say. You're a soldier. You've been in battle. I'm just an English teacher."

"Oh, really? The other day you were bragging about how you were a bodyguard too. You change your tune from day to day."

He walked across the bedroom and pulled Aidan into his arms. "I will protect you, sweetheart. You know that."

Aidan nestled his head against Liam's shoulder. "I know."

Liam stood there with Aidan next to him, and he knew that he'd do anything, go anywhere, sacrifice what he had, to protect Aidan and the life they had together.

He pulled back from Aidan. "Your grandparents left Russia when they had to, didn't they?"

Aidan nodded.

"And my family left Ireland and England and Germany and wherever else for the United States. We're lucky—we're a lot more portable than they were back then. We can get on a plane and go back to the States, or anywhere else we want. Between us we speak a couple of languages, and we have a wide range of skills. I have a lot of contacts from my days as a SEAL. If we have to leave Tunisia, we will."

"You'd do that?" Aidan asked.

"If we can't live safely and comfortably in this country, we'll find one where we can."

Aidan hugged him again, then leaned up and kissed his cheek. "As long as we're together," he said.

7 – Dinner in La Manouba

Aidan was reassured by Liam's conviction that they would be fine wherever they went, but he couldn't help worrying, and his dreams were confused and uncertain. He and Liam were on a ship crowded with refugees, and he didn't know where they were going. There were a lot of elderly people around, dressed in the kind of clothing Aidan had seen in sepia-toned photos of his grandparents and great-grandparents.

Then suddenly they were in the desert again, as they'd been on their first adventure together. The old Jews were on camels, and Liam, holding a rifle, led the train. They crossed a rise and were engulfed in a demonstration like the one he'd been caught in outside the cathedral.

When he woke, he was tired and hungry, and Liam had already left the guesthouse. After a quick shower, he dressed and walked over to the house, where he found Hakim preparing waffles as Leila sat at the counter watching him. They were speaking Arabic but stopped abruptly as Aidan walked in.

"Please to try and convince Miss Leila to eat a waffle," Hakim said to Aidan. "She has not seen such food before."

"My mom used to make waffles for us on Sunday mornings," Aidan said. "I had to go to Sunday school, and it was the only way she could get me to wake up. She put chocolate chips in them because she knew I would eat anything sweet."

"You went to school on Sundays in the United States?" Leila asked.

Out of the corner of his eye, Aidan saw Hakim turn to the cabinet and pull out a bag of chocolate chips. "Religious school," Aidan said. "At the synagogue. We read stories from the Bible, sang songs, and played games. Do you have something like that here?"

"When I was little, I went to an Islamic kindergarten," Leila said. "It sounds like that, only we studied the Koran."

Hakim poured batter into the waffle iron, and Aidan inhaled the smell of eggs and chocolate. "The Bible and the Koran have a lot in common, don't they?" Aidan asked. "I mean, doesn't the Koran include a lot of the same stories as the Bible? Cain and Abel, the story of Abraham, Noah and the flood?"

"Yes," Leila said. "But the way of the Koran is the true one."

Aidan nodded. Hakim opened the waffle iron and lifted the golden-brown waffle onto a plate. "Will you try, please?" he asked Aidan.

"Can you split it in two? Maybe Leila will try one half, and I'll try the other."

Hakim split the waffle and passed the two plates to them. "I like to put some butter on mine," Aidan said, helping himself as Leila stared at the plate before her.

Aidan cut a piece of his with a fork, then ate it. "Wow, that's good," he said to Hakim. "Even better than my mother's."

It was true; his mother hadn't been the best cook, but she had tried. Hakim's waffle was light and fluffy with an underlying taste of eggs, butter, and cinnamon, complemented by the gooey richness of the chocolate chips.

Leila finally took a bite of her waffle as Aidan ate. She looked up. "It is good."

"Allah be praised." Hakim began making more waffles.

Within a few minutes James, Farid, and Liam joined them in the kitchen, sitting around the oak table. When breakfast was over, James and Farid left to check the groves, Leila went back to her room to read, and Aidan followed Liam back to the guesthouse. "What's on our agenda today?" he asked Liam.

"I don't know. I can't install the security system myself—we have to wait for the company to come from Tunis. And they won't be able to get out here while there's so much going on. All we can do is hang around and be watchful."

Hanging around was not something Liam did well, Aidan thought.

Liam began pacing the living room of the guesthouse, which was tough because there was so little room. Aidan was relieved when there was an abrupt knock on the door, and Liam stopped pacing to open it.

"There has been another act of sabotage," James said. "Someone has destroyed one of our most productive trees."

Aidan and Liam walked back down to the grove with James. The sun was already high in the sky, and it was hot, though very dry. The slight breeze wicked away any sweat before it could have a cooling effect.

As they approached, Aidan saw the denuded trunk surrounded by branches on the ground. It was almost painful to see such a beautiful old tree destroyed—not to mention the waste of all the unripe fruit on the branches.

Farid joined them. "Who would do such a thing?" he asked, shaking his head. "This tree is hundreds of years old."

Liam knelt down to examine a branch. "Looks like a hacksaw," he said. "Same kind that was used to destroy the pump, probably."

"This is unacceptable," Farid said, his voice high. "These trees have been entrusted to my family for generations. I cannot let them be destroyed."

"I know," James said, putting his arm around Farid's shoulder. "It's a terrible thing. But what can we do?"

Farid turned to Liam and Aidan. "You must do something. We cannot have any more trees destroyed."

"You could hire men to watch the groves at night," Liam suggested. "If you can find me two men for each grove, I can train them today, and they can work tonight. It won't be much, but it could discourage more of this kind of damage."

James and Farid strode back to the house to make calls, and Aidan and Liam followed. "We'll need to get them supplies," Liam said. "I'll make a list. You should be able to buy everything we need in Tebourba."

The rest of the day passed in a haze of activity. Liam walked around the groves and talked to the workmen while he waited for the watchmen to arrive for training. Aidan drove the Jeep down to a general store in Tebourba with a shopping list from Liam.

Some of the Arabic words were unfamiliar, and he struggled to pronounce them. He was forced to pantomime certain actions, which was very amusing to the shopkeeper and other customers. But he tried to roll with their laughter rather than resent it, and eventually, a young boy who had studied some English in school became his unofficial translator. Together, they assembled a clutch of heavy-duty flashlights, miner's headlamps, walkie-talkies, and batteries. The boy helped him carry everything out to the Jeep, and Aidan tipped him a few dirhams, which the boy accepted with great delight.

He drove the long, dusty road out of Tebourba with the cool breeze in his face. Back at the Ferme Deux Hommes, he brought all the gear down to the grove and helped Liam train the night security. Liam had a natural authority that the men responded to, and soon they were clear on their responsibilities.

When Liam was confident, he sent them home to sleep, and he and Aidan went up to the house, where they found Farid and James in the pool. Farid was still upset about the desecration of the olive tree.

"The watchmen know what they're supposed to do," Liam said.

"Good," James said. "Come, join us. Help me distract my partner."

They put on their swimsuits and returned to the pool. Though the air was cool, the sun was bright and the shimmering blue water was welcoming. They waded in from the shallow end, and Liam began swimming laps. Aidan walked over to James and Farid.

"How is Leila?" Aidan asked.

"She doesn't speak," Farid said. "She sits and reads her Koran or plays with your little dog. She is a very confused little girl; on the one hand, she believes in every Hadith about homosexuals—yet she ignores those in which Muhammad commanded that dogs be killed."

"We have to give her time to adjust," James said. "There are too many terrible things happening. Let her be on her own, if that's what she wants. When she needs us, she'll come to us." He smiled. "And you never know, maybe if she decides she likes dogs, homosexuals will be next."

Aidan doubted that would be the case.

After Liam had finished a dozen laps, he surfaced next to them. "Either your workmen don't know anything, or they're not saying." He leaned back against the wall of the pool, letting his legs rise.

Aidan was sorry that James and Farid were there; he would have liked to have gotten himself between Liam's legs and… Well, that would have to wait until evening.

"I told you, our workmen are loyal," James said. "Whoever is sabotaging us is someone from the outside."

Liam went under water and began swimming again.

Liam's cell rang, and Aidan hopped out of the pool to answer it. When Liam surfaced, Aidan handed it to him, along with a towel. "It's Faisal."

Liam climbed out of the pool and turned away. After a hushed conversation, he turned back to Aidan. "Faisal can't get out of Tunis, but he wants to meet us at six, at a restaurant called El Bar across from the train station in La Manouba."

Aidan looked at his watch. It was four o'clock; if they left quickly, they could make the drive with time to spare. They explained where they were going to James and Farid, then hurried into the guesthouse to shower and change into khaki slacks and loose-fitting, short-sleeved shirts that would cover the guns at their hips.

"You think it's necessary for us to go in armed?" Aidan asked.

"I have no idea what kind of trouble we might run into on the road to La Manouba, or in town itself, so I think it's best to be prepared. You have a problem with that?"

Aidan held his hands up in front of him. "No problem."

The road toward Jedeida, where they would pick up the P7 toward Tunis, was nearly deserted, and that made Aidan uneasy. It was lined with cultivated rectangles in alternate shades of green and brown, with only an occasional man with a tractor in a field.

Aidan had given up his old life with barely a backward glance, swept up in his love for Liam and the desire for a new adventure. But now, over a year later, was he losing his nerve? Was love enough to keep him in this wild new world? In his darker moments, he feared that he would never be a very good bodyguard, and that his lack of musculature or combat training would lead him—or some innocent client—into danger. That Liam would realize one day that Aidan could never be his full partner and would kick him to the curb, just the way Blake had.

He pushed those doubts aside and focused on the highway. Once they passed Jedeida, they were surrounded by the usual run of commercial traffic. This part of Tunisia was more fertile than the southern desert, and as they got closer to the capital, the small towns were closer together, clusters of one- and two-story buildings, warehouses and gas stations, and all the commercial detritus of modern civilization.

As they approached La Manouba, they saw police cars but no demonstrations. They parked the Jeep a block from the train station and reached the restaurant just before Faisal arrived.

He was a high-ranking officer in the Tunis police, with the latitude to choose the cases he worked. Faisal was in his mid-forties, perhaps ten years older than Liam, and he had worked his way up through the police hierarchy. His tan face was unlined, his black hair lush. There were dark circles under his eyes, his normally dark skin looked sallow, and his uniform was wrinkled. "Tough day?" Liam asked.

"Very bad. I have never seen Tunis so disrupted. You are wise to stay in the country."

"Not wise, just lucky."

The three of them sat down at a table by the streaked window and ordered. When the waiter was gone, Faisal said, "So. You have an interest in Khadija Mansoor."

"We were hired to bring her daughter out of Tunis, to her uncle's in Tebourba." Liam explained how they had been introduced to James and Farid at dinner and initially turned down the job offer.

"Louis Fleck," Faisal said, nodding. "I am not surprised he is involved here."

"But why?" Aidan asked. "What does the United States embassy have to do with Khadija?"

"I am well aware of Fleck's position at the embassy. He keeps tabs on the important opposition groups. One of those is the Muslim Leadership. With Omar Mansoor in France, his wife is the public face of the organization. Her death is a very sensitive one."

"How did she die?" Liam asked.

"She was in custody at the Mornaguia Prison, in a holding cell with a dozen other women. When her identity was verified, she was transported to a single cell." He opened a pocket notebook. "Sometime between midnight and six a.m. she was killed by a homemade knife."

The waiter brought their platters, and Liam waited until he was gone to ask, "A prison guard?"

"I hope not," Faisal said. "That would be very dangerous for the police and the government—whoever is in charge." He picked at a piece of lint on his uniform shirt, then smoothed the creases along his shoulder. "The choice of weapon makes it look like another inmate was the murderer. And the security in the women's wing is lax; sometimes the women trade sexual favors with the guards for freedom of movement. It's possible another woman lured Mansoor to the bars of her cell and then stabbed her."

"Do you think her daughter is in danger?" Aidan asked.

"In a word, yes. With Khadija dead and Omar in France, the Muslim Leadership could choose to make the girl the group's figurehead. Or someone could use her for leverage with her father.

You must watch her carefully."

"I'll call James and tell him to keep a close eye until we get back," Liam said. "What about Khadija's brother—Burhan?"

"He is in protective custody right now. But as we have seen, that was not enough to protect Khadija."

"We'll have to do a better job with Leila," Aidan said. The girl was a pill, but Aidan thought that was mostly the result of indoctrination, and most recently, the loss of her mother.

As they drove back to Tebourba in darkness, the road ahead lit only by their headlights and the spangle of stars above, Aidan thought back to his own mother's death, some five years before. She had concealed the seriousness of her illness from Aidan for a long time. By the time she told him she had been diagnosed with pancreatic cancer, she had only a few months left to live.

Aidan had commuted back and forth from Philadelphia to Trenton several times a week, driving her to doctors, making sure there was food in her house and that she ate what she could. Blake had been cranky about Aidan's frequent absences, but there was little he could say.

Blake had a morbid fear of funeral homes and cemeteries. He insisted that he had mild psychic powers and that the spirits of the dead bothered him. Aidan accepted the fact that Blake wouldn't come to the funeral or the cemetery. *"I don't know anything about that Jewish mumbo jumbo anyway,"* Blake had said. *"I'd just be in the way."*

Liam would never have said something like that, Aidan thought. Liam approached adversity head-on, believing the only way to get through trouble was to face it. And he had a deep well of compassion; Aidan could see that in everything Liam did. He lived lightly on the earth, doing his best not to hold in anger, to destroy or resent. It was a characteristic Aidan responded to at his deepest levels.

He turned to look at Liam's profile as his partner drove. Liam's face was handsome, yet lived-in; there were faint lines beside his nose, and his chin was stubbled with shadow. Aidan felt an almost overwhelming surge of love for Liam as a truck passed them on its way toward the city, its headlights washing over them.

Liam felt his gaze and turned to him. "What?"

Aidan couldn't find the words to describe how strong his love for Liam was and how much he appreciated this chance at a new life in a new place. So all he did was shrug and say, "Nothing."

When they reached the Ferme Deux Hommes, Aidan was still feeling sentimental, and he stopped to stare at the sky. He was struck by how many stars he could see overhead. He stood there a moment, looking up, and Liam came around the side of the Jeep to stand beside him.

"Up there? That cross-shaped constellation? That's Cygnus, the Swan, with Deneb shining brightly at its tail," Liam said, pointing. "And that cluster of four stars? That's Crux, the Southern Cross. Because you can't see it from the Northern Hemisphere, there's no mythology associated with it. But navigators use it to point south."

He took Aidan's hand and squeezed. "There's a place for us somewhere under those stars. "Don't you worry about that."

Aidan smiled. Once again, Liam saw into his soul and knew just what worried him. They walked hand in hand up to the house, where they found James and Farid in the living room. In broad strokes, Liam sketched out what Faisal had told them. He left out Louis Fleck's role in case James and Farid didn't know that Louis was CIA.

"This is very bad," Farid said when Liam was finished. "Leila is just a girl. And how can we protect her here, when we cannot even keep our machinery safe?"

"That's what we're here for," Liam said. "Farid, you should talk to your brother about what he wants us to do with Leila, and then we'll have to sit down with her. She's willful, and he's the only person she listens to. Whatever we decide has to come from him." He looked at Farid. "And it's up to you to convince him that her safety is important—even more than his politics."

8 – Rue Mongi Slim

Aidan looked at Leila over more waffles during breakfast the next morning. From the part of her face visible under her wraparound scarf, he couldn't tell why she was scowling. Was it her mother's death? Her father's exile? The fact that she was stuck out in the countryside with four gay men she hardly knew?

He could only imagine how he'd feel at thirteen if his world had been turned upside down. At Leila's age, he had been an ordinary teenager, concerned with schoolwork, friends, and imagined slights at the bus dock. He had completed his bar mitzvah and been able to stop attending Hebrew school two afternoons a week, though he continued in religious school on Saturday mornings for the rest of the year.

His parents were happily if tumultuously married. His part of suburban New Jersey was quiet to the point of dullness—no one protesting in the streets or throwing stones at the police. His father's political activism stopped at being the president of the neighborhood association. His mother was a businesswoman who had never seen the inside of a jail cell.

Like Leila, he was an only child, but he fell right in the middle of a broad range of first and second cousins. At every family event, he was surrounded by kids who shared his blood. Leila had no one now beyond her father and her uncles. That must be the hardest of all, he thought; no one to commiserate with, to play with, to argue with.

He'd had some progress in breaking through her shell on Sunday morning, bonding over the chocolate-chip waffles, but as soon as the meal was over, she had retreated to her room, just as she did that Monday morning when she finished eating, picking up Hayam from a sunny spot on the tile floor and carrying her away.

When she was gone, the four adults moved to the living room. "I spoke with my brother last night," Farid said. "Omar would like Leila to come to him in Marseille, at least for now. He hopes to return to Tunisia someday. Or perhaps when Burhan is released, Leila can live with him and his mother."

"I think sending Leila to Marseille is a good idea," Liam said.

Farid nodded. "Omar is very worried about Leila's safety. If your friend in the police is correct and someone truly wishes to harm the Muslim Leadership, then it would not be a good idea for Leila to travel to Marseille alone."

He paused. "When I mentioned to my brother that we had a pair of trained bodyguards here with us, he was most relieved. He would like you to escort Leila to him in Marseille."

"How soon does he want Leila there?" Liam asked. "Because we still have some work to do here for you."

"Could one of you take her, and the other stay here?" James asked. "I keep hoping that the security company will show up and get to work, and I need someone who knows what should be done to supervise them."

Liam looked at Aidan. "Suppose I stayed here, and you flew to Marseille with Leila and delivered her to her father?"

Aidan had done a couple of jobs on his own before, chaperoning women around Tunis. But he'd always had Liam close, had always been able to see him at night and ask his advice. It was a big step to take a client out of the country on his own.

"I'm not sure. What do you think?"

"You can handle it. You'll fly over, drop her off, and be back here by dinner."

Aidan wasn't sure if that was an acknowledgement of his abilities or merely diminishing the job to one that even Aidan could manage. "What does Leila think?"

"I haven't told her yet," Farid said.

Liam sat back against the sofa. "Then I think it's time you did."

Farid stood up. "I'll get her."

Aidan said, "I can take Leila to Marseille, but only if she's willing to go. I can't manage keeping her under control and watching for trouble at the same time. I'm worried about her modesty, though. Does she have a female relative who could go with us?"

James shook his head. "Burhan is not married, and his mother is too old and in poor health. Perhaps some cousins. But with the unrest in Tunis, I'm not sure any of them could be persuaded to travel."

Farid and Leila returned, with Hayam trailing behind, and the girl sat down on one of the sofas by herself. Her headscarf had been pulled down low over her forehead, and Aidan had the sense that she was trying to hide behind it.

Liam explained to Leila what he had learned from Faisal. "My friend is worried about you," he said gently. "We don't know why your mother was killed. But if it was a strike against your father and his political group, it could mean that you're in danger too."

Leila sat on the sofa, her arms crossed over her copy of the Koran. Hayam jumped up on the sofa next to her, but she didn't respond. Aidan felt sorry for Leila—but she was no longer just an annoying girl, she was a client, and she needed to be protected. "Would you like to go to your father in Marseille?" he asked.

"If it is what my father wants," she said, looking down.

Aidan stood up. "I'll get my laptop and check on flights." He returned with the computer, and while they waited for it to boot up, he asked Farid, "Does Omar live in Marseille itself, or somewhere nearby?"

"I will have to check. I believe he lives in the city, but we have not discussed it."

Aidan checked an online travel site. "Good news. There are direct flights on Air France from Tunis to Marseille. There's one tomorrow morning at eight ten, but I think that's too early. It would mean leaving Tebourba before sunrise."

"I don't think Leila would like that," James said. He smiled, but Leila would not look at him.

"We could get a flight this evening at five forty, but that arrives in Marseille at eight fifteen tonight," Aidan said. "That's too late. We want Leila to be settled with her father before dark. Oh, there's one tomorrow just after noon. That gets into Marseille at two forty in the afternoon. Just right. Kind of like Goldilocks and the three flights."

Farid and Leila looked baffled, and Aidan didn't bother to explain. "Leila, will you need to go back to your mother's apartment in Tunis and pack some more before we can leave?" he asked.

"How long will I be gone?"

"We don't know that now," Aidan said. "So perhaps you should take anything with you that matters to you."

She nodded.

"Why don't you pull up the news from Tunis," Liam said. "Let's see if we can get Leila into the city today to do her packing."

Liam made a couple of phone calls while Aidan checked the Internet. The second provisional government had crumbled, and there were random gun battles between the military and protesters around the city. It appeared, however, that the complexion of the crowd in the streets had changed. Whereas the protesters demanding Ben Ali's resignation had included many from Tunisia's more affluent classes, those who followed included a higher percentage of trade unionists and supporters of outlawed Islamist parties like the Muslim Leadership.

"We'll consider this a sort of commando raid," Liam said. "We'll drive in to the Rue Mongi Slim, get Leila's stuff, and get out. We'll come back here to stay overnight, and then in the morning, we'll head back to the airport."

Aidan closed the laptop, and they prepared to leave. "Do you want one of us to come with you?" Farid asked.

Liam shook his head. "We can manage. And more people with us is just more people we have to protect."

Farid looked to Aidan like he didn't like that idea, but that was tough. Leila was a thirteen-year-old girl; she would be most comfortable with her own clothes and her own things around her. Yes, they could put her on the plane with what she had with her, but the risks that they would run into trouble seemed slight compared to the benefits.

Aidan drove, with Liam literally riding shotgun—or at least handgun. He sat in the front passenger seat with his semiautomatic in his lap, his gaze constantly searching the road and the area around them.

Sometimes he couldn't get inside Liam's head, Aidan thought as he drove. His partner was the strong, silent type, and there were times when Aidan could use less silence and more communication. He was secure in Liam's love—but his respect was something else altogether. Sometimes, in the middle of an operation, Liam treated him like an ornament—pretty but fragile and useless except for decoration. Then there were other times like the night before, when Liam was able to look deep into Aidan's heart. And occasions in the field, when Liam respected Aidan's skills—his ability to talk to people, to research, to keep his head in a crisis.

Aidan knew he'd never be as strong, as skillful, or as resourceful as Liam. His partner had physical strength and years of SEAL training and conditioning behind him. But sometimes that held Liam back. He wasn't as able to think outside the box as Aidan was, because his brain was too full of options and complications. With less training, Aidan could come up with solutions that were so off-the-wall—yet workable—that they would never have occurred to Liam.

He kept his eyes on the road as he drove, but his mind was on Liam. His partner was more sexually adventurous; he knew that if he offered Liam the chance for a threesome, for example, Liam would probably accept. Was he making a mistake in leaving Liam alone with two gay men who seemed equally receptive? He had noticed James ogling Liam's physique, and he'd bet that his and Farid's pillow talk involved speculation about Liam's hidden assets.

But Liam knew how Aidan felt about fidelity. Aidan was strictly a one-man kind of guy, and the thought of sharing Liam made him angry rather than horny. One of his faults, he knew, was this tendency to overanalyze, to create drama and complications where there was none. He took a deep breath as they exited the Route Nationale 7 in Tunis, and focused on navigating the local roads to get to the Rue Mongi Slim. The usual angry buzz of scooters, panel trucks, and luxury sedans kept him on alert.

To Aidan's eye, there was nothing unusual in Leila's neighborhood. A young mother carried a baby in a sling around her neck, and an old woman tugged a broken cart filled with vegetables. The aroma of roasting lamb and the spicy, smoky scent of *harissa* hung in the air. Someone played tinny Arabic music through a window. A group of teenage boys loitered at the edge of an empty lot smoking cigarettes, a soccer ball at their feet.

Aidan found a parking spot a block from Leila's apartment, and they walked there, keeping Leila between them. A middle-aged woman in a business suit with shoulder pads that would have been fashionable in New York ten years before passed them, looking curiously at Leila in her jeans and silver head scarf.

The front door of the building was still broken, and the small, tiled lobby smelled of burned rice and cumin. Aidan noticed dustballs in the corners he had missed the last time they were there, cracks in the stone stairs, and water stains along the walls. They climbed to the apartment Leila had shared with her mother and her uncle. "Can I help you pack?" Aidan asked once they were inside.

"I will manage," Leila said.

"Probably afraid you'll sneak a peek at her undies," Liam whispered once Leila had gone into her room.

"As if," Aidan said. "The last girl whose undies I cared about was Michelle Gotowski, and I was more interested in how her bra held up her boobs than in the boobs themselves. I think we were both fifteen then."

"That's my Aidan." Liam began looking around the living room, picking up papers, leafing through books.

"What are you looking for?" Aidan asked.

"Not sure. But it seems like it would be a waste not to snoop while we can."

Aidan stood near the door to Leila's room, ready to alert Liam when she was finished packing. He was sure that she wouldn't appreciate anyone looking through her family's belongings. He noticed Liam pocket a jump drive, and that made him wonder if there was a computer anywhere in the apartment. He didn't see one in the living room.

"Liam," he whispered. He beckoned his partner over. "Why don't you check the other bedrooms while Leila's finishing. See if there's a computer."

"That was my next move," Liam said.

While he waited, Aidan opened the refrigerator. There wasn't much food there, just some expired yogurt and a couple of bottles of water. What did the family eat? Did Khadija make dinner for them every night, or was she too busy with political agitation?

"What are you doing?" Leila asked, appearing behind him.

"Looking for something to drink," Aidan said, pulling out one of the bottles of water. "You want one?"

"Those bottles belong to my family."

"May I have one?" he asked. "It's pretty hot out."

Leila waffled. Aidan knew that hospitality was important in Islam; many Muslim Tunisians believed that sustenance was a right rather than a gift. He was pretty sure that the story of Abraham presenting food and drink to the angels, who would later announce that Sarah would have a child, was in the Koran as well. But she was such a strange and willful girl, he wouldn't put it past her to refuse.

"Yes, please," she said finally. "Anybody who believes in Allah and the Last Day should serve his neighbor generously."

"Thank you." Aidan held a bottle out to her, and she took it, and they both drank. There was something sweet in that shared gesture, he thought, and hoped it meant that Leila was continuing to warm up to him.

"My suitcase is very heavy," she said when she stopped drinking.

"Do you think you could carry it for me?"

"Certainly." She led him into her room, and he noticed that the closet was empty and so were the two drawers of the bureau. Did she have so little, he wondered? Or had she just jammed everything she owned into the case?

The suitcase had to weigh over fifty pounds, and it was old and worn. No wheels to help transport it. He lifted it by the handle and carried it out to the living room, where Liam was waiting for them.

"Ready to go?" Liam asked.

"You carry the suitcase," Aidan said. "I'll take point."

Liam looked at him, but then hefted the case. "Wimp," he said, but he picked it up easily and walked to the door.

Leila paused for a moment as she was ready to close the door behind her. "You'll come back here," Aidan said quietly. "And you'll see your father soon, and your uncle Burhan. And until then, Liam and I will take care of you."

"I am not worried," she said tartly. "I was just trying to make sure I had not forgotten anything."

Whatever, Aidan thought. "Then let's go."

He heard the rumble of the crowd as they walked down the stairs. It was a low sound of chanting and rock throwing that got progressively louder. A door on the first floor slammed shut as they passed, and Aidan heard windows creaking and latching.

The air crackled with static electricity. "Can we make it to the Jeep?" Aidan asked Liam as they got to the ground floor. Leila was between him and Liam, and Aidan longed to be the one next to his partner, a place he had always found safe.

Liam peered out the front door. "There's a small crowd marching this way, but they're still a block away. Can you run, Leila?"

She looked frightened. "Yes," she said in a small voice.

"Then let's go." Liam pushed the door open and grabbed her suitcase, holding it in front of him with both hands. Then he took off at a run down the street, dodging an elderly woman in a long dress and a hijab who was hurrying herself.

Aidan looked left and saw a group of young men with posters approaching, with police in riot gear and Plexiglas shields on either side. The men yelled angrily in Arabic, and they hefted stones in threatening gestures, occasionally letting one off at a police shield. The sun had hidden behind a screen of clouds, and the air felt heavy.

"Take my hand," Aidan said, reaching for Leila.

"I cannot."

"I'm not arguing with you." He grabbed her hand and began to run after Liam. Reluctantly, Leila came along with him. A rock hit a storefront just in front of them, and the glass shattered. Leila gasped and began to run in earnest.

Aidan pulled the key fob for the Jeep from his pocket as he ran, beeping it open. Liam reached the Jeep first and opened the back gate, heaving Leila's suitcase inside. Then he opened the passenger door and pushed the seat forward so that Leila could jump in.

By the time Liam was in his seat, swinging the door closed, Aidan had the engine started and had pulled out into the street.

A couple of the protesters at the head of the demonstration had identified them as non-Arabs and began chasing them and shouting. A rock bounced off the Jeep's back gate.

Aidan gunned the motor, fishtailed a bit, then took off down the Rue Mongi Slim. The demonstrators were coming from the direction of the city, so Aidan couldn't take the quickest way back to the Route Nationale 7. Instead, he followed the road down past the sports grounds on the left, where there were already men and women gathering.

He turned left on the Boulevard du 7 Novembre 1987, circling past the open fields, concentrating fiercely on the road and the surroundings. Young men stood in small clusters, waiting for the demonstration to catch up, and shop owners were rapidly shutting their metal gates. The air smelled of gunpowder and automobile exhaust.

Liam had his gun out again, his gaze scanning from right to left and back again. Leila cowered in the backseat, her hands on the ends of her head scarf.

A police car rushed past them, sirens blaring and lights flashing, and once it passed, Aidan saw the entrance ramp for the highway, and he accelerated onto it. He let out a breath he didn't realize he had been holding.

"We're not out of trouble yet," Liam said. "Stay focused."

Aidan looked over at him and nodded slightly to the back of the Jeep. Liam took the hint and turned back to Leila. "Are you all right back there?"

In the rearview mirror, Aidan saw Leila nod, though she didn't say anything.

The traffic leaving the city was heavy, and every time Aidan found a gap he could accelerate through, he ended up behind another line of slow-moving vehicles. But at least they kept moving.

A crowd milled around the Hippodrome de Ksar Said, though the highway was far enough away that they didn't feel any danger. The day was still overcast, but there was no hint of rain. They passed too quickly for Aidan to be able to read any of the Arabic script on the signs they held, but he was sure the messages were angry.

A shaft of sunlight pierced the sky ahead of them, glinting off the car in front. "Jacob's ladder," he said to Liam, pointing.

"What?"

"Those beams of light shining through low clouds. They're called Jacob's ladder, after the Bible story."

"Focus on driving, Aidan."

Aidan pursed his lips but didn't say anything. They passed the train station in La Manouba and the café where they had met Faisal, and everywhere Aidan looked, he saw young men, and a few women, either protesting or waiting for something to happen.

There were more crowds outside the Palais de Justice, standing before the spike-topped wrought-iron gates with signs written in Arabic. Past the neighborhood of Cite des Oranges, the road opened, with farms and fields on each side, and Aidan felt a tightness in his chest become looser. He was confident they had left the demonstrations behind. At least until they had to return to the city, and the airport, the next day.

9 – Scared is Good

They reached Tebourba late in the afternoon. "You think we could go in for a swim?" Aidan asked Liam as they pulled into the driveway of the Ferme Deux Hommes. "I could use some relaxation."

"Let's get Leila situated first."

"I would like to go to my room," Leila said. She smiled as Hayam came rushing out to greet her, and Liam carried her suitcase for her once again, the dog following.

Aidan walked into the office to find Farid and James looking over plans. "The security company hopes to come out tomorrow," James said.

Aidan explained about their narrow escape, and Farid left immediately to find Leila. Liam came to the office, and then the two of them walked back to the guesthouse. "Tough day," Liam said. "But you were a champ. Great driving."

The praise created a warm spot in his chest. "Thanks. I was scared when that rock hit the Jeep."

"Scared is good," Liam said. "Adrenaline is good. The day we stop being scared is the day we get into trouble."

Liam swam his laps again, but Aidan relaxed in the pool, trying to empty his mind of danger, protesters, and the uncertainty of leaving the next day to deliver Leila to her father in Marseille. The logical thing would have been to force Leila to stay in Tebourba until the property was secure. Then Aidan and Liam could take her to Marseille together. Or Aidan could have gone home to Tunis while Liam made the delivery.

He wasn't sure how Liam felt about him going—was it just a business decision? Or was he getting tired of having Aidan around? Liam seemed to take their relationship for granted sometimes. He assumed that Aidan would take care of certain things, like the shopping and meals. That Aidan would always be there when needed but stay quietly in the background when not.

Aidan continued to brood as the sun gradually sank down on the western horizon, illuminating the sky with shards of red and orange, and a restless breeze swayed the two palm trees that stood sentinel next to the guesthouse.

Dinner was quiet and somber. Leila ate her couscous quietly and without argument, with Hayam curled protectively around the leg of her chair. When they were done eating, they watched the TV news together once more. There was no specific mention of a protest in the Rue Mongi Slim, but there were small uprisings all over the city.

After the report, Liam stretched and said, "I think we'll call it an early night. Aidan has a big day tomorrow."

Aidan looked over at him. He was expecting that they'd all spend some time together, talking perhaps of the next day's trip, but he trusted Liam's instincts. They were both quiet until they reached the guesthouse.

"Time to fire up the laptop," Liam said. "Let's see what's on this jump drive I found."

"You don't want to tell James and Farid about it?"

"Nothing to tell till we know what's on there."

Neither Liam nor Aidan was that proficient in written Arabic. Liam was better; he could figure out that one file was a list of supporters of the Muslim Brotherhood. The rest of the drive, however, was a mystery.

"I'm going to send this to Faisal. Maybe it can help him figure out who had a motive to kill Khadija," Liam said.

"You're sure that's a good idea?"

Liam looked at him. "Why not?"

"Suppose it was someone in the government. Faisal might suppress the evidence."

"I trust Faisal."

Aidan liked Faisal, and he had proved himself trustworthy in the past. But this was the Arab world, and loyalties shifted like the sand of the Sahara. "I think we should send the file to Louis Fleck."

"Fine. We'll send it to both, if that makes you happy."

Liam sent separate messages to both Faisal and Louis. Then he pushed the laptop back to Aidan. "I want to take a walk through the groves. See the watchmen and make sure they're doing a good job. Come with me?"

"Sure." Aidan shut down the laptop while Liam found them a couple of high-powered flashlights. They didn't turn the lights on at first; there was enough moonlight as they walked down the slope toward the river and the groves.

Aidan was always surprised at how many stars he could see

whenever he was away from the lights of the city. The heavens were a canvas of brilliant points of light; he could make out a few constellations he recognized, and the swirl of the Milky Way. "It's beautiful out here, isn't it?" he said.

"You're such a romantic," Liam said. "Used to be, when I looked up at the stars it was just for navigation purposes. But then I met you. Now I can't help noticing how amazing the world is." He reached over and took Aidan's hand. "I'll bet you still wish on stars, don't you?"

"I used to," Aidan said. "Didn't see many when I lived in Philadelphia, but I'd always try and wish on the first one I found."

"What did you wish for?"

Aidan squeezed his hand. "You."

"Come on," Liam said. "You didn't know me. You didn't even know I existed. And besides, you were involved with Blake all those years."

Aidan had loved Blake and thought Blake loved him. But somewhere deep in his heart, he knew that there had to be more to life, and love, than Blake could provide. When Blake kicked him to the curb, he finally set out to find what he had been wishing for. He landed in Tunis and fell in lust at first sight, spying Liam showering naked in the courtyard behind the Bar Mamounia. That lust had blossomed into the love he had never found back in Philadelphia.

"Yeah, but after the first year or two with Blake, I started to think about other guys," Aidan said. "Not like I wanted to go out and get laid with some random trick. But I kept hoping that some knight in shining armor would sweep me up and take me with him."

"You read too many romance novels."

"I used to. But now I feel like I'm living in one. I don't need them anymore."

"You're a sweetheart, you know that?" Liam leaned down and kissed him. Aidan wrapped his arms around Liam and pressed him close, feeling his dick unfurl and his heart race.

Then they were both startled by a bright light. They backed apart immediately, and Liam spoke in Arabic to the watchman. "At least we know he's on duty," Aidan grumbled under his breath.

They walked around with the watchman, Aidan only half listening to the conversation. All he wanted to do was get Liam back to the guesthouse and pick up where they had left off. Liam was conscientious, and it was a half hour before they were alone once more, in the bedroom.

"Did you book a return flight from Marseille?" Liam asked, kicking off his sandals.

Aidan unbuttoned his shirt and placed it in a laundry pile for Hakim. "I thought I'd wait to get the lay of the land in France. Make sure Leila is all right. Maybe even see if I could talk to Omar about what might have caused Khadija to get killed."

"You're not a private eye or a police detective," Liam said, pulling his polo shirt over his head. "You don't need to do any snooping."

There was that attitude again, Aidan thought. Diminishing anything Aidan was able to contribute. "But if we discover why someone killed Khadija, we help neutralize any threats against the client." He unbuttoned his shorts, toed off his deck shoes, and dropped the shorts and boxers to the floor.

"You don't want to disobey me," Liam said, coming over to him as he bent over to pick up the shorts. Liam jabbed his index finger up Aidan's butt, and he yelped in surprise. "You know what the consequences are."

For a second, Aidan's anger flared. Then he realized that Liam was teasing him. "The consequences of staying too long in Marseille are being away from you," Aidan said. He wiggled his ass and pushed back against Liam's finger.

Behind him, he heard Liam spit, then felt him remove his finger from Aidan's ass. Before he could turn around, though, it was replaced by Liam's dick.

They had long since stopped using protection when they had sex. Both were disease-free and committed to monogamy. Aidan loved the feeling of skin on skin, the sense that there was nothing between them. It was an emotional thing—the breaking down of borders, a sharing that was complete.

Liam reached around Aidan's waist and pulled his partner toward him, impaling Aidan deeper on his dick. He leaned down and kissed Aidan's neck as Aidan began bucking his ass back and forth. Liam picked up his rhythm, pulling back as Aidan went forward, then slamming in as Aidan came backward.

Aidan closed his eyes and focused on the pleasure of his lover's dick in him, stroking his anal walls, pressing against his prostate. He felt Liam reach around and grab his dick with his rough hand. "Ow!" he said. "Lube, Liam."

"Sorry." Liam breathed into the back of his neck. He pulled his mouth away from nibbling Aidan's skin to spit in his hand a couple of times, then put his hand back on Aidan's dick. That was much better. They moved in sync, back and forth, and Aidan felt the pressure of his orgasm rise. He began panting and whimpering as Liam fucked him faster and faster, stroking his dick with the same speed.

Aidan yelped with the pressure of his orgasm, and squeezed his ass around Liam's dick, putting him over the edge as well. Liam sagged a bit but stayed inside him, his hand still wrapped around Aidan's dick. "You make me crazy, you know that?" Liam said softly.

"Back at you, bud," Aidan said.

"You can't stay in Marseille too long."

"I won't."

They pulled apart, and Liam flopped down on the bed as Aidan got a damp towel. When they were both clean, Aidan nestled beside his partner, his head on Liam's broad chest. Hayam jumped up onto the bed with them, circling around three times until she settled. Who knew what the next day would hold? For now, at least, they were together.

10 – Transactions

Liam woke the next morning at sunrise and left Aidan asleep, Hayam snoring at the foot of the bed. He used the bathroom, then pulled on a bathing suit and walked out to the pool deck and began exercising. He was about halfway through his routine when Aidan joined him for some sit-ups and jumping jacks.

Aidan exercised for a half hour, then went inside to get showered, dressed, and packed for the trip to Marseille. James had reached out to Louis Fleck, who had helped secure a tourist visa for Leila so that she could enter France to be reunited with her father, who had temporary residency there. Omar had written a letter authorizing Aidan to escort Leila and faxed it to the office at the Ferme Deux Hommes. As a US citizen, Aidan didn't need anything more than his passport.

After a quick breakfast, they were ready to drive to Tunis Carthage airport. Farid insisted that Leila dump her antiquated suitcase and take one of his. He had also procured a new pink backpack from somewhere, which Leila shyly accepted.

As they were loading the Jeep, James came up to Aidan and handed him a couple of hundred euros. "In case you need walking-around money," he said.

Liam wanted to leave extra early in case there were protests on the road or at the airport itself, but the morning was strangely calm. The area around the airport was commercial, with broad avenues and multistory office buildings, and it seemed like business as usual there. Aidan recognized the logo of many American and European companies on what looked like warehouses, though often the logo was represented in Arabic script instead of Roman.

Liam nosed the Jeep up to the curb in the departure lane, and Aidan got out and pulled the seat forward for Leila. While she climbed out, he and Liam unloaded the bags from the back. The air seemed more humid close to the Mediterranean, layered with the smells of jet fuel and automobile exhaust.

"You be careful," Liam said.

"You too. My job's the easier one." Aidan struggled to maintain a light tone, despite his fear and his unwillingness to leave Liam. "I'll deliver Leila to her dad and probably be back tomorrow."

Neither of them was willing to hug or kiss in public. Aidan stuck his hand out, and Liam took it. "I love you," Liam said.

"I love you too, sweetheart. Now get the Jeep out of here before you get a ticket."

* * *

After he dropped Aidan and Leila at the airport, Liam called Faisal's cell, reaching him at an investigation at the Bab el Khadra train station. "Any news on the death of Khadija Mansoor?" he asked.

"Once again, what I have to say should not be said over the phone," Faisal said. "Can you meet me here?"

"How are the roads?"

"No significant demonstrations that I know of," Faisal said. "But you never know what will happen. Stay away from the main streets and squares."

"I'll be there in a half hour," Liam said. He parked a block from the train station and jogged over to where Faisal stood, smoking a cigarette.

"What's the case?" Liam asked.

"Acid throwing." Faisal took a long drag from his cigarette. "Open and shut. A man dropped his girlfriend for a younger, prettier woman, and the girlfriend took her revenge against her replacement."

"Why is a senior police official here, then?"

"Because the man involved is another senior police official." Faisal dropped his butt to the pavement and ground it out. "About Khadija Mansoor."

"Yes?"

"I am increasingly certain that there was no police involvement in her death. Which is good news for me but not for you."

"Why not?"

"Because it means that there must be some conflict, either within the Muslim Leadership, or between it and another group. Which leaves the Mansoor girl in danger."

"She's on her way to her father in Marseille," Liam said. "Aidan is chaperoning her."

Faisal raised his eyebrows. "And you are still here?"

"We're working for Omar Mansoor's brother as well. Someone is sabotaging the olive groves he owns in Tebourba."

"You think there is a connection? Is the brother political as well?"

Liam shook his head. "The brother has no interest in politics. But he's gay, and he and his partner are shaking up production techniques. They think someone wants to see their business fail."

"Attitudes in the country are not as liberal as they are in the city."

"Did you get a chance to look at that spreadsheet I e-mailed you? The supporters of the Muslim Leadership?"

"There were some names there I did not recognize," Faisal said. "So it was interesting in that regard. But none of the women on the list were in Mornaguia Prison at the same time as Mrs. Mansoor. So the list is a dead end as far as I am concerned."

He looked up. Though he was not a short man, he was still several inches shorter than Liam. "Have you asked Louis Fleck?"

"I e-mailed him. Haven't spoken to him yet."

"He may have some additional insight." Faisal's cell rang, and he turned away from Liam to answer.

While Faisal spoke, Liam looked around. Life had returned to normal in Tunis; there was a new government in place, and people were tired of the endless demonstrations and riots.

Faisal finished his call. "I must go back to headquarters. Always something new. You will let me know if you find out anything I should know?"

"You bet." Liam walked slowly back to where he had parked the Jeep, dialing Louis Fleck's cell as he did.

Louis didn't bother with formalities. "Liam. Interesting e-mail you sent. I'd like to talk to you about it."

"I'm near the Bab el Khadra train station. Can we meet?"

"So you spoke to Faisal first. I'm hurt."

Not for the first time, Liam was impressed with Louis Fleck's connections. He knew about the acid-throwing incident and surmised that it would require a senior investigator like Faisal on the scene. From Liam's position, he intuited that Liam had already spoken to Faisal.

"Just working through my list," Liam said.

"I can be at the coffee shop in the Hotel Africa in an hour," Louis said. "Can you?"

"Your wish is my command, Master."

Louis laughed. "Save that kind of talk for Aidan." Then he hung up.

Liam stopped by the Bar Mamounia on his way to meet Louis. Of course, the first person he saw as he walked through the beaded curtain was Abdullah, the young Tunisian he had fooled around with a few times before he met Aidan.

"Liam!" Abdullah said, rushing up to hug him.

Once again, Liam regretted ever fucking the mocha-skinned queen. He had been horny and drunk, and Abdullah had fawned over him, kissing his cheek and stroking his crotch until Liam couldn't resist. He remembered picking the skinny man up and carrying him across the courtyard to his king-size bed, where he had fucked Abdullah's succulent ass and…

He realized his dick had sprung to attention, and he backed away. "Where's Fadi?" The bald-headed older man was usually behind the bar in a white T-shirt, polishing something or serving up drinks.

"He had to go out to buy supplies," Abdullah said. "He left me in charge."

Liam looked around the dim bar and realized that he and Abdullah were alone there. "Where is everyone else?"

Abdullah shrugged. "They are frightened to go out. Even to have a drink." He put his arm around Liam's waist. "It is just you and me, Liam," he said, stressing the first syllable. "Won't you make love with me like we used to?" He pressed his palm against Liam's erection. "Your dick wants me."

Liam's mouth was dry. Yes, his dick did want to plow Abdullah's ass again—but his head, and his heart, said no. "Sorry, Abdullah. You know I'm in love with Aidan. He's the only one who gets my dick these days."

Abdullah pulled away and pouted. "Such a waste, Liam. You are such handsome man. I can make you feel very good."

"I know you can. Listen, when Fadi comes back, tell him that Aidan and I are out of town on a job. We took Hayam with us. He just has to keep an eye on the house."

Abdullah sat on a barstool. "I can tell him. But what do I get for my trouble?" He spread his legs seductively.

Liam had treated sex as a transaction before he met Aidan. Two men who both wanted something. He could return to that with

Abdullah. The queeny Tunisian would do whatever Liam wanted in exchange for some quality naked time.

Before he could think further, Liam crossed the room to Abdullah. He lifted the lithe young man up and cupped his butt under one hand. He wrapped the other behind Abdullah's head, then leaned in for a deep kiss, his tongue probing Abdullah's. With the index finger of the hand holding Abdullah up, Liam stroked the Tunisian's butt crack through his slacks, and Abdullah shivered with ecstasy. He placed one slim, cool hand on Liam's chest and fingered a nipple ring.

Then Liam gently sat him back down on his bar stool. "That's what you get for your trouble. And now, if you'll excuse me, I have a meeting."

He turned and walked out through the beaded curtain, leaving Abdullah slumped against the bar.

The streets of Tunis normally teemed with businessmen, tourists, and average citizens—some hurrying, others lingering. But that morning, the streets were nearly empty, and traffic flowed smoothly through intersections. Few people were on the sidewalks, and those he passed seemed eager to get where they were going.

Fifteen minutes later, he was walking into a very different kind of room: the coffee shop at the Hotel Africa. The restaurant was immaculately clean, filled with the discreet buzz of low-voiced conversations and the clink of silverware on china. Louis Fleck was already there, at a table at the back, with a tiny cup of espresso in front of him.

Liam couldn't help comparing him to Abdullah—they were such opposites, though both were gay men. Louis was a burly, hairy, butch guy; Liam hadn't even realized he was gay until Aidan had pointed it out.

Liam slid into the chair across from Louis and motioned to the waiter for another pair of espressos. "So, your list," Louis said.

"My list. Anything on it that might relate to Khadija Mansoor's murder?"

Louis shook his head. "Not that I can see. But Faisal probably already told you that."

"He did. But he suggested you might have some additional insight."

The waiter brought the coffee and then faded away. "What do you know about the Muslim Leadership?" Louis asked.

"Not much. Just what you told us at dinner the other night."

"And imagine all that has happened since that dinner. It was what, a week ago? How many governments have fallen since then?"

"Three? Four?" Liam asked.

"Something like that. Omar Mansoor's brother-in-law Burhan Deeb was released from prison yesterday, and he's right there in the mix, scrapping away, trying to make a place for the Muslim Leadership. They're an Islamist party, but not as conservative as the Muslim Brotherhood, for example. They want a return to religion, but they don't want to force it down the country's throat."

"Does that make them a better ally?"

Louis shrugged. "You know politicians. They say one thing and do another."

Liam looked at his watch. Aidan's flight was still in the air. What would he discover when he got to Marseille?

"We'll see that soon." Liam explained that Aidan was delivering Leila to her father.

"I doubt they'll stay in France long," Louis said. "As soon as the government stabilizes, we'll see recognition for some of these smaller parties, and with legitimacy comes the chance for Mansoor to come back."

"Faisal thought that Khadija might have been killed as part of an internal struggle within the Leadership or by someone from a rival group. What do you think?"

"I doubt it's coming from within the group. Omar Mansoor is the big cheese; Khadija and her brother were his right hands. There isn't anyone else I know of who could try and take over." He passed a piece of paper across the table to Liam. "But there are a couple of other groups that could benefit if the Muslim Leadership falls apart, especially now, when things are so uncertain. I'd check them out, if I were you."

Liam took the paper but said, "Why me? Why not give this list to Faisal?"

"I'm sure he already knows about these groups. And once he's finished dealing with a country in total uproar, perhaps he can get back to the murder of one political activist. Hopefully before whoever killed Khadija goes after her daughter or her husband."

Liam frowned. "I'll see what I can do."

He thought about stopping back at the Bar Mamounia on his way out of town, to make sure that Abdullah had passed on his message to Fadi. But that wasn't a good idea; Abdullah would still be there, and another encounter with him could only lead to trouble.

11 – IDENTIFY THE PROBLEM

As the Jeep drove away, Aidan shouldered his duffle bag and picked up the handle of Leila's suitcase. Liam always said that Aidan wore his emotions openly, so he was determined not to reveal the turmoil he felt inside—to Liam or to Leila.

She carried her backpack, and they walked into the airport. The Air France flight was on schedule, so they checked the two bags to Marseille and went through security.

"Do you want anything to eat or drink?" Aidan asked.

Leila shook her head.

"I'm sure they have something *halal*," Aidan said. "A bottle of water?"

She shook her head again.

"Well then, let's sit down." He led her to a row of hard plastic seats. "Is this going to be your first time on a plane?"

She nodded.

"I was just about your age the first time I flew anywhere," he said. "Maybe a year older. My parents sent me on a summer study program in France sponsored by my high school. I was kind of scared, but at least I had a whole bunch of other kids around me. I guess it's tougher for you."

She didn't say anything, just sat there with her hands in her lap and the pink backpack at her feet.

"You're not scared, are you?" Aidan asked. "Because you know, flying is safer than any other kind of travel."

She said, "I'm not scared," but there wasn't much conviction in her voice.

The television mounted on the wall above them switched to a news station. The anchor announced in Arabic that there was a new government in place in Tunis, and that there were only sporadic protests.

"I will protect you, you know," Aidan said. "I've been trained as a bodyguard. I can shoot and use a knife, and I understand the principles of hand-to-hand combat. No one is going to hurt you as long as I'm around."

She looked up. "Why? Why are you protecting me? I don't even like you."

"Liking has nothing to do with it. Your uncle hired me to deliver you safely to your father. You're my client, and it's my job." He took a breath and looked out the window to where their plane was taxiing up. "It's also the way I was raised. You may not agree with my religious beliefs, but I was brought up to care about people who were less fortunate or needed my help. My parents used to give me a quarter, which I handed in at Sunday school, for this thing called *keren ami* in Hebrew, charity. They wanted me to learn early to give to other people."

"I would like a bottle of water, please," Leila said.

"Sure. Let's walk over there together." They stood up, and she put her hand in Aidan's. He smiled.

* * *

Leila sat in the window seat, and she marveled at the land and then the ocean below her. Aidan relaxed in his seat and tried not to think about Liam. It was going to be the first night they had spent apart in the nearly two years they'd been together, and he was missing Liam already. But Liam was too much of a professional to miss him—even now, he was probably back at the Ferme Deux Hommes, inspecting the groves or working with the new security company. He had the ability to compartmentalize—he had put Aidan in a box at the back of his brain, to come back to later. Aidan wished he could do the same thing.

The flight was smooth, and Leila was impressed at how big Marseille was from the air. It took a while for their bags to arrive and then to go through customs. Since Leila was on a Tunisian passport and Aidan on a US one, they could both go through the same line for non-EU citizens.

When they walked out into the main terminal, its white ceiling supported by a series of round metal trusses, Leila suddenly cried, "*Abi!*" and took off, her backpack swinging on her shoulders. She skidded into a tall man with a dark beard who leaned down and gathered her in his arms.

Aidan hurried after her, sorry he hadn't told her in advance that she should stay by his side until they met her father.

She stepped back as Aidan approached. "This is Aidan. He's my bodyguard," she said to her father in Arabic.

"I am Omar Mansoor," he said in English, extending his hand to Aidan. "Thank you for taking care of my daughter."

"My pleasure." Aidan noticed a large bodybuilder type hovering behind Omar and said in a low voice, "Do you know the man behind you?"

Omar turned. "Yes, this is Benoit. He is my bodyguard." He introduced the two men, and they shook hands. "We have a car waiting," Omar said and turned to walk out of the terminal. Aidan was almost jealous when Leila took her father's hand.

Aidan tugged Leila's suitcase as well as his own duffle as he followed Omar, Leila, and Benoit out of the terminal. Benoit led them to a large SUV in the parking garage. Aidan loaded the luggage in the back, feeling more like a porter than a bodyguard, but he was determined not to say anything. Seeing that Omar had his own security reassured him that he'd be able to return to Tebourba quickly.

Omar got into the backseat with his daughter, and Aidan took the front seat beside Benoit. Omar and Leila chatted away in Arabic as they got onto the A7 highway toward the city. Aidan thought perhaps by speaking in French he could get to know the other bodyguard. "How long have you worked for Mr. Mansoor?" he asked the big man.

Benoit stared straight ahead. "I am not at liberty to speak of my employment."

Interesting, Aidan thought. "Are there any specific threats I should be aware of?"

"I am not at liberty to speak of my employment."

Omar leaned forward and spoke in French. "You must forgive

Benoit. He takes his job very seriously. There have been some threats against my life, but no one has taken action."

"Yet," Benoit added.

Omar sat back and continued his conversation with his daughter. Benoit left the highway when it ended and then negotiated the narrow streets of the city. Eventually they were on a broad avenue called the Boulevard de la Liberation, and Benoit pulled the car up at a tall apartment building with a luxurious green lawn.

Aidan wondered how Omar Mansoor could afford such a fancy building when his wife and daughter lived in a small apartment in Tunis. But he said nothing, just got the luggage from the back of the SUV and followed Benoit, Omar, and Leila up to the seventh floor.

The apartment was spacious and open, with big glass windows that looked down the street toward the ocean. The floor was lushly carpeted, the furniture the kind of old-fashioned dark wood that Aidan associated with his grandmother's home. He noticed empty places on the walls where art must have hung; the only decoration was a calendar of Muslim holy days.

Omar led them down a hallway to a small bedroom, where he said, "For my daughter." A narrow bed with a white spread and a single pillow was pushed against the wall. There was a low dresser, a night table, and an incongruous poster of a French rock band on the wall. Leila would probably take that down immediately, Aidan thought.

He deposited Leila's suitcase on the bed and turned to Omar. "Is there somewhere I can stay overnight? I'll get a flight back to Tunis in the morning. Or I can stay at a hotel, if that's easier."

"No, no, you should stay here," Omar said. "There is a second bed in Benoit's room. And I would like you to stay for at least a few days."

"Let me put my bag down and we'll talk," Aidan said.

"When you are ready, please come to the living room."

He walked away, and Aidan turned to Benoit. "Can you reveal the location of the room we're sharing? Or is that confidential too?"

Benoit frowned. Then he turned and walked down the hall. "Mr. Mansoor's room," he said, pointing to the right. Then he opened a door opposite, next to Leila's. "This is my room."

Either Benoit had brought little with him, or he was very neat. There was nothing visible on the bureau or the bedside table. The closet and bureau doors were closed. Both beds were so neatly made Aidan had no idea which bed was to be his. "You can have that one," Benoit said, pointing at the farther of the two. Then he turned to leave.

"Bathroom?" Aidan asked.

"Next door. We will have to share with the girl."

Aidan sat on the bed after Benoit left. He didn't want to have to stay in Marseille for a few days without Liam. He missed his partner already, and he hadn't realized how scared he would be on his own, without Liam there to back him up. Who did he think he was, anyway? He wasn't really a bodyguard, despite the course he'd taken in the States and the year he'd spent working with Liam and learning from him. He didn't have the strength, the determination, or the ability to focus that Liam had.

He looked down at his right hand. It was shaking, and he focused on calming it. That's what Liam would do, he thought. Identify a problem, then direct all his resources toward a solution. Not sit there and mope like a scared schoolgirl.

His hand stopped shaking, and he dug his phone out of his pocket and turned it on. He waited while it found service in Marseille, then dialed Liam's cell. "We're here. Omar lives very nicely in a high-rise with an ocean view. He wants me to stay for a few days."

He was worried that his voice shook.

"Why?"

Liam sounded preoccupied, or irritated, as if this twist was somehow Aidan's fault.

Aidan struggled to keep his voice even, his tone light. "Don't know yet. He has a bodyguard of his own. Says there have been threats, but nothing concrete."

"What does the bodyguard say?"

"That he is not at liberty to disclose the details of his employment. He's a regular Mr. Personality."

"If there's already a guard there, why does Mansoor need you?"

The irritation finally rose. "I don't know, Liam. I just got here, and I wanted to let you know we arrived safely. I don't have your ability to assess a situation immediately. It takes me a while to find my way."

"I'm not blaming you, Aidan," Liam said, and Aidan noted the use of his name, rather than one of the usual endearments. "I'm just trying to understand what's going on."

"I'm about to talk with Omar. I'll call you when I know. How are things there?"

"Nothing new. Security company is still stalling. Now they're saying tomorrow. But it does seem like the city is settling down." Aidan heard Liam speak to someone near him; then his partner was back. "Gotta go. Talk to you later."

No mention of love or other endearment. Aidan didn't even get to say good-bye before the connection was severed.

He sat there for a moment longer, trying to analyze the conversation. Liam was busy, he thought. He loved Aidan, he missed Aidan, but he wasn't the type to say those things out loud too often, even if Aidan wished he was.

He sighed, then stood up and walked out to the living room. Omar Mansoor was on the phone, but he motioned Aidan to a chair across from him. He spoke rapidly in Arabic, and Aidan couldn't understand enough to know what he was talking about.

When he hung up, he switched smoothly back to English. "I will be out at meetings until late today. Sadly, that is my life; I am not at leisure to spend much time with my daughter. Benoit must accompany me, but I cannot take Leila. I would like you to stay with her until we are able to return to Tunis."

"How long are you talking about?" Aidan asked.

"Perhaps a week. Things are moving very quickly, and I hope to be able to go back to my country and to my party now that the government has changed."

Aidan did not relish the thought of babysitting Leila for a week. And to be away from Liam for so long? Not a good idea. He had a feeling that his self-confidence would begin to crumble the longer they were apart, and he worried that in his absence Liam might figure out that he could get along just fine on his own once more, as he had for years.

"My brother tells me you are a teacher as well," Omar said.

Aidan nodded. "I have a degree in English as a Second Language. I do teach now and then, but most of my work is in personal protection."

"It is perfect. You can help Leila with her English, particularly her English writing. It is a skill that will be very important to her."

Aidan hesitated. He did love to teach, and he thought he might be able to break through more of Leila's reserve if they worked together. Teaching was what he was good at.

But to stay in Marseille without Liam?

Omar ignored his hesitation. "And perhaps you can show Leila around Marseille as well. It is a very cosmopolitan city, and I would like her to become more comfortable around Europeans and Americans."

"I thought your party was strongly Islamist," Aidan said.

"I cherish my religion and use it as a guide in my daily life. But I am a realist as well as a politician. We cannot ignore our less religious citizens if we take control of the government, nor can we force them to pray. Many of the most important countries are already suspicious of us. We must be citizens of the world as well as worshippers of

Allah."

It sounded very reasonable to Aidan. But then, in his experience, politicians had the knack for making almost anything sound palatable. "I'll have to check with my partner," he said. He didn't know what he wanted himself, so he thought he'd leave the decision to Liam. "Let me call him and then come back to you."

Omar looked at his watch. "I must leave now. But you will stay until I return?"

"Of course."

Omar and Benoit left, and Aidan took his cell phone out to the balcony that looked down toward the ocean. He relaxed on a lounge chair and started to feel better about the idea of staying. There were worse places to be stuck for a week; perhaps he would get that vacation he had hoped for. And he could help Leila improve her English and broaden her world view.

Besides, he needed to prove to himself, and to Liam, that he could function on his own. Back in Tunis, when Aidan worked as a bodyguard, it was always with Liam by his side. Liam worked some jobs on his own, and occasionally, as he had mentioned to Omar, Aidan picked up teaching jobs, as a substitute or a short-term private tutor.

The more he thought about it, the more determined he was to stay. Maybe Liam would appreciate him more if he wasn't there to satisfy each of Liam's needs. He could handle an assignment without Liam by his side. And he could prove to himself that he could manage on his own, if he had to.

He had gone directly from Blake to Liam, with no more than a week between the two. He had never thought of himself as someone who had to be in a relationship, though as soon as Blake kicked him out, he had found and fallen in love with Liam.

Or was the speed at which they had fallen in love something more? A need on Aidan's part to belong to someone, a need Liam didn't even know he had to connect with someone else. Had they both been conveniently what the other needed? If their relationship was strong, wouldn't it survive a week apart?

He picked up his phone and pressed the speed dial for Liam. When his partner answered, he sketched out the details of why Omar wanted him to stay.

"I don't think it's a good idea," Liam said. "We don't know anything about what kind of threats have been made against Omar. You don't have any connections in Marseille. If anything happens, you're on your own."

There it was again, Aidan thought. Liam's belief that Aidan couldn't function without having his hand held. "Honestly, I think he's paranoid," Aidan said. "He needs a babysitter for Leila. I'll have the chance to teach her a few things, I'll get to spend some time in Marseille, and I'll be out of your way back in Tebourba while you finish up."

He waited for Liam to say he wouldn't be in the way at all, but instead all Liam said was, "Tell me about this other bodyguard."

"Benoit? Not much to tell. Looks like a bodybuilder. Doesn't talk. Haven't seen his balls."

"Excuse me?" Liam asked.

"It was a joke, Liam. You know, ben-wa balls?"

"I have no idea what you're talking about. But you'd better not be looking at this guy's balls."

"Don't worry. I'm sure he's straight. And even if he was gay, he's not my type. I prefer a man with a brain."

"Try and keep things professional, all right? He works for an agency, or freelance?"

The conversation was not going well, Aidan thought. Once again, he was trying to make light of something, to skate along the surface of danger because he didn't have the ability or background Liam did. And that was just making Liam angry.

Aidan took a deep breath and forced himself to focus. "I don't know. I'll try and find out."

After he hung up, Aidan got his laptop and discovered that he could get a wi-fi signal. He logged on, checked his email, then did a search for ben-wa balls. He was amused to see that they were also called Benoit balls. He sent the link to Liam with a note that said, "I'll have to introduce you to these."

He shut down the laptop and went to find Leila. Depending on her mood, it could be a good week—or a very bad one.

12 – An Ex-Soldier

Liam looked at the list Louis had given him. There were three organizations listed on it: the *Parti de Liberation*, or PL; a group whose Arabic name translated to something like the Arabic Front, or AF; and the Islamic People's Party, or IPP.

He sighed. He preferred to leave the research up to Aidan, but with his partner en route to Marseille and out of the picture for at least a day or two, he had no choice. Then he realized that Aidan had taken the laptop with him to France.

He resisted the urge to utter a couple of choice curses he had learned in the Navy. Instead, he drove to an Internet café in the Bou Choucha neighborhood, near the P7, and laid down a few dinars for the use of a computer. It was a comfy if run-down place, the gleaming new computers a direct contrast to the peeling sand-colored paint on the walls, the chipped tile floor, and the rickety tables and chairs.

There were half a dozen other people in the room, and Liam took a table in the corner, away from everyone but a dark-haired young Arab woman in a high-necked blouse and long, flowing skirt. The waitress came over while the computer was booting up and he ordered mint tea and a *brik*, an egg fried in a thin pastry envelope filled with vegetables.

Once he had online access, it was easy to dispose of the PL. It was too small and insignificant, he felt, to mount any kind of real challenge, either to the government or any of its rivals. It consisted of a handful of older men who had supported President Habib Bourguiba and still resented his overthrow by Ben Ali in 1987. Their primary objective seemed to be to topple Ben Ali, not to assume power themselves. They did have a history of violence, which was probably why Louis had included them on his list.

The waitress returned with his brik and placed a small cup on the table. She held the pot of mint tea high and let the liquid flow down, creating a froth. She finished off the tea with a fresh mint leaf and smiled at Liam.

He thanked her, then picked up the cup of tea and took a sip. "It's very good," he said in Arabic. As she smiled again and returned to the kitchen, he noticed the young woman at the next table staring at him. He ignored her and went back to his computer.

In contrast to the PL, the Arabic Front was a group of university-educated young men and women, the kind who had initially filled the streets during the Jasmine Revolution. They had a professional-looking Web site, and he realized that a video had been loading at the bottom of the screen once it began to play.

He quickly turned off the speaker, though not before the whole café had been treated to the beginning of a diatribe against the government. He kept his head down and ignored the curious looks of those around him.

The AF talked a good game, Liam thought, as he read through a rough translation of their Web site. They had specific ideas and recommendations, and they cited numerous experts in foreign relations and economic development.

He nibbled on the brik as he read the rest of the Web site. The food and the tea were good, he thought, though they would have been better had Aidan been there to share them.

The idea surprised him. He'd always been so self-sufficient and prided himself on being able to handle any assignment on his own. But since Aidan had entered his life, that had changed. He liked having a partner, both in business and in life.

Sure, it was easier now that Aidan handled the domestic stuff like meals and laundry. Liam was willing to admit he hated handling those boring, routine details. But more important was the way he had come to rely on Aidan's insights. He looked at the world in a different way, and sometimes he saw things Liam missed.

He smiled. Aidan was easy on the eyes too, sexy in bed and funny, sometimes when it wasn't appropriate. He couldn't imagine life without Aidan by his side.

He looked up and realized that the young woman was still staring at him. Had she heard the beginning of that video? Pegged him as a supporter of a different group? He met her gaze, searching for her motivation.

She smiled at him, then looked down briefly, then back up.

Oh. She was flirting.

He'd always been aware of his good looks. When he was a little boy, his mother used to beam as she combed his wheat-blond hair and told him how handsome he was. Then when puberty rang in and boys and girls began to notice each other, he was one of the most sought-after for dates and parties. He had always been athletic, and he picked up the basics of dancing quickly.

Girls seemed to like him because he was polite. He never pressed a girl toward sex, though now he realized it was because he didn't have the internal desire. Back then he had thought he was being a good Catholic. In the locker room, he never bragged about conquests, and the other boys assumed he was getting laid and didn't need to boast.

"You are American?" the young woman said in accented English, bringing Liam back to the present.

He glanced over, said, "Yes," and then returned his attention to his screen. The Arabic Front were well-organized and in direct opposition to the Muslim Leadership. But his final assessment was that they were just too earnest, smart, and even naive to consider murdering a woman in her jail cell on the off chance that it would help them achieve power. Maybe that was naïveté on his own part, he thought, but his gut told him to move on.

"I want to go to America," the girl said.

He didn't look up. "It's a big country."

"You are living here, in Tunisia?"

He glanced over at her again. "Sorry, I have a lot of work to do."

She switched to Arabic and began a litany of complaints, about men in general and then American men. Liam looked up and caught the waitress's eye.

She walked over to the girl and spoke to her in hushed Arabic. The girl complained, then finally grabbed her purse, stood up, and walked out.

It was such odd behavior for a young Tunisian woman, he thought, as she slammed the glass door of the café behind her. Most of the young women he knew were demure and shy, especially when it came to men they didn't know.

He smiled at the waitress again, who shrugged. Then he switched his attention to the IPP, the Islamic People's Party. They seemed like strong suspects. Their leadership was a mixed bag of hardened politicians, many of whom had served in the parliament, along with tough young activists who were often detained by the police. They looked to him like a bunch of loose cannons, with only the barest sense of organization.

They had a rally scheduled for that afternoon, and Liam thought it would be worthwhile to attend and see what they had to say. The rally was called for two o'clock in the waterfront park between the Mediterranean and the Sortie Ouest highway. He spent another few minutes reading e-mail, and when his time on the computer expired, he returned to the Jeep and drove out to the numbered streets to the west of the city. He parked a few blocks inland from the Sortie Ouest and walked toward the ocean. The air was heavy with the smell of automobile exhaust and the faint traces of salt water.

Young people crowded the streets, laughing and joking and singing snatches of songs. It was as if they were on their way to a rock concert rather than a political rally. He found his chechia in his back pocket and kept his head down to blend in with the crowd.

A makeshift stage stood at one end of the park, and the crowd clustered around it. Liam stayed toward the edge of the crowd, close enough to hear but with an easy exit in case things got rowdy.

Two o'clock came and went, and there was no action up on the stage. The crowd began to get restless, and Liam made out numerous shouts, mostly from young men holding signs printed in rough Arabic—ACTION NOW and DOWN WITH THE RULING CLASS.

He was about to give up when a middle-aged man mounted the steps to the platform. The crowd quieted as the man took the microphone and began to speak.

Liam could carry on a basic conversation in Arabic, could watch most TV programs and get the gist, yet he was nowhere near fluent. The man on the dais was speaking very quickly, and Liam could only catch bits and pieces of what he said.

What he did hear, though, disturbed him. The man seemed to be urging the crowd to violent action—and not just toward the current government, but against all outside forces who sought to destroy Tunisia and Islam. He spouted the same kind of rhetoric Liam had been hearing for years, but the crowd loved it, chanting slogans back to the speaker, waving their arms and their signs.

He was about to turn and leave when, without warning, he felt his right arm grasped and twisted behind his back. A rough voice spoke into his ear in Arabic, the man's breath redolent of onions and garlic. "If you struggle, the crowd will come after you."

Liam tried to turn around to see who had him immobilized, but the man grasped Liam's neck with his other hand and forced him to face ahead. "What are you doing here?" the man asked.

"Observation," Liam said. He was not about to reveal his true purpose, especially since he had no idea who was holding him. He thought that if he could stall long enough, the man would lose focus, and Liam could turn the tables on him. "I read about the Islamic People's Party online and wanted to see what they stand for."

"Why?"

Liam continued to face forward, looking as far left and right as he could without moving his head. The people around him did not seem to notice he was being held. But given the crowd's anti-American sentiment, he didn't think it was a good idea to attract their attention.

"I live and work in this country," Liam said. "I have a right to know what's going on with the government."

"I know what kind of work you do," the man said. "Are you protecting someone in the government?"

The man knew he was a bodyguard? How? "I'm not working for anyone," he said. "This is strictly on my own."

"And your partner?"

Liam tried to focus on the voice. Clearly the man knew him and Aidan. But who was he? Liam had to tread very carefully, figuring out just how much to reveal.

"My partner is in Marseille, protecting a teenage girl," he said.

"Without you? I thought you were the muscle."

"Who are you?" Liam said. "How do you know me?"

The man released his grip and spun Liam around to face him.

"Nusrat?" he said, when he saw the man's face.

Liam had met Nusrat Khan when he was a SEAL and Khan was a liaison officer with the Tunisian military. Liam knew that he had retired, but that was all.

The ex-soldier still maintained a military bearing. He was about forty-five, with dark hair in a brush cut and a scar along one cheek.

"I was watching the crowd on a security monitor when I saw you," Nusrat said. "You do not blend in with this crowd very well."

Liam was insulted. He prided himself on his ability to blend in, to shrink his posture and mimic the movements of those around him. But as he surveyed the crowd, he realized Nusrat was right. He was taller and lighter-haired than anyone around him. He'd never pass as a Tunisian here.

"Come with me," Nusrat said, putting his hand on Liam's shoulder. "We should talk."

Nusrat led him away from the edge of the crowd and then across the highway to a small café, about as run-down as the one where Liam had spent the afternoon, but without the advantages of the shiny new computers. They sat at a spindly round metal table with a terrazzo top, and Nusrat ordered them both bottles of Celtia beer.

"What's your connection with the IPP?" Liam asked.

"I help out with security." He tipped his bottle against Liam's. "To old comrades," he said as the bottles clinked. He drank, then said, "Now, tell me why you are here."

"The girl Aidan is taking to Marseille is Omar Mansoor's daughter." Liam was curious to see what kind of reaction he would get from Nusrat; that would tell him how much more he could reveal.

"Ah," Nusrat said. "You are investigating the murder of her mother?"

"In a way," Liam said. "To identify any potential threats to her or her father."

Nusrat nodded. "And that brings you to the IPP. You think someone from this group could have arranged for her death."

"That idea did cross my mind."

"Well, you can let it keep crossing," Nusrat said. "I know these people. They wish to gain power—but not through such means."

"You're sure?"

"If there were such a plan, it would go through me," he said. "And I can assure you that I had nothing to do with Mrs. Mansoor's death."

Liam lifted the beer to his lips and drank. He had always found Nusrat Khan to be truthful when they had worked together, and there was no reason to doubt him now. But if none of the Muslim Leadership's political opponents had arranged for Khadija's death, then who had?

13 – Dinner in Noailles

Omar was busy in meetings all day Wednesday, so Aidan was left with Leila. She spent the morning reading her battered copy of the Koran, but by lunchtime, Aidan was antsy and wanted to get out of the apartment.

"Your father told me he wants you to be more comfortable around Europeans," he said as he prepared a quick salad for them to share. "So this afternoon, we're going to go out and see something of Marseille."

"I want to stay here."

Aidan shook his head. "You won't learn about France by sitting in your room reading the Koran. You don't want me to tell your father that you disobeyed him on your first day here, do you?"

She frowned. She was wearing her black-and-silver hijab again, and Aidan was nervous about walking the city streets with her; he wasn't sure how she would be received in her Muslim getup. But there was only one way to find out.

When they finished lunch, they took the elevator downstairs, then walked past the open door of the concierge's apartment and out onto the street. It was a crisp, sunny day, much cooler there than it had been in Tunisia, and Aidan was glad he had brought long pants and a lightweight jacket with him.

"What do you like to do for fun back in Tunis?" Aidan asked.

"What do you mean?"

"On the weekends. What did you do with your mom, or with your parents, when your dad was there?"

"My parents are very important people. They were always busy, even on the weekends."

"Surely they took you to the park sometime. Or the zoo or museums."

She shook her head. "I have never been to any of those places."

No wonder she was such a sour girl, Aidan thought. Well, he could try to change that. He kept up a steady chatter as they walked, pointing out features of the Belle Epoque architecture, the wrought-iron balconies, and tall multi-paned windows. They passed an ornate gilt merry-go-round in a park, with small children bobbing up and down on carousel horses to a jaunty tune. From the way Leila looked straight ahead, he knew she wouldn't consider riding it.

He tried to interest her in items in store windows, and people they passed. No one seemed to notice them, and they saw men and women whose dark skin marked them as North Africans, though Aidan suspected most were Moroccan rather than Tunisian.

He had become accustomed to life in Tunisia—street signs and ads in flowing Arabic script, the constant sense of being a foreigner. Though Aidan had a Mediterranean complexion, with slightly olive skin that took a tan well, he was several shades lighter than most Tunisians.

In France, he felt more comfortable walking on the street, and his French was strong enough that at a glance he could understand almost every sign he saw. He loved the sun, even though it was cooler there, and the sense that they were close to the ocean. He could smell the salt water, and as they neared the Vieux Port, he relished the sounds of boat motors and halyards clinking on sailboat masts.

He was so happy to be there that he almost forgot he was working. Even Leila seemed to be warming up; she began looking around more, tugging on Aidan's arm so that he would stop to look in a store window.

"Women are so much more fashionable here than back in Tunis," she said, as a tall, leggy model type with oversize sunglasses walked past. She wore a tight knee-length skirt and a man's long-sleeved shirt, with impossibly high heels.

"They created fashion here in France," Aidan said.

"So many of these women are dressed improperly." Leila shook her head, but Aidan thought he could sense a hint of envy.

They walked down the broad avenue of La Canebière toward the port, passing brand-name shops selling clothing, jewelry, and leather goods, as well as a McDonald's. "You have to understand that each culture has its own beliefs," Aidan said. "For these women, it's not improper to dress the way they do."

"But men will look at them!"

"So? In many cultures, that's a very positive thing. Women dress to impress men, and men reward them with comments and wolf whistles."

"What is that?"

"A wolf whistle?" Aidan laughed, then demonstrated.

A very attractive woman swiveled her head at the sound, looked Aidan over, then smiled and walked on.

"See?" Aidan said. "She wasn't offended. She's not calling her husband to come and kill me because I whistled at her."

"You think that is what we do?" she asked. "Kill men for such things?"

Aidan stopped at a wrought-iron bench overlooking the harbor and sat down, motioning Leila to sit next to him. "You have to admit, Islam is not the most tolerant religion," he said. "Look at all the news reports. Not just things like blowing up the World Trade Center, but women being stoned for adultery, thieves having their hands cut off."

"That is not true Islam." Leila began a long speech about the principles of her religion, and Aidan's mind wandered. He looked around the old port, at the row after row of sailboats docked on finger piers, at the apartment buildings clustering the waterfront, and the massive fort up on the hill. It was all so different from the world he had become accustomed to, and he wondered if he could just pick up and leave Tunis so easily.

Leila stopped talking. "Were you listening to me, Aidan?"

He smiled. "Of course, Leila." He stood up. "Come on, let's walk some more." They went to the Quai des Belges at the end of the harbor, and Leila wrinkled her nose at the smell of the fish market there. They stopped at a series of street food vendors, and Aidan bought himself a *pissaladiere*, an individual pizza covered with sautéed onions, olives, garlic, and anchovies, along with a rounded bottle of orange soda.

Leila agreed to try a *panisse*, a delicate, fried cake made of chickpea flour, which she seemed to like, with a cola.

As they returned home along La Canebière, they saw flashing blue-and-white police lights. Two uniformed officers confronted a small group of young men and women with animal rights slogans, who were protesting in front of a couturier furrier. He put his hand on Leila's shoulder and steered her across the street.

"Are you frightened of them?" Leila asked. "They're just silly people with signs."

"I've had enough of silly people with signs in Tunis," Aidan said. "From signs people move on to rocks and grenades, and then the police start firing their guns. My job is to keep you safe—from everything."

Omar and Benoit returned to the apartment soon after Aidan and Leila did. "Did you have a nice day?" Omar asked his daughter in Arabic.

Aidan was in the kitchen with Benoit.

"Very nice, thank you, Abi." She explained about the walk they had taken, down the Canebière to the old port, and all the strange people and things she had seen.

"You should not take her out on foot," Benoit said to Aidan. "It is too dangerous."

"Since you refuse to tell me what kind of dangers there are, I don't see any reason why she should be a prisoner in this apartment. You heard her father. He wants her to experience French culture."

"From the television," Benoit said.

Aidan didn't bother to argue. Benoit wasn't his boss, so he figured he didn't have to bother much with the Frenchman.

"Gentlemen!" Omar called from the living room, and Aidan ushered Benoit out of the kitchen ahead of him. "I have arranged a dinner this evening with some friends who have children Leila should meet. We will leave for the restaurant at eight."

Privately, Aidan thought eight o'clock was late for a dinner with kids, but he assumed that the children of Omar's friends were as meek as Leila was. He walked out onto the balcony with his cell phone and called Liam. "How are things back in Tebourba?"

"Quiet," Liam said. "Security company finally showed up and started installing the alarms. It's going to take them a couple of days. How's Leila?"

"Warming up a little. We went walking through the Vieux Port. Did you hear anything from either Faisal or Louis?"

"Yeah. Got the names of a couple of organizations, and I checked them out. Couldn't come up with anything, though."

They talked for a few minutes, and by the time he hung up, Aidan was missing Liam fiercely. He went into the room he shared with Benoit to find the big man lying on his bed, reading a bodybuilding magazine. Aidan plugged the headphones into his phone and lay back against the bed. As he listened to the music, he thought of Liam.

It felt strange being so far from Liam, separated by the Mediterranean Sea. Aidan hadn't been on his own like this since the day he walked away from Blake and boarded the plane at Philadelphia International Airport, the one that brought him to Tunisia and to Liam.

He remembered the thrill of seeing Liam naked that first time, as he was showering behind the Bar Mamounia. His confusion when he thought Liam was pursuing him, and the despair he'd felt when he realized it had been a case of mistaken identity.

Then the electricity of their first kiss, the feel of Liam's muscular body against his, the sense that he could find love, shelter, and happiness in Liam's arms.

After that, things had settled into a sort of complacency, he realized. Was he taking Liam for granted? Their sex life was still exciting, but had they both taken the time to build their emotional connection? Sure, they expressed their love for each other every day, but was that enough? Liam wasn't the type for hand-holding walks along the beach, but what did romance mean to him?

Aidan couldn't answer that. Did Liam think of romance when they made love? When they were apart? At any of those small moments during the day? Aidan resolved that when they were together again, he would try to answer those questions.

Promptly at eight, the four of them took the elevator downstairs. The air was even cooler than it had been during the day, cold to Aidan.

"We walk to Quartier de Noailles," Omar said. "It is the Arab section of the city. There are many wonderful restaurants there. Only a few blocks away."

Aidan rubbed his upper arms; his light jacket clearly wasn't enough for the weather. But Leila's long-sleeve shirt and the suits worn by Omar and Benoit seemed to keep them all warm. Walking in a different direction than the one he and Leila had taken earlier in the day, Aidan saw the area change complexion—literally and figuratively.

Most of the people around them were darker-skinned, and from the signage he saw, he assumed they were a mix of Algerians, Egyptians, Moroccans, and Tunisians. They followed a narrow, cobbled street away from a central square, past small, dark, cluttered shops selling tea sets and spices. Aidan saw signs for everything from meat and seafood to Middle Eastern pastries, pistachios, crystallized fruits, and tubs of olives and dates.

His mouth began watering. Men in cotton robes sat at outdoor cafés, talking loudly over bracingly strong demitasses of coffee. They passed a woman wearing a *sifsaris*, a white one-piece cloth with loose folds that covered her head and body down to the knees.

The quarter was a kaleidoscopic mélange of colors, sounds, and smells: rotting produce, incense, sizzling kebabs of chicken and lamb, and the comforting aroma of baking flatbreads and sugary almond cookies. They turned a corner onto a narrow pedestrian street festooned with lines of triangular flags and tiny colored lights, then stopped in front of a glass-fronted restaurant called Café Raoued.

The restaurant was small and dark, only about thirty feet wide and perhaps twenty feet deep. Posters of the island of Djerba, off the Tunisian coast, and the ruins of the ancient city of Carthage hung on the plaster walls. Most of the square tables had been pushed together to form a U-shape, and they were already filled with adults and children all talking loudly in Arabic and French.

It appeared that Omar had reserved the whole place, as he seemed to know everyone. He kept Leila by his side, introducing her to many people, and she was very shy, hardly speaking. Aidan felt sorry for her; he imagined she was overwhelmed. When she was finally released to join the other kids at a separate table at the back of the restaurant, she looked quite relieved.

Aidan sat with Benoit at a table in the corner. Benoit was not happy to have so many people around, or to be separated from Omar, and Aidan wanted to tell him to lighten up—but he knew it wouldn't matter.

He kept an eye on Leila. Only two other girls wore hijabs, with very fashionable long dresses. The others wore American jeans or midcalf skirts; they were demure but still stylish. The teenage boys were all older than Leila, loud and randy, joking with each other and horsing around. Leila looked like a little mouse among frolicking cats.

Aidan was disappointed that he wouldn't get to eat real French food. The closest he could get was the *mahjouba*—a giant, rectangular-folded crepe filled with sautéed tomato, red pepper, onion, and harissa. Benoit refused to order anything beyond a fizzy water, which he insisted be delivered in an unopened bottle.

Aidan missed Liam. How much more fun he would have with his partner—even if they were working. He liked the Arabic music playing in the background, the good food, and the sound of laughter rising and falling around him. Working with Benoit couldn't duplicate the easy connection he had to Liam, the way everything they did seemed better because they were doing it together.

It was after eleven by the time dinner was over, and Aidan could see that Leila was falling asleep as she leaned against her father. Omar said his good-byes to those still in the restaurant and walked outside with his daughter. Benoit and Aidan were right behind them.

The cold mistral swept down the street, and as Aidan stepped into it, he was buffeted backward.

When he connected the booming sound, and then the breaking glass, he realized it wasn't the wind at all; they had stepped into a bomb blast.

14 – Jean-Luc Derain

Because he was so close to the restaurant, Aidan was pushed backward against the stone building front. He stayed upright, though. Omar, Leila, and Benoit were all knocked to the ground by the force of the blast.

Aidan's first instinct was to reach for Leila. He grabbed her under the arms and pulled her back out of the street. There was chaos everywhere—people shouting, car alarms going off, breaking glass, and the smell of smoke. A woman next to Aidan screamed for her husband, who was inside the restaurant, and Aidan realized the blast had blown out the plate-glass window. He heard someone crying behind him.

Leila was in shock. Aidan wrapped his arm around her and pulled her close. Then he looked for her father.

He could just make out Omar's legs coming out from beneath Benoit. The big bodyguard must have been trying to protect Omar and fallen on him. Aidan turned to the crying woman. "Please hold Leila." He pushed the girl toward the woman, who reluctantly embraced her. Leila began crying as Aidan stepped out into the street.

He leaned down to Benoit and pressed his fingers against the bodybuilder's neck. There was no pulse. Under him, he heard Omar groaning. With a huge effort, Aidan pushed at Benoit's body. The man hardly moved. "Someone help me, please!" he called in French, and a Tunisian man joined him. Together they managed to free Omar from beneath Benoit.

The high-low whoop of police sirens added to the chaos as Aidan and the other man helped Omar to his feet. He looked back to the restaurant, his face streaked with grit and his suit jacket torn, and saw Leila. She broke free of the woman holding her and rushed to him.

The blue-and-white police lights flooded the street as Aidan shepherded Omar and Leila back inside, stepping carefully over the broken glass. He led them around upended tables and chairs to a booth at the rear. Omar sat close to his daughter, with his arm around her shoulder.

Aidan pulled out his cell phone and stepped back. "There's been an incident," Aidan said when Liam answered. "I'm fine and so are Omar and Leila. But the other bodyguard, Benoit, is dead."

He realized that his voice was quavering, and he took a deep breath as Liam asked, "What happened?"

"We were at dinner at a restaurant in the Arab quarter," Aidan said. "Looks like someone set off a bomb as we walked out into the street after the meal."

"What kind of bomb?"

"I'm not a munitions expert, Liam," Aidan said, his voice raising an octave. "A big bomb."

"Okay, calm down," Liam said. "You're all right, and so is the client. That's terrific. But I need you to give me some more details."

Aidan took another couple of deep breaths, then began describing what had happened, in as much detail as he could remember. "Sounds like a pretty small blast," Liam said when he was finished. "We'll have to see if the police can tell if it was on a timer, or if someone set it off as Omar was leaving the restaurant."

"The police are here," Aidan said as a couple of uniformed officers walked in. "I'll have to call you back."

The officers didn't speak to anyone, just kept the dozen remaining guests in the restaurant until ambulances had taken away the wounded. Aidan noticed two of the teenage girls texting on their cell phones as if they'd just seen an exciting movie. Leila dozed in her chair, her head resting on her father's shoulder. A plainclothes detective came inside, and began sequestering people individually to speak with them.

It was well after midnight by then, and Aidan was exhausted. Whatever adrenaline he'd felt after the blast was gone. He could barely keep his eyes open. The police made quick work of the other people in the restaurant, until only the Mansoors and Aidan were left.

"You will come with me, monsieur?" An officer stepped up to Aidan and escorted him across the room to where the inspector sat.

"I am Marcel Christophe," the inspector said. "You are?"

Aidan gave his name, then handed the man his passport and sat down. "You are American? You speak French?"

"Yes." Aidan explained that he was a bodyguard, based in Tunis, that he had been hired to escort Leila Mansoor to Marseille and keep an eye on her while her father was in meetings.

"Yes, Omar Mansoor," Christophe said. "What can you tell me about him?"

"It's a complicated story."

"It may be late, monsieur, but I can handle complicated."

Aidan nodded. "I'm not sure I can, though. But I'll try. My involvement began when my partner and I were introduced to Omar Mansoor's brother Farid." He stepped through being asked to investigate the situation at the Ferme Deux Hommes, and their initial reluctance. "Then when Leila's mother was arrested, Farid asked us to pick Leila up and bring her out to the farm."

Christophe took notes as Aidan took him through their arrival in Marseille the day before. When he finished, he asked, "Do you think this was an attack on Omar Mansoor?"

Christophe shrugged. "It is too early to say anything yet. But I would advise Monsieur Mansoor to get a new bodyguard as soon as possible."

"I'll tell him."

When he returned to where Omar and Leila sat, he discovered that Omar had already called the company that had supplied Benoit. "The man in charge of the branch here in Marseille will be here soon," he said. "He will take over for Benoit until he can find someone else."

"You're sure about this agency?" Aidan asked.

"You think Benoit was involved in his own death?"

"I don't think anything. I'm just trying to be careful."

"I could wonder the same thing about you," Omar said. "I was very safe here in Marseille until you arrived."

Aidan yawned. "I'm happy to return to Tunis when you want."

Omar looked at him. "No, I must ask you to stay. My daughter is precious to me. She must be protected, no matter what. I have seen how you care for her."

An officer appeared to escort Omar to speak with Christophe. Leila woke as her father shifted away from her, and Aidan reached out to put his arm around her. It was cold in the restaurant with the windows blown out, and she snuggled up close to him, all her formal reserve dissipated. Aidan made sure her jacket was zipped up, and she drifted back to sleep.

They huddled together until Omar returned from his conversation with Christophe. As he sat down, a tall Frenchman with tousled black hair appeared at the door of the restaurant. He showed his ID to the police officer and was granted access. He walked immediately to the table where Omar, Leila, and Aidan sat.

"Monsieur Mansoor? I'm Jean-Luc Derain. I'm the regional manager for the agency. Are you and your daughter all right?"

Omar nodded. "Benoit was very brave. He put himself at risk to save me."

"He was a good man," Jean-Luc said. "I'll make sure that his family knows how he died."

"He had a wife? Children?" Omar asked.

Jean-Luc shook his head. "No. He has a brother back in the countryside where he came from."

"I wish he had spoken more," Omar said. "I spent a great deal of time with him, but I did not know him at all."

"Benoit was a professional." Jean-Luc looked across the room at where Inspector Christophe was conferring with one of the uniformed officers. "Let me see if I can take you back to your apartment yet."

Aidan was surprised that he hadn't asked who Aidan was or what he was doing there. The Frenchman left them to speak with Inspector Christophe, and when he returned, he said, "I have a car outside. Monsieur Mansoor? Leila? Monsieur Greene?"

They all stood up. Jean-Luc did know who Aidan was. "There are flics everywhere, so I believe we are safe, but you will please be watchful."

Jean-Luc took point; Leila held her father's hand and walked beside him, and Aidan took the rear, doing his best to stay alert for any possible dangers. There were indeed cops everywhere, including a crime-scene van, and they had to pass a mobile bomb unit to get to Jean-Luc's four-door sedan, parked a block from the restaurant. Aidan was glad to reach it and settle into the front seat, allowing Omar and Leila the privacy of the rear.

"I'm going to take over for Benoit for the next few days," Jean-Luc said to Aidan. "I was able to retrieve his copy of the key to the apartment before he was taken away. I hope you will be as helpful to me as you were to Benoit."

Aidan turned to look at him. "I hardly spoke to Benoit."

"Still, he was very observant, and he reported everything to me."

Jean-Luc parked the sedan in the garage of the apartment building. He pulled a duffle bag from the trunk, then led them all upstairs. He wasn't as big or as muscular as Benoit, but he had a quiet air of authority that Aidan respected.

"I'll show you to the bedroom," Aidan said when Leila and Omar had gone to their rooms.

"I'd like to do a quick recon of the apartment first, if you don't mind," Jean-Luc said.

"No problem." He led the man around, pointing out the double-lock on the front door and the vulnerabilities he had identified. "Someone with a long-distance scope could get a clear shot at anyone on the balcony from that building over there," he said, pointing to a lower building a few hundred yards away.

"Yes, Benoit mentioned that he had warned Monsieur Mansoor to stay off the balcony."

When they had done a complete circuit of the apartment, they ended up in the bedroom Aidan had shared with Benoit. The bodybuilding magazine he had been reading was lying open on his bed. That was when it finally hit him, that Benoit, who had been alive just a few hours before, reading that magazine and probably dreaming of competitions or repetitions, was dead.

He knew he should call Liam again, but it was very late, and he could barely keep his eyes open. He used the bathroom, and when he returned to the room, Jean-Luc had already packed Benoit's belongings into his bag and unpacked his own. Aidan stripped down to his shorts and climbed between the sheets and was asleep almost immediately.

15 – Looking for Intel

Liam walked down the hall to the master bedroom and knocked on the door, which was ajar. A moment later, James opened it fully, wearing a lightweight cotton robe. Behind him, Liam saw Farid sitting up in bed. Lamps next to both sides of the bed were lit, and it appeared both men had been reading.

"There's been a bombing in Marseille," Liam said. "Aidan, Omar, and Leila are all fine, but the other bodyguard was killed."

"My God," James said, looking stricken. "I knew there were people who didn't like Omar, but I never considered…"

"You are sure that my brother was the target?" Farid asked.

Liam shook his head. "Nothing is sure yet." He explained about the dinner and the bombing. "I'll check with my contacts, but most likely we'll have to wait till the morning to hear what's going on."

"Thank you, Liam," Farid said. "And please thank Aidan for us too. I'm very glad you are both here to help."

Liam went back to his room. Aidan had taken his clothes with him to Marseille, and the room felt empty without his clutter. He lay down on the bed, on the side he usually slept on, then turned his head on the pillow, trying to catch a trace of Aidan's scent on it. He looked around for the netbook and once again remembered that Aidan had taken it with him to Marseille.

He went back to the main house, moving quietly so that he wouldn't disturb James, Farid, or the manservant, Hakim, who slept in a bedroom next to the farm's office. He turned on the desktop computer and surfed the Internet, looking for news of the bombing. It took a while, because he didn't know any of the specifics, but eventually, reports began to surface. The restaurant was called Café Raoued, after a beach just north of Tunis, and it was in the Noailles quarter of Marseille, where there was a concentration of North Africans.

Once he had those specifics, he narrowed his search. He found a couple of photos taken by a teenage girl who had been in the restaurant with her family, which she had posted to her Facebook account. Through the blown-out front window, Liam could see the blue-and-white police lights captured in mid-swivel by the camera's shutter. There was a lot of glass on the floor, which indicated to him that the bomb had been set off outside.

He downloaded the four pictures, then opened them in Photoshop and enlarged them. The quality was poor, but in the background of one shot, he saw Aidan, Leila, and a man who must be Omar Mansoor.

From the way the tables and chairs had been overturned, he could tell the bomb hadn't hit the restaurant straight on; the force of the blast had come at the front window from the right. Logically, the bomb couldn't have been on a timer, because there was no guarantee that Omar Mansoor would leave the restaurant at a particular time. The bomber would need a place to stay out of sight, but with a clear view of the front door of the café, to know when to detonate.

He opened a new document and began making notes. He pulled

up Google Earth and looked at the surrounding buildings. It was hard to tell for sure, but there was a fruit-and-vegetable vendor's stall at the entrance to an alley, catty-cornered to the restaurant. He'd bet money that the bomb had exploded there.

The street was a narrow one, with multistory apartment buildings lining both sides. He found a photo of the Café Raoued in a user's photo album on Flickr and analyzed it. A dark green awning hung over the front, with metal piers framing two big windows. The building was painted a dark tan, with light blue shutters and a couple of slim balconies overlooking the street. He imagined that the police would be canvassing everyone who lived there about suspicious activity and hoped that there was a nosy old man or woman who might have noticed something.

The windows of the shop across the street had been painted bright green, with an overlay of Indian gods and goddesses. Up above, pennants had been strung from the second-floor level across the street. In the pictures he found on Facebook, several strands hung loose, while others pooled on the pavement. One of the green windows across the street had also blown out.

He yawned. It was after one by then. He assumed Aidan was still caught up at the scene of the bombing and couldn't talk. He saved the document he'd been working on to the desktop, then turned off the computer and returned to the guesthouse, though he was so accustomed to having Aidan beside him that it took him longer than usual to drop off.

* * *

When Liam woke the next morning, the first thing he did was check his phone for missed calls. There were none. It was still early, so he kept the phone with him as he exercised on the pool deck. Working out had been the one constant in his life since he was a teenager, the opportunity to master his body and build his strength. When he reached puberty, he didn't understand the feelings he had and the way his body reacted to the sight of other naked boys. He focused on controlling what he could, building his muscles and pushing the limits of his endurance. It was a strategy that had served him well in the SEALs.

Since Leila was gone and there were no women on the property to be scandalized, he reverted to his usual custom of working out wearing only a jockstrap to keep his dick and balls in place. He loved the fresh air and sunshine on his skin, and he was proud of his body. Even though the morning was cool, almost cold, he quickly worked up some body heat, and the air was refreshing rather than chilling.

He finished his clap pushups, looked up and saw James in the doorway of the house, holding a mug of coffee and watching him. "Don't let me disturb you," James said as Liam stood up.

"No, I'm finished for today."

"Pity. I was enjoying the view." James wore the same cotton bathrobe, in a blue-and-white stripe. If he had anything on underneath, it was only a very skimpy pair of briefs—but there was probably nothing there.

Before he'd met Aidan, Liam would have taken that comment as an invitation, walking up to the man, taking the mug from his hands, and putting them somewhere much more useful. But instead he said, "Then you won't mind if I take a quick swim."

He dropped the jockstrap to the ground, then dove into the deep end of the pool and swam forward. He surfaced near where James was standing.

"Aidan is a very lucky man," James said.

Liam could see the older man's stiff dick pressing against the fabric of his robe and was embarrassed to feel himself responding similarly. He turned and began his laps, focused on the water and his movement through it, and when he pulled himself out, James was gone.

He showered after his swim. Then he donned a pair of multi-pocketed shorts, sandals, and his leather vest. He hadn't bothered to remove his nipple rings because they had left Tunis in a hurry, and looking at himself in the guest-room mirror, he decided to leave them in. He thought they made him look tougher.

The security company returned as Farid, James, and Liam were finishing breakfast. Liam met the two workmen at the front door and began walking the property with them, pointing out places where he wanted cameras and enhanced locks. It was already ten degrees warmer than it had been when Liam woke, and in the distance, he heard the low grinding noise of the olive press.

Once he had showed the two men around, he returned to James's office, turned on the computer there, and began making phone calls. The first one was to Aidan.

"What time is it?" Aidan said, yawning.

"Nearly nine here. You're not up yet?"

"We had a late night."

Liam tapped impatiently on the desk as he waited for the computer to warm up so he could pull up the notes he'd taken the night before. "What about Omar and Leila?"

"Don't know. I just woke up. But Jean-Luc's probably with them."

"Jean-Luc?"

"He's the manager of the agency Benoit worked for," Aidan said. "Fifty-something, very professional. He showed up at the restaurant last night and drove us back here. Looks like he slept in Benoit's bed."

"You asked him for his ID, I hope."

"He just walked in the restaurant and took charge. He knew who we all were. And he had a car to drive us back to the apartment."

"You got into a car with the client and a strange man?" Liam felt his voice rising, but he couldn't help it. "How stupid can you be?"

"He showed an ID to the police officer at the door of the restaurant," Aidan said. "They wouldn't have let him in if he wasn't legit."

Liam took a couple of deep breaths. The computer had booted up by then, and he opened the document he'd begun the night before. "Here's what I want you to do. Get up and very carefully look around the apartment. Assume that this guy Jean-Luc is not legit and see if you can find Omar and Leila." He thought but did not add, *and hope that they're both still alive.*

Though if this Jean-Luc had truly been there to kill the clients, he would have killed Aidan as well; no need to leave a witness around. But Liam held his breath as he heard what sounded like Aidan getting dressed, then walking out of his room.

Then he heard Aidan say, "Good morning, Omar. Leila. Jean-Luc. Let me just finish up this call."

Liam let his breath out. "Everything's fine here," Aidan said. "Omar and Leila are having breakfast. Jean-Luc is talking on his phone."

"Give me his last name and the name of the agency."

"Hold on. I'll get a card from Jean-Luc for you."

Liam resumed his online search while he waited. There were a couple of brief reports about the incident, but nothing more than he already knew.

"His name is Jean-Luc Derain, and the company is called Agence de Securité."

Liam added it to the file. "I want to come out to Marseille, but I need to stay here at least one more day until the security system is finished."

"I'll be fine here, Liam. Jean-Luc seems like a real professional."

Liam was not reassured. "You take care of yourself. I love you."

"Love you too," Aidan said.

Liam sat back against the padded chair. His heart had skipped a couple of beats at the thought of Aidan in danger. That bothered him.

He'd never worried about a partner before. Not that he didn't trust Aidan, within the limits of his ability. But if something happened to him... Liam didn't know how he would react, how he would cope. He had to face facts. Love had made him its bitch, and there was nothing he could do about it.

Well, not quite nothing. He could do what he was trained to do. He turned back to the computer and found the website for Agence de Securité. His French wasn't as strong as his Arabic, so he hit the button for automatic translation and waited impatiently for the site to appear in English. The company looked like a reputable, professional organization, and Jean-Luc Derain was listed as the regional manager for southern France, based in Marseille. There was even a photo of Derain, a good-looking Frenchman in his mid-fifties.

Liam's next call was to Louis Fleck. "You hear about the bombing in Marseille?" he asked when Louis answered his cell.

"No. Anyone we know involved?"

"Farid Mansoor's brother Omar, his daughter Leila. And Aidan. I'll e-mail you what I know—can you see what you can dig up through your channels?"

"Aidan all right?"

"Yeah, he's great." Liam logged into the web client for their e-mail provider, opened a new e-mail message, and attached the document. "It's on its way."

"I'll see what I can find. Gotta go—another call coming in."

Louis hung up, and Liam put the phone down. He wanted to know more about the bombing, but he knew he'd just be spinning his wheels. Louis Fleck had access to a lot more intel than Liam ever would. He had to wait for the CIA agent to get back to him.

He e-mailed all his documents to himself and copied the message to Aidan, then went back outside, where the security company was working. He was too restless to stand around and watch them, so he drove down into Tebourba. A goat grazed on the sparse grass by the roadside as he approached the town. The land was flat, with the occasional olive or palm tree, and Tebourba was a large town compared to many Liam had visited in the Tunisian countryside. The buildings were white stucco that shimmered in the bright sunshine, trimmed with the same bright blue paint found all over Tunisia.

He stopped at the police station, a one-story building with the Tunisian flag flying from the roof. He introduced himself to the officer at the front desk in Arabic and asked to speak to someone about the incidents at the olive groves. "That would be Lieutenant Issa," the officer said. "I'll call him."

He turned his head and yelled, "Lieutenant! Someone here to see you." Then he turned back to Liam. "You can have a seat."

Lieutenant Issa was a short, compact, dark-skinned man. Liam introduced himself once again. "The owners have hired me to supervise a new security system. I would like to know if there have been similar incidents at other groves in the area."

Issa shook his head. "No, the Ferme Deux Hommes is the only one that has experienced trouble. But that land has had many problems."

"Perhaps I could buy you a coffee and you could tell me?"

"There is a café just down the block," Issa said. As they walked, he said, "You speak very good Arabic for a foreigner. You have been here in Tunisia long?"

"A few years. I'm based in Tunis, where I provide executive protection services."

Issa nodded. "You were a soldier before that?"

Good, Liam thought. The man was perceptive and paid attention. "Yes. Never based here in Tunisia, but I had some contacts here who helped me get set up."

They talked about the political unrest, which fortunately had bypassed Tebourba. When they were both seated in a corner of the café with iced coffee, Liam asked, "You said there have been problems with the farm in the past."

Issa nodded. "The Mansoor property was once only half as large. Ten years ago, the old man, Mr. Mansoor, bought his neighbor's land and doubled the size of his groves."

"And that was a problem?"

"He acquired the land at a bargain price, and the heirs of his neighbor were not happy."

"Those heirs—they're still around?"

Issa pulled a notebook from his pocket. "You read Arabic as well as you speak?"

"Not really."

"I will write in English for you, then. The man you need is called Ayham Samaha. He is a person known to the police. A troublemaker, you might say. It was his grandfather's land, and he is still very angry about the situation."

He tore a sheet of paper from his notebook and handed it to Liam. "Here is his address. And now if you will excuse me, I have a meeting to attend. Thank you for the coffee."

He stood up and walked out. Liam remained at the table, sipping his coffee. He decided to return to the Ferme Deux Hommes and ask Farid what he knew about the Samaha family before searching the man out. He just might be able to solve the problem in Tebourba and get to Marseille to help Aidan very soon.

16 – Follow the Money

After Aidan finished his call to Liam, he sat on his bed and thought. He had been foolish the night before to accept Jean-Luc Derain without asking for any proof. He wasn't thinking like a real bodyguard and anticipating problems. He was just reacting as things came up.

Well, it was time to start behaving like he knew what he was doing.

Liam had taught him to ask questions and then seek out the answers. The first question he thought of, as he looked around the room, was where the money was coming from to fund Omar Mansoor's life in Marseilles. It had to be expensive to live in this fancy apartment building and hire a bodyguard 24-7. Who was paying for it?

He picked up his cell phone and dialed. "Morning, Richard," he said when his British hacker contact answered.

"Morning, Aidan. Always a pleasure to hear from you blokes. Got something interesting for me to nose into?"

Aidan gave him the information he had on Omar Mansoor. It wasn't much. "I want to know where his money comes from," he said.

"Blimey, you don't want much, do you?"

"If you can't do it..."

"Didn't say that, mate. But it'll be tricky."

"You do tricky very well," Aidan said. "E-mail or text me when you have something. I'm in Marseille with the client, so I may not be able to talk."

Aidan went back out to the kitchen, and Jean-Luc motioned him out to the balcony. "I've managed to convince Monsieur Mansoor to stay close to home today," he said. "That means he's going to be conducting his meetings here in the apartment. You and I will take turns manning the door. We'll check IDs against a list of who's expected."

"No problem."

"The first guests should be arriving in about half an hour. I'll take door duty for an hour, then switch off with you."

Aidan went back to his room and opened his netbook. He checked his e-mail and responded to a couple of messages, then did some Internet searching on Omar Mansoor. He discovered that Omar and Farid had been born at a hospital in Tunis forty-two years before. Both boys had graduated from the Université de Tunis, where Omar had begun his political career as president of the student government. He had worked in several government ministries before founding the Muslim Leadership six years before.

He began speaking out against President Ben Ali and was arrested several times for minor offenses. He had decamped to France about a year before, leaving his wife and brother-in-law in charge of the movement.

That was all Aidan could find. Many of the pages online were in Arabic script, and his command of the written language just wasn't good enough. When he used the automatic translation system to render the pages into English, they made little sense.

Frustrated, he went back to the links he had found for Farid. He had been a successful interior designer in Tunis until closing his business a year before and moving out to the Ferme Deux Hommes.

Aidan sat back against the bed's headboard. Was there a connection between Omar's departure from Tunis for France and Farid's leaving the city for Tebourba? Had the two of them been involved in something that forced both to leave? What if Farid really was more involved in the Muslim Leadership than he let on?

He had told Aidan that he and his brother were estranged. Aidan had assumed it was because Farid was gay. But what if there was something more to it?

"Need you at the front door," Jean-Luc said, sticking his head into the bedroom. "One meeting is breaking up, and another's going to start."

Aidan spent the next couple of hours alternating with Jean-Luc as people came and went. When he was on duty, he stood near the front door so he could hear everything that was being said in the living room. Just before noon, he admitted a middle-aged Frenchwoman with dyed red hair and a tight-fitting black suit. Her name was Micheline Allange, and the card she gave Aidan indicated she worked for a travel agency.

Omar greeted her in French, kissing her on both cheeks, and Aidan followed most of the conversation.

"There are flights available daily to Tunis direct from Marseille," she said, sitting on the sofa across from Omar, who was wearing dark slacks and a white dress shirt, open at the neck. "I can get you on a flight with just a few hours' notice."

"Very good," Omar said. "You'll be able to arrange the priority boarding?"

"Of course. The airport is always very accommodating to diplomats."

"I am not quite a diplomat yet," he said, smiling. "At least, not until the next election."

That was interesting, Aidan thought. Omar was going back to Tunisia and running for office. What kind of office, though? President? The Tunisian Parliament had two houses: the Chamber of Deputies, elected by popular vote, and the Chamber of Advisors, comprised of regional representatives and official nominees. Did the Muslim Leadership have enough support to elect a president? Aidan doubted it.

But he could see Omar winning an election to the Chamber of Deputies, either from Tunis or from the electoral district encompassing Tebourba.

The Frenchwoman left, and Jean-Luc took over at the door. Aidan returned to his room, where he found an e-mail from Richard. The rent on the apartment in Marseille was being paid by a United States corporation called Gardiner Holdings LLC, which was in turn owned by James Gardiner. Gardiner Holdings also made charitable contributions to the Muslim Leadership and paid Omar Mansoor a substantial salary.

All that had begun at about the same time that James and Farid moved to the farm, and Omar left Tunisia for Marseille.

Aidan forwarded the e-mail to Liam. He wanted to talk to Liam about it—but not from the apartment. He walked back from the bedroom to where Jean-Luc lounged by the front door. From there he could see yet another meeting going on in the living room, this one with several men in *djellabas*, the loose-fitting robe favored by Moroccans.

"Everything all right?" Jean-Luc asked.

"Do you think I could slip out for a few minutes? I need some fresh air."

Jean-Luc looked at his watch. "This group should be here at least another hour."

"Great. Thanks."

Aidan took the elevator downstairs and walked around the corner to a café he had noticed the day before. Once he was seated there, with a cappuccino on order, he called Liam's cell.

When Liam answered, Aidan heard an electric drill in the background, which faded as Liam spoke. "How are Omar and Leila holding up?"

"Leila's been in her room all morning, still freaked out by what happened last night. Omar has been in meetings all day in the living room. I overheard a conversation he had with a travel agent. Sounds like he's getting ready to go back to Tunisia and run for office."

"The sooner the better," Liam said. "I want you back here."

"Did you get the e-mail I forwarded from Richard?"

"Not yet. Since you have the laptop, I've had to adapt and use the computer in the farm's office. I haven't checked it since early this morning."

"I knew you had to have some kind of access because I got the files you e-mailed me." Since they almost always worked together, they hadn't invested in a second computer. "You can read and send e-mail from your phone too, you know. I called Richard this morning and asked him to look into where the money comes from to fund Omar's lifestyle here in France. Guess where?"

"No idea."

"James Gardiner."

"So? He's doing it for Farid."

"I'm not so sure." The waitress delivered Aidan's coffee, and he smiled at her. "Farid said he and his brother were estranged, remember? And that he hadn't seen Leila in years."

"Maybe James is paying Omar for his share of the farm," Liam said.

"Possibly. The payments only started when Omar left Tunisia and James and Farid moved to Tebourba. I'm thinking maybe something happened in Tunis between the brothers that drove them apart. And James is paying Omar off."

"You have a very active imagination, Aidan," Liam said. "But I'll sniff around and see what I can find out about what might have gone down between the brothers." He paused. "How's the new bodyguard?"

"Jean-Luc? Very professional. I feel like I can learn from him. I see the way he moves and the things he notices."

"What? I'm not a good enough teacher for you anymore?"

"Of course you are, Liam. But it's always good to learn from different people—you know that." He laughed. "You're not jealous, are you?"

"That depends. Is this Jean-Luc gay?"

Aidan laughed again. "Nope. He's straight, and he smokes Gauloises. Definitely not my type."

"Good. I don't love the idea of you sharing a room with any man other than me."

"I'll keep that in mind. What's new in Tebourba?" Aidan sipped his cappuccino.

"The security company is working steadily—at least as steadily as anybody works in this country. I think they'll have everything in place in the next day or two." Liam paused. "And I might have a lead on who's doing the sabotage."

"Really? Who?"

"Local bad guy whose family used to own the land next door. Omar and Farid's father bought it cheaply, and the guy may hold a grudge."

"Sounds like a good lead. What are you going to do?"

"I'm waiting to sound out Farid before I go any further."

"Can you pass the information on to the police?"

"That's where it came from. I'm not sure whether I should go out and confront this guy or wait for him to try something else."

"Didn't you tell me yourself we're bodyguards, not investigators?

That means you protect the client and try to neutralize any threat. Not that you go off confronting crazy Arabs."

Liam laughed. "I take it back. You are listening to me."

Aidan drained the last of his cappuccino. "I should get back to the apartment. I want to spend some time with Leila this afternoon, see how she's doing."

"Take her some candy," Liam said. "Maybe you can sweeten her up. She's awfully sour for a girl so young."

"She's almost a teenager. Trust me, there are lot like her out there."

They hung up after mutual declarations of love, and Aidan walked back to the apartment. As he did, he passed a trio of young girls, not much older than Leila, laughing and horsing around, and once again he was sorry for his charge, who didn't seem to know how to enjoy life.

Most of his career had been focused on teaching adults. Back in Philadelphia, he had worked for a technical college, helping recent immigrants learn enough English to pass their certification exams. But on occasion, he'd taught younger students too, most recently at a summer institute in Bizerte, on Tunisia's north coast.

They were strange creatures, teenagers, teetering between childhood and the adult world, not sure where they wanted to stand. They wanted their independence, yet they were beholden to their parents for financial and emotional support. They wanted to be treated like adults, yet they also needed routine, rules, and regulations.

Leila seemed like a young twelve-year-old to him. She could

quote the Koran and the Hadith like an imam, but she had no sense of the outside world, and that was dangerous for a girl on the brink of womanhood.

That was, Aidan thought, if she could survive her father's political opponents.

17 – Birthright

As Liam was walking up the driveway at the Ferme Deux Hommes on his way home from his coffee with Lieutenant Issa, his cell rang. "Louis. Did you find out anything?"

"Basic pipe bomb. Gasoline in a glass container, with plastic bags dissolved into the gas. You've seen that, I'm sure."

"Consistency of melted marshmallow? Yeah. Don't you add gun cotton to it?" Gun cotton was a form of nitrocellulose used in explosives.

"You've got it. Whoever mixed it up added nuts, bolts, and screws along with gunpowder and a couple of M-80s, making it the equivalent of a Molotov cocktail."

"But worse. Those metal fragments can be nasty. They'll go right through a brick wall when you detonate."

"And that's exactly what happened. Somebody tossed the bottle when Mr. Mansoor walked out of the restaurant. Fortunately for your client, the thrower was a lousy shot."

"Guess American baseball hasn't taken hold in France."

"Assuming the thrower was French. It's equally possible it was thrown by an Arab immigrant who disagreed with Mansoor's politics—or was paid to do it."

"The police have any leads?"

"Not that I can find out. But I'll keep my ears to the ground."

"Thanks, Louis. I'm sure Farid and James will appreciate

anything you can do."

He hung up and then walked around the property, checking the work being done by the security company. His first instinct had been to secure the house, but James had insisted that so far there had been no danger to either him or Farid, and he wanted the groves protected first. The workmen were installing a series of cameras around the perimeter of the property, to be linked to a computer in the study where James could watch what was going on. There would be motion sensor triggers as well.

It was late afternoon by the time he ended up by the pool, sipping sangria with Farid, who had been supervising the olive harvest.

"You see, it is not easy making olive oil," Farid said.

"You work hard. I understand why your brother doesn't want to work the land too."

"Omar was always more interested in politics and city life." Farid sipped his sangria, looking thoughtful.

"But you must have been close once."

Farid nodded. "When we were boys, we were inseparable. Omar was the leader, and I was the follower. Our father scolded us many times for climbing the trees before the olives were ripe. We swam in the river when it was high enough; we stole candied dates from the kitchen when our mother had her back turned. It was a wonderful childhood. I'm sorry Leila hasn't been able to have one like it."

Liam drank some of his sangria. "Were you still close in college?"

"Not so much. Omar made many new friends, and so did I. I began to understand that I preferred men to women. Omar met Khadija, and they socialized with other couples, ones who agreed with their politics."

Farid sighed. "After we graduated, we both remained in Tunis. Omar and Khadija married, and I moved in with a male friend. My brother was angry when he discovered that the man and I shared a bed."

"Is that what forced you apart?"

"Only one of many things. Our mother died when we were in college, but our father stayed out here on the farm, growing olives and grinding them into a cheap olive oil he and the rest of the farmers in the area sold to a big collective. One year there was a drought, and because my father was very smart and used the resources of the river well, he succeeded where others failed. He was able to acquire the neighboring farm at a low price. Their groves are a substantial part of our acreage now."

James joined them, bringing a fresh pitcher of sangria.

"Do either of you know a man named Ayham Samaha?" Liam asked when James had refilled all their glasses.

"Never heard of him," James said.

Farid cocked his head. "The name is familiar, but I am not sure where to place it. Does he work here?"

"Not as far as I know. I checked the payroll records, and his name doesn't appear there." He explained what Lieutenant Issa had told him earlier that day.

"Ah, yes, the man whose property my father bought was called Samaha. But even though our properties were adjacent, we did not have much to do with them. I remember the father was not a good Muslim. He beat his wife and children."

"After your father bought the groves, where did the Samahas go?"

Farid shrugged. "I believe the mother had already died by then, and it was just the father and a few children. I assume they moved into the town."

"Did you ever get any threats from them?"

"You think perhaps this Ayham Samaha is the one who has been causing us this trouble, because of how my father treated his?"

"It does seem like a good hypothesis. And he has a police record."

"What will you do? Will you confront him?"

"I'd rather catch him in the act of doing something, because then it becomes a police matter. The lieutenant gave me his address. I'm going over there tonight, and I'll watch to see if he tries to come over here."

"Isn't that dangerous?" James asked.

"That's what you pay me for," Liam said.

James drained the last of his sangria and stood up. "I'll see how Hakim is coming with dinner."

Farid sipped his sangria and looked at Liam. "You have family, back in the US?"

"Two younger sisters. One married, one divorced, both with

kids. We aren't angry at each other—we just live very different lives. I talk to both of them now and then and send gifts to my nieces and nephews."

"I feel very sad that I have missed time with my brother and his family. Omar would bring Khadija and Leila here, but only when he knew I would not be visiting as well. I saw him for the first time in ten years when our father died. Just when I thought we might establish some rapport, he left for Marseille, and I moved here with James."

Liam remembered the conversation with Aidan, who had noticed that synchronicity. "Why did he leave? Did you two fight?"

Farid shook his head. "His leaving had nothing to do with me. He had been arrested several times for his political activism—always minor offenses, you understand, but he was taken into custody, held for several days each time. One day he simply announced that he was going into exile in France. And then he left."

"Who owns the farm now? Both of you?"

Farid shook his head. "My father was very traditional. He believed that the farm was Omar's birthright, because he was the eldest. The house and land went to him. He wanted to sell it immediately to fund his political aspirations, and James bought the property from him." He smiled. "For me. The farm is now in both our names, and we share everything."

Liam sipped his sangria. It didn't appear that Farid knew James was still paying Omar—or supporting him in Marseille. That was interesting. Why would James keep it a secret from his partner? Had

Omar made threats against Farid, and James was paying him off? Or was there more to the real estate transaction than Farid knew?

"Dinner's ready," James announced from the doorway. Farid and Liam rose and followed him into the dining room.

Liam missed Aidan most acutely as they ate. He had grown so accustomed to his partner's charm and ready smile that the meal seemed gloomy and dim without him. He wondered if Aidan felt the same way, or if he was cheerfully enjoying a great French meal.

"I'm starting to think this security company is a bunch of clowns," James said, bringing Liam out of his reverie. "Have you seen the work they're doing?"

"I'm watching them," Liam said. "They aren't the sharpest knives in the drawer, but they know their equipment. The camera guy surprised me with some of the features of the system."

"I'll take your word for it," James said. "I'm still having some trouble getting into the third-world lifestyle. Back in California, if I snapped my fingers, things happened."

"How did you end up here?" Liam asked.

Farid giggled. "Tell him, James."

James looked embarrassed. "After I sold my business and came out of the closet, I found a couple of like-minded buddies, and we went on a sex tour of the world. The Philippines, Thailand, Morocco. Sampling the wares, if you will. We were passing through Tunis for a couple of days. One of my buddies knew this gay club, very upscale but underground. I didn't even want to go out that night, but he dragged me along."

"And our eyes met across the crowded room," Farid said. "It was very romantic."

"We were both horny," James said. "Farid came back to my hotel room with me, and we must have stayed in bed for three days, living on sex and room service."

Liam could just imagine the distinguished-looking James, with his touches of silver hair and his businesslike bearing, walking into a gay club and spotting the willowy, dark-skinned Farid across the room, probably dressed to the nines.

"I managed to convince James to stay in Tunis for a while," Farid said. "After a week, he gave up his hotel room and moved into my apartment. And here we are, years later."

"How did you and Aidan meet, Liam?" James asked.

"By mistake." Liam pushed his empty plate away. "I was supposed to meet a client at a bar, and Aidan matched his description. I walked up to Aidan and started talking. I was dressed pretty much like this, and I could almost see his mouth watering. But at that time, I thought he was the client, and I draw the line at sex with anyone who's paying me."

"Too bad," James said.

"James!" Farid said, laughing.

"Liam knows he's attractive. Look at the way he flaunts his body in that vest." He smiled wolfishly. "It never hurts to let one's interest be known."

"Aidan and I are happy together," Liam said. "No need to bring anyone else into the mix." Liam realized that the three of them had probably drunk too much sangria, and he tried to bring the conversation back to business. "On another note, I've gotten some more information about the bombing in Marseille." He told them, in layman's terms, what Louis had relayed to him.

"But the police have no suspects?"

"Not that we've heard," Liam said. "And Aidan says that Omar may be coming back to Tunisia soon. Apparently, he was meeting with a travel agent today."

Farid and James exchanged a look that Liam could not interpret. Perhaps there was something to Aidan's suspicions, and his clients weren't being completely honest with him.

18 – Hacksaw

As soon as dinner was over, Liam got into the Jeep and drove toward Tebourba, looking for the address Lieutenant Issa had given him for Ayham Samaha. It was a small stucco building in a row of similar homes, on the outskirts of Tebourba, across from a closed gas station. As his headlights swept the building, he saw a weather-beaten scooter leaning against one wall.

He drove another block and pulled up behind the ruins of what looked like an old olive press, its millstone cracked and resting in the midst of dried weeds. He turned the Jeep's engine off, and after it finished ticking, the night was soundless. There was almost no ground light, so the stars above shone brilliantly.

A bird of prey—hawk, kestrel, or falcon, he couldn't tell in the dark—soared above in search of rats, gerbils, or jerboa, a long-tailed hopping rodent with cartoonishly large long ears. The wind shifted direction, rustling the fronds of a single palm tree. A barn owl's drawn-out hissing scream disturbed the stillness, lingering for a few seconds, then dying away.

It was eerie out there, far from the lights and noise of the city. Nice enough for a vacation, but give him urban bustle and decay any time.

The best route from Samaha's house to the olive groves was a straight run, past the Sidi Gharsallah cemetery to the main road that ran past the entrance to the farm. Liam couldn't follow the man from his home; there was so little traffic out at night, he was sure to be spotted. He decided he'd leave the Jeep at the house and borrow a bicycle from James and Farid. Then he could hide near the driveway and be able to follow the scooter if it came near the property.

He turned the Jeep back on and drove back to the Ferme Deux Hommes, passing only a single beat-up minivan on the way. The gap-toothed driver grinned and waved, and Liam returned the gesture.

From the garage adjacent to the house, he collected a coil of rope, a miner's light he could mount on his forehead, his gun, and a few other tools, and got into position.

Shifting clouds alternately hid and exposed the half moon. There were hundreds of stars out in the clear night, and Liam kept his mind busy identifying constellations. He had learned some celestial navigation as a SEAL, and it was a good skill to keep up. Unlike Aidan, however, who only looked at the beauty of the stars and the romance of travel to other worlds, he counted on those points of light to ground him firmly in this world.

Shortly after eleven o'clock, a low rumble approached from the direction of Tebourba. He mounted the bicycle, tensed and ready to follow. But it was a truck, not a scooter, and it didn't even slow down as it passed the farm's entrance. It was another hour before he heard another engine—this time with a much lower sound, with backfires. Once again he prepared to follow, and as the scooter passed, he slid quietly in behind it.

The man didn't go far; he soon slowed and stopped at the edge of the road, a few meters from the first olive trees, and left the scooter leaning against a speed sign.

Liam pulled up a hundred meters behind the man and carefully laid the bicycle on the ground. He watched as the man pulled a hacksaw out of a canvas bag on the back of the scooter. He was skinny and about five-seven, wearing a T-shirt, shorts, and sandals. Liam followed him silently across the road, toward the trees, waited until the man had reached a tree and grabbed a branch, preparing to cut it off.

"Stop right there," Liam said in Arabic. "I have a gun." He turned the miner's light on Samaha, who was frozen in position. Liam walked carefully up to him as Samaha turned to face him. He was about twenty-five, with a thin, drawn face and wiry arms. "Hold out your hands."

"Don't shoot me. This is all a mistake."

"Don't bother to talk. At least not yet." Liam tied Samaha's hands together with the rope, then pushed him forward as they climbed the slope up to the house.

Samaha kept talking in Arabic, alternately protesting his innocence and pleading for mercy. Liam ignored him. When they reached the front door of the house, he rang the bell. Hayam's short, high-pitched barks responded.

After a minute or two, the outside light came on, and James Gardiner opened the front door. "I found your saboteur," Liam said, holding up the hacksaw.

"Bring him inside," James said, stepping back.

They all walked into the living room, where they were joined by

Farid. "This is Ayham Samaha," Liam said. He led Samaha to a chair by the wall and motioned him to sit, holding his roped hands in front of him. Hayam stayed close by Liam, but he could tell she had her eye on the captive.

As he and James sat down opposite Samaha, Farid peered at him. "Is your father's name Mohammed?"

Samaha nodded sullenly.

"I remember him from when we were children," Farid said, leaning back. "He lived on the next farm."

"The farm your father stole from my grandfather," Samaha said.

Farid shook his head. "My father was an honorable man. He would not have stolen."

"It was almost a theft—your father paid so much less than the property was worth."

Farid turned and translated to James.

"It was worth nothing back then," James said. "Those olive trees hadn't been properly tended in years. There was no irrigation. Even today, you can tell which trees belonged to your grandfather—they are the stunted ones, the poor producers."

Farid repeated the information to Ayham in Arabic. They began to argue until finally James held up his hand and said, "Enough. Ask him how much money he wants to leave us alone."

"You can't pay him off," Liam said, standing beside Samaha. "He's a criminal. We have to turn him over to the police."

"James is right," Farid said. "Though I believe my father did nothing wrong, it is enough that Mr. Samaha believes it so. If we don't do something positive, there will be bad blood in the land. Allah will keep the trees from bearing fruit and will ruin the crop."

He turned to Samaha and returned to Arabic, negotiating a price. Once they agreed, Farid said, "Liam, can you please remove the rope from Ayham's hands?"

"I think you're making a mistake," Liam said.

James left the room and returned a moment later carrying a checkbook. He sat down at the desk and wrote a check, which Farid carried to Ayham. "From now, you will no longer bother us?" he asked in Arabic.

"The debt between your family and mine has been repaid." Ayham took the check and stood up. "I am sorry for any trouble. But I had to satisfy my family's honor."

"Yes, I understand," Farid said.

Ayham turned to Liam. "My saw?"

Liam shook his head. "You've got enough money to buy a new one if you need it."

Ayham frowned, but said, "*Ma'a as-salaama*," and bowed slightly.

Farid said, "*Allah ysalmak*," and walked him to the front door.

Liam turned to James. "If it's all right with you, I'd like to fly to Marseille tomorrow and see how Aidan is doing."

"Now that the security company is here, and they know what they have to do, I can keep tabs on them. I appreciate everything you've done. And consider yourself still on the clock—I know Farid would want his brother and his niece protected."

"What are you talking about?" Farid asked, returning to the

living room.

"I'm going to Marseille tomorrow," Liam said. "I want to help Aidan take care of Leila and Omar."

"Thank you. For everything you have done so far, and for what you will do for my family," Farid said.

"I'll have to ask you something in return. Can Hayam stay here? I could drop her back in the city on my way to the airport, but it means leaving an extra hour early."

"Of course."

"I don't want to get into the hassle of carrying our guns into France. I'll leave them in a bag for you too."

James nodded. "I'll take good care of them."

Liam went down the hall to the office, Hayam on his heels. He went online and booked the early morning flight to Marseille; then he picked up the little dog and carried her outside. "Do you miss Papa Aidan?" he said into the dog's pointy ear. "I do." He put the dog down, and she scampered over to a spiky aloe. Carefully avoiding the spines, she sniffed around, found a good place, and squatted to pee.

He ushered the dog back into the guesthouse ahead of him. Then he began packing everything they had left there. He found himself smiling, even though he knew it was foolish; even with Samaha taken care of, there was still a lot of danger. And yet, the idea of being with Aidan again made him happy.

He'd served with many straight men as a SEAL, and he had listened to many hours of maudlin sentimentality as they reminisced about their wives and mistresses and girlfriends. He had dismissed them all as drunken rambling because he'd never missed anyone that much. But then again, he'd never had such a deep emotional connection to anyone as he had with Aidan. Missing him was like a physical ache, an empty spot somewhere near his kidneys that was only satisfied when Aidan was close.

He forced himself to concentrate so that he didn't leave anything behind. Then he slept for a few hours, waking at sunrise. He dressed in khaki slacks and a close-fitting polo shirt that pressed his nipple rings against his skin in a way that was mildly sensual. He thought of taking them out but then imagined sex that night with Aidan, his partner's teeth on a gold ring, twisting, and his rapidly stiffening dick convinced him to leave them in.

He brought Hayam into the kitchen of the main house and settled her on a blanket on the floor by the stove, kissing her goodbye on her cold, wet nose. He left a note for James and Farid with the two guns, promising to call once he reached Marseille, and drove to Tunis, the highway busy with early morning truckers and tour buses.

He left the Jeep in long-term parking. He went through security quickly and then dozed on the plane. While he waited in line at customs, he called Aidan. "I'm here in Marseille," he said. "Just waiting to finish up at the airport. Where are you?"

"At the apartment. Omar is leaving in a half hour for the Friday prayer at a local mosque, but he wants Leila to stay here. I'm staying with her. You can get a cab at the airport to bring you here."

Liam wrote down the address and hung up, then moved forward

in the line. He knew that the only special feature of the Muslim Friday "Sabbath" was the midday prayer, which Muslims were encouraged, almost mandated, to do communally.

An hour later, he was walking in the front door of the apartment building off La Canebière. He greeted the concierge and explained where he was going, and the elderly woman waved him on.

Aidan opened the door at his knock, then jumped into Liam's arms. "I missed you," he said into Liam's neck.

"Missed you too." It felt so good to have Aidan's body pressed against his own. They had only been apart for three days, but it seemed much longer. He pulled back. "Tell me what's been happening."

"Nothing much. I spent yesterday afternoon with Leila. She's still not the happiest camper in camperland, but she likes being with her father. Omar has been in nonstop meetings. I think he's very close to returning to Tunis, though." He stepped back into the apartment. "Come inside, I'll show you around."

They left Liam's duffle bag on Aidan's bed and walked through the apartment. Liam was surprised at how luxurious the apartment was, even though Aidan had told him about it. He nodded when they came to the balcony, and Aidan pointed out the adjacent building where a shooter might be placed.

Liam felt more relaxed now that he had seen Aidan and the apartment. Though he loved and trusted his partner, Aidan was still a novice when it came to security, and Liam was pleased to see he was learning.

When they came to Leila's door, Aidan knocked. "Leila? Liam is here."

She opened the door. She looked much the same as she had in Tunis; the same long-sleeved T-shirt and long pants, with a blue scarf wrapped around her head. She did manage a brief smile, though.

"I'm glad you're here," she said. "Did you know that a bomb blew up on Wednesday night?"

"Yes, I did. As soon as I caught the man who was destroying your uncle's olive groves, I came right here."

"That's good." She turned and went back to her bed and picked up her Koran, and Aidan and Liam walked out to the balcony. Aidan closed the door behind them.

The balcony faced down the broad avenue of La Canebière to the old port. The sailboat masts were a close-set forest of skinny poles, the blue-green water of the harbor sparkling in the morning sun. "Nice digs," Liam said. "Be tough for Omar to go back to that poky little apartment after this."

"Who knows, maybe he'll be moving into the presidential palace," Aidan said.

"Not at first, at least." Liam leaned against the balcony rail. It was cooler than in Tunis, but it felt great. "Tell me what's been going on here. As much as you can."

Aidan sat on one of the waffle-weave chairs and Liam joined him at the other. Aidan went back through everything that had happened since Tuesday, with Liam stopping him periodically to ask for details. When he finished, he said, "Now you. What happened?

You caught somebody?"

Liam spread his long legs out and explained about Ayham Samaha. "I'm still not happy that they didn't call the police. I've seen this before. Americans walk into third-world countries and think that if they spread enough money around, they solve every problem. But it doesn't work that way. These families have probably been sparring for decades, if not centuries. Giving Ayham Samaha a few grand isn't going to change that."

He heard the apartment door opened and turned to look. "Guess the client is back."

The first person through the door was a middle-aged Frenchman with dark hair, who met him and Aidan halfway through the living room. "You must be Liam," the man said in English. "I'm Jean-Luc."

They both sized each other up. "You are everything Aidan described," Jean-Luc said. "Pleased to meet you."

"The same," Liam replied.

"Let me introduce you to Monsieur Mansoor." He turned to the Tunisian man behind him and made the introductions. Omar didn't look much like Farid; he was stockier and more masculine in bearing but did have a similar dark skin tone. There was a second man with them, introduced only as Ali.

"Monsieur Mansoor met Ali at the mosque," Jean-Luc said. "He has some interesting information. Let's all have a seat."

Omar turned to Ali. "Can you please tell them what you told me? In French, if you please, so everyone can understand?"

Ali nodded. "I told Mr. Mansoor to be very careful. There is someone in Marseille who is trying to hurt him."

"How do you know this?" Jean-Luc asked.

"I hear many things. I own a small café in the Noailles section, and many people come there to gossip. I am a very peaceful man, and I do not like to hear rumors of people doing evil things. When I can, I pass what I know to the police."

"Did you know about the bombing at the restaurant before it happened?" Liam asked.

Ali shook his head. "No, but that made me think the rumors I was hearing had more strength than just idle gossip."

"Where do these rumors come from?" Jean-Luc asked. "Who wants to see Monsieur Mansoor harmed?"

"All I know is that there is money on offer for anyone who can hurt Mr. Mansoor—or his daughter." He looked at Omar. "Your wife? She has been killed?"

Omar nodded. "While she was in police custody in Tunis."

"It was not the police. I believe her death was connected to the threats I have heard here in Marseille. Whoever wishes you harm has very long tentacles."

"Can you give us any lead to follow?" Liam asked. "Anyone we should talk to who might know more about where these threats are coming from?"

"There is a young man who comes to the café. His name is Pierre Badou—his father is Moroccan, his mother French. He is the kind of man people ask to do dangerous and illegal things."

Jean-Luc asked, "Where can we find him?"

"He does deliveries for the *boulangerie* on the Rue St. Bazile. But you must not mention my name. Please."

"Of course," Jean-Luc said.

Ali left soon after, and another man arrived for a meeting with Omar. Aidan, Liam, and Jean-Luc went back out to the balcony to talk.

"Should we give this man's name to the police?" Aidan asked. "This Pierre Badou. They can bring him in for questioning."

Both Liam and Jean-Luc shook their heads. "Can't bring the police in yet," Liam said. "We don't know enough. For all we know, this guy could be trying to date Ali's daughter, and Ali just wants to get him in trouble."

"I think we should speak with him ourselves." Jean-Luc pulled out his cell phone and began punching keys.

"Liam," Aidan whispered, while Jean-Luc was turned away. "You really don't think we should bring in the police?"

"I don't know anyone in Marseille. How do we know who to approach?"

"Why don't we start with the detective who's investigating the bombing? He seemed like a good guy."

"Everyone seems good to you, Aidan. What if he turns out to be involved? Suppose he asked for this assignment just to sabotage it?"

Aidan frowned. "Now you're starting to sound paranoid."

"Just because you're paranoid doesn't mean they're not out to get you."

Jean-Luc turned back around. "Badou is at the boulangerie. If we go over there quickly, we can catch him before he leaves. Aidan, can you stay here and watch Mansoor?"

Aidan looked at Liam. "Sure, go for it. I'll stay here and play nanny."

Fresh from his triumph the night before, Liam was eager to wrap up the assaults on the Mansoor family. "Let's do it, then."

19 – Fresh Bread

Liam followed Jean-Luc Derain downstairs and out to La Canebière. "You were a US Navy SEAL?" Jean-Luc asked in English.

"Yup."

"What took you to Tunisia?"

"I left the military under the Don't Ask, Don't Tell policy," Liam said. "I bummed around for a while, trying to find my future, and then a contact in Tunisia put me in touch with a client who needed a bodyguard. I liked the work and liked the country, so I stayed."

They walked down the broad avenue, passing stylish French women in tight skirts and high heels and grizzled old pensioners pushing metal shopping carts. As they approached the Noailles quarter, he saw more Arab men and women wearing scarves.

"How about you?" Liam asked. "How'd you become a bodyguard?"

"I worked in the French police for thirty years," he said. "Got my pension and retired at fifty-two. My wife told me she'd kill me if I didn't go back to work. I started picking up the occasional job from Agence de Sécurité, and when they opened an office in Marseilles, they asked me to be the boss."

The French pop star Joe Dassin sang from a clothing store's speakers about the Champs Elysees, and Liam smelled a mixture of salt air, perfume, and cooking oil. "What's it like working for an agency?"

"Sometimes it's a pain. I don't have control over who I work for, as you and Aidan must."

"We don't get enough business to be picky," Liam said.

"Here, there's more than enough business. We turn down jobs occasionally because no one on my staff speaks much Arabic, for example. And it's hard to hire men who have much intelligence, sadly. Poor Benoit, for example. A hard worker, very strong and very disciplined." He tapped his head. "But no initiative."

He pointed ahead. "There is the Rue St. Bazile. The boulangerie is halfway down the block. How are you as an interrogator?"

"Not my specialty," Liam said. "I know how to ask questions, though."

"I'll take the lead, then."

Jean-Luc opened the door of the boulangerie, and Liam smelled the rich aroma of baking bread. His mouth watered at the array of loaves on the shelves. He hadn't had good French bread in years.

Jean-Luc flashed what looked like a police badge and asked the plump woman behind the counter where he could find Pierre Badou. She nodded her head toward a door that led to the rear of the bakery, and Jean-Luc pushed through it; Liam followed.

The warm, buttery aroma was even stronger in the hot kitchen. The walls were lined with ovens, while the center of the room was filled with metal cooling racks loaded with brioches, baguettes, round boules, and flat *fougasses*. One tray was filled with snail-shaped *kouign amann*, another of *pain au chocolat*. At the back of the room, a handsome young man with well-tanned skin and an Elvis-style pompadour loaded paper-wrapped baguettes into delivery boxes.

"Pierre Badou?" Jean-Luc said, once again flashing what looked to Liam like a badge. "I'd like to speak with you."

Badou looked up at them, then dropped the box on the floor and ran out the back door. Liam darted around the trays, though he couldn't help knocking into one full of chocolate brioches, and reached the back door seconds after Badou had exited. He saw the man rushing down a back alley and gave chase.

The cobblestones were rough and littered with debris—browning lettuce leaves, crumpled pastry wrappers from the boulangerie. Badou slipped on an oily patch on the pavement, and Liam was on top of him immediately. He pressed him to the ground in a wrestler's hold until Jean-Luc joined them.

"Why do you run, Pierre?" Jean-Luc asked, leaning down. "I just want to ask you some questions."

One side of his face pressed against the stones, he muttered, "I don't talk to flics."

Jean-Luc nodded to Liam, who stood up, still keeping a firm hand on the man's shoulder. Then he transferred his grip to the Frenchman's wrist.

"What makes you think I am a flic?" Jean-Luc opened the badge. "This?" He held it up to Liam and Badou, and Liam could clearly see it was a fake. "Just a conversation opener. I'm not a flic. I work for the Agence de Securité."

"So?" Badou sneered, and Liam was struck by the uncanny resemblance to a young Elvis—although one from Morocco rather than Mississippi.

"So I have been hired to protect Omar Mansoor, and someone set off a bomb recently, trying to kill him. I don't like it when things like that happen."

"I didn't do it."

"No, you probably didn't," Jean-Luc said. "But you're the kind of guy who hears things, aren't you? The kind who knows who's who and what's what." He opened his wallet and pulled out a hundred-euro note. "What do you know about the bombing?"

"Have your thug let go of my arm and maybe I'll tell you."

Liam was insulted. A thug? He had to admit he did look menacing, with his chest pressing against his shirt and his biceps bulging. But a thug? No.

Jean-Luc nodded to him, and he released his hold on Badou's arm but remained poised to chase the man if he ran again.

"There is a man," Badou said. "He asked me if I could do the bombing, but I said no. I'm no good with that kind of thing."

Jean-Luc held up the note, with its green-and-gray picture of a baroque archway. "His name?"

"You won't tell him I told you?"

"Of course not."

"Serhan Rimidi. He's a bouncer at the Bar XX in the Cours Julien district." He reached for the note, and Jean-Luc released it.

"How will we recognize him?" he asked.

"As tall as your thug here, but with a shaved head and tattoos on his biceps. I wouldn't mess with him, though." He looked from Jean-

Luc to Liam. "Am I finished here?"

Jean-Luc nodded, and Badou walked back down the alley to the bakery. "You mind if we stop back in the front before we go back?" Liam asked. "I'd love to get my hands on some of that bread."

"I wouldn't mind a kouign amann myself."

They returned to the apartment with a bag of assorted breads and pastries. Omar was still meeting with the same man, so Liam, Aidan, and Jean-Luc went out to the balcony with their boulangerie purchase. Liam dug into a baguette, relishing the crisp crust and the light, fluffy inside. As he expected, Aidan pounced on one of the chocolate croissants.

Liam filled Aidan in on their interrogation. "He called me a thug," he said.

Jean-Luc laughed. "This Bar XX. It is a gay bar."

"I guessed that from the name," Liam said. "You want Aidan and me to check it out?"

"I think you'd blend in better there than my wife and I."

"We can do that," Aidan said.

They heard a loud knock on the front door. "Who's that?" Liam said. "I thought you said Omar didn't have another meeting till four o'clock."

"I'll see." They watched Jean-Luc cross the living room and look through the door's peephole, then open it. He ushered in a Frenchman in a dapper navy suit. Omar Mansoor and the man he'd been meeting with stood up, and as Aidan and Liam entered from the balcony, Omar was making his apologies to the man.

"Inspector Christophe," Jean-Luc said, presenting the man to Liam.

"I have come to tell you the results of our investigation so far," Christophe said. Liam showed Omar's guest to the door and made sure it was locked and then joined the rest of them in the living room.

It was pretty much as Liam had guessed—a crude pipe bomb, tossed at the restaurant as Omar Mansoor walked out. "You are very lucky, monsieur," he said to Omar.

"Benoit was not so lucky." Omar turned to Jean-Luc. "You've spoken to his family?"

Jean-Luc nodded. "I expressed your condolences as well as those of the firm. And we maintain a generous life insurance policy on our employees, so their families will be taken care of."

"Have you found the person who threw the bomb?" Omar asked Christophe.

The policeman shook his head. "We have some persons of interest but have not made an arrest yet."

Omar leaned forward. "Who are these persons of interest? Someone who was at the dinner?"

"I'm not at liberty to reveal the names of our suspects at this point. It wouldn't be fair to do so until we know for certain."

"But should I be worried? Suppose I continue to meet with this person, and he tries to kill me again?"

"That is what you have bodyguards for," Christophe said. "What are your plans, Monsieur Mansoor? Will you be remaining in

Marseille?"

"Through the weekend at least. But beyond that, I am not certain. I hope to return to my country, but I must be sure of my safety and that of my daughter."

"Of course." Christophe rose. "Thank you for your time. I see that you are in capable hands, but if you should need anything, please call me."

After the policeman left, the four of them sat in the living room again. "With Liam here, I think I may return to my office," Jean-Luc said. He turned to Liam and Aidan. "Unless you feel you need additional help?"

"That depends on Mr. Mansoor," Liam said, turning to the client. "Will you be staying in the apartment? If you go out, we may need additional help."

"I would like to take Leila out this weekend," he said. "Perhaps you could come back then, Jean-Luc? You know this area better than Aidan and Liam."

Jean-Luc nodded. "I'll leave you all my numbers. If anything happens, call me, and I'll be right here. But first, I think we should talk about our strategy."

"I have some time before my next appointment," Omar said, standing. "I will spend it with my daughter."

He left the living room. "I assume you had a reason for not giving Serhan Rimidi's name to the police," Liam said to Jean-Luc.

"Not yet. I would like you and Aidan to go to the Bar XX tonight and see what you can discover. Then we will pass the name to

Christophe. That way we will be sure not to involve Pierre Badou."

"You'll have to come back and stay with the Mansoors while we're out," Liam said.

"Yes, I'll do that."

"And you'll be available if we have to speak to anyone else over the weekend?"

"Of course. I'm not abandoning you. The Agence de Securité will still be involved. I'll ask some questions of my old colleagues on the force and see what I can find out about the bombing investigation as well."

They talked about logistics, and then Omar's next meeting arrived. Aidan manned the door while Jean-Luc packed and Liam stood in the living room by the doors to the balcony. He didn't know what was going to happen next, but at least he and Aidan were back together.

20 – Alarm Service

Once Jean-Luc was gone, Liam returned to the bedroom and called Richard. "Got another little job for you," he said. "The man's name is Ayham Samaha, and he lives in Tebourba, Tunisia. He should be depositing a big check into his bank account today. I'd like to know where that check is drawn."

Liam wasn't sure why, but he thought there might be a clue there.

"That's all you have?" Richard asked.

"I can tell you who wrote the check, if that helps."

"Just a name and a city? You don't want much, mate. But I'll get on it and see what I can find."

When Liam returned to the living room, he heard Omar's cell phone ringing. He watched as Omar made an excuse to the group he was speaking with and stepped out onto the balcony to take the call. Liam immediately crossed the room to the glass windows and checked to make sure there was no one on the adjacent balconies who might be taking aim at the client.

He couldn't hear the conversation through the thick glass, but he could tell Omar was upset—he saw the man brush a tear away from his eye. When he came back into the apartment he said, "That was my brother-in-law, Burhan. He has been released from custody."

"That's good," Liam said.

"He wishes to begin preparations for Khadija's funeral."

"Will you go back to Tunis for it?"

Omar nodded. "Yes, Leila and I will go. I don't know if we will stay or return to Marseille, but we will go."

Liam and Aidan spent the rest of the afternoon alternating door duty. Every time he passed Aidan, Liam felt a frisson of sexual attraction, which irritated him. Was he so dick-whipped that all he could think about was hot monkey sex with his partner? It had been what, three days? Before meeting Aidan, he'd gone for months, even a year, without sex, and it hadn't ruled his life.

He longed to reach out and touch Aidan, place his palm over his partner's crotch and feel him react, nibble on his ear and feel Aidan tug at his nipple rings. His dick stiffened uncomfortably against the tight khaki slacks, and he forced himself to focus on the job at hand.

Just before five o'clock, while Aidan was at the door, Liam's cell phone rang. The number was protected, which probably meant Louis Fleck.

"Got some more information for you," Louis said. "Not sure how good it is, though. The police in Marseille are tracing the materials used in the bomb, but they don't have much hope for success. They've also been making inquiries in the Arab community."

"So have we," Liam said. "Did the name Serhan Rimidi come up?"

"Not that I've heard. Who is he?"

"Right now all we know is that he's a bouncer at a gay bar with a bad reputation."

"Sounds like fun."

"We'll see tonight. Aidan and I are going to the bar to check him out."

"You guys get all the plum assignments," Louis said. "Call me if you hear anything I can use."

"You do the same."

"And Liam? Be careful."

"Always," Liam said and hung up. Omar ordered them dinner from a Moroccan restaurant, delivered by a boy no older than Leila. The four of them ate together at the table in the kitchen, and Leila was the most animated Liam had ever seen her, chatting and laughing with her father. After dinner, she led him to her bedroom to talk more, and Aidan and Liam went back to their bedroom.

"Do you like France?" Aidan asked, sitting down on his bed.

"Sure. I speak enough French to get by. Love the food and the wine. And it's nice to be out of the third world for a few days."

"Speaking of the third world." Aidan leaned back against his pillow. "You think you want to stay in Tunisia forever?"

Liam sat down across from him. "What brought that on?"

"The demonstrations in Tunis freaked me out," Aidan said. "And I see how intolerant Leila is—I feel sorry for her; she just lost her mother—but she's not a very nice girl. What if people like her and her father take power in Tunisia? Will there still be a place for us?"

"You're jumping the gun, Aidan. Omar seems like a pretty nice guy. And nothing's going to happen overnight."

"I hope you're right," Aidan said. They snuggled again and lay down together on Aidan's narrow bed. Liam felt as horny as a teenager, and he understood what his high school classmates meant when they talked about blue balls. His were so tight with longing for the intimate touch of Aidan's body that they ached. But they still had work ahead of them, and Liam was resolved not to start anything they couldn't finish quickly. And when he did have his way with Aidan, it would be anything but quick.

Jean-Luc returned at nine-thirty and knocked on the bedroom door. Liam rose to meet him. "We'll go soon," he said. "I want to get there early enough to be able to talk to this bouncer before the club gets busy."

Jean-Luc agreed that was a good plan. As Jean-Luc walked down the hallway, Liam turned back to Aidan, who had peeled off his polo shirt and was rummaging in his suitcase. He pulled out a low-cut V-necked sweater and slipped it on. It fit him like a second skin and exposed the curly black hairs that clustered at the base of his throat.

Liam was immediately jealous. "You're wearing that?"

"Got to dress to attract," he said. He reached back in the suitcase and pulled out a sock, which he stuffed into his pants.

"Aidan. Really."

"Some of us are not as generously endowed as others."

"What exactly are you planning to do tonight?"

Aidan cocked his head and looked at him. "Get friendly enough with the bouncer that he'll spill his secrets."

"Christ. You don't have to seduce him for that."

"You can try things your way, and I'll try them mine."

Liam wanted nothing more than to strip his partner naked, and take Aidan over his lap and spank that sexy ass until he agreed that he would not flaunt his body for anyone other than Liam. But that was a jealous, Neanderthal attitude, especially when Aidan was just trying to help in his own way.

He took a deep breath. "I guess I should wear my old blue T-shirt, then," he said, referring to an old faded one that was too tight as well as strategically ripped to show off his right nipple ring.

"That's the idea," Aidan said. "And think of how much fun we'll have taking these clothes off each other later."

That was exactly what Liam was thinking of, though he hated the idea of waiting at all. As they walked to the Club XX, his dick was so stiff and leaking precome that he was afraid he'd arrive with a big wet spot at his crotch. Fortunately, the cold air and the need to stay alert tamped down his eager dick.

The bouncer at the door looked nothing like Serhan Rimidi had been described. He was short and squat, with flowing dark hair and pockmarked skin. They walked past him into the club, where colored lights spiraled around a nearly empty dance floor. The DJ was playing French dance music, and the few men in the club that early clustered around the bar or stood singly by the walls.

Liam walked up to the bar and motioned the bartender. He ordered a pair of French beers for himself and Aidan, then asked, "I'm looking for Serhan. He around?"

The bartender, a skinny Frenchman with a goatee and tattoos around his neck, said, "No, Serhan works Saturday night."

Liam paid him and took the beers. He turned back to Aidan and handed him a bottle. "We might as well drink the beer before we go back."

"Or we could stick around," Aidan said, putting his arm around Liam's waist. "We haven't had much time together in a while."

"Jean-Luc is watching the clients," Liam said. "He's not expecting us back quickly."

Aidan lifted his beer to his lips and drank. "You want to dance?"

"With you?"

"No, with that loser over by the wall. Of course with me."

"Well, when you put it that way." Liam took his bottle and Aidan's and put them on a table, and then led his partner to the dance floor.

Liam had never danced much before he met Aidan. As a teenager, he was too shy around girls, and he didn't have the hormonal drive that would have forced him to be more sociable. Then as a Navy SEAL, he was surrounded by men, and when the team would go out to bars, they'd be intent on drinking and carousing rather than dancing.

But Aidan loved to dance, and he'd turned Liam on to the pleasure of swaying with another man's body close to his. He enjoyed the almost military strategy behind formal dances—the way a certain step was accompanied by a movement of the hips, the repetitive patterns, the opportunity to use his body in a different way than accustomed.

Aidan had been a good teacher, and in the privacy of their little house, they had practiced slow dancing first. Aidan would rest his head on Liam's shoulder, one arm snaked up behind to his partner's neck, the other resting chastely on his hip—though sometimes the hand roved farther south.

After a few initial stumbles, Liam had mastered the art of slow dancing, and they'd moved on to the samba, the fox trot, and the mambo. From there, they'd begun improvising, imitating moves they saw on music videos, practicing synchronization.

The midtempo music had a recurring rhythm of drums and hi-hats, and he and Aidan improvised, moving with the beat into their own routine, laughing as they touched hands and bumped hips.

The club was hot and dark, and at first most of the men there seemed to stick to the shadows, checking each other out. But gradually groups arrived together, and the dance floor became more crowded.

They danced for an hour as the club filled up, both of them keeping an eye out in case Serhan Rimidi showed up on his night off. He didn't, and before midnight, they gave up and returned to the apartment, downing bottles of water on the walk home.

Jean-Luc met them at the door. "Mansoor and Leila are both asleep. Call me tomorrow morning, and let me know what you're going to do."

When he was gone, Aidan said, "I may not know what we're doing tomorrow yet, but I know what we're doing right now."

Liam leaned down and kissed him. "I like the way your mind works." Aidan led him into the bedroom, then pulled the tight-fitting sweater over his head.

"Mmm," Liam said, leaning down to take one of Aidan's nipples in his mouth. Aidan moaned as Liam licked around the areola and then took the nipple between his teeth.

"Keep your voice down," Liam said through his teeth.

Knowing the client was in the apartment gave an extra bit of the forbidden to their lovemaking. He unbuckled Aidan's pants, and they fell to the floor, where Aidan kicked them off. Quickly, they were both naked, and Aidan was lying on his back on the bed, his dick sticking straight up in the air. "This isn't going to work," Liam said. "There's not enough room for both of us. Get up."

Aidan looked disappointed, but he got up from the bed, and Liam took his place. His own dick was stiff too but didn't stick up as straight as Aidan's. "Now come straddle me," Liam said.

Aidan stepped gingerly over Liam and then settled his ass on Liam's groin, Liam's dick resting in the groove of Aidan's ass. Then he leaned down, and they kissed.

Liam wrapped his arms around Aidan and pulled him close. He wondered sometimes at the depth of his love for his partner. It wasn't something he thought about a lot, but every now and then they'd be away from each other during the day, and Liam would feel something in his heart, a longing to be near Aidan. And then sometimes they'd be together, like this, and Liam couldn't imagine how his life could be any better.

Aidan rubbed his stiff dick, leaking precome, against Liam's stomach, then rose and lay flat on top of Liam, his weight pressing down. Both of their dicks were slippery by then, and they rubbed back and forth, suppressing any sound, until they were moving quickly, both of them pressed onward by urgency. He heard Aidan make a very quiet yelp beneath him, and felt the spurt of his partner's come, and that was enough to drive him over the edge as well.

When Aidan tried to slide off Liam and lie next to him, he fell off the bed entirely, and both of them burst into stifled laughter.

* * *

Liam woke Saturday morning to the ring of the cell phone. "Richard?" he said. "Do you know what time it is?"

"What am I, your bloody alarm service? It's after eight in the morning. You're not awake yet?"

"I am now. What did you find?"

"It's curious. I'm e-mailing you the results so you can see for yourself. I found the big transaction you asked about, going into Ayham Samaha's account. But it's not the first one he's received."

"You mean James Gardiner has been paying him?"

"The money has been coming from a different account. I tracked it back to a man named Seif Mansoor. He connected to Gardiner?"

"Gardiner's partner's name is Mansoor—but Farid, not Seif. You're sure it's not Farid?"

"See what I sent you. And there's a bill with it, by the way."

"Thanks, Richard."

Aidan was already awake and had their laptop open. "I'm

assuming he sent us something."

"You're assuming correctly. You ever hear Farid talk about someone named Seif Mansoor? Another brother?"

"I'm pretty sure there's just the two of them, Omar and Farid," Aidan said. "But we can ask Omar over breakfast. And that may mean that we haven't really solved the problem back in Tebourba at all."

21 – Family History

Liam took a quick shower and dressed while Aidan downloaded the file from Richard. When he walked back into the bedroom, a towel wrapped around his waist, Aidan called him over.

"Look at this." Aidan pointed to the screen. "There's a pattern of transfers from Seif Mansoor's account to Ayham Samaha's. First some small amounts, then getting larger."

"I'll bet those would correspond with the dates when things were happening at the farm," Liam said.

"You'd win that bet. Now, see here—the most recent was the day before James Gardiner's transfer."

"And that night I caught Samaha trying to cut down another olive tree." Liam nodded. "You'd better get in the shower, and then we're going to have to show this to Omar."

When Aidan was dressed, they carried the laptop out to the kitchen. Leila was buttering some of the bread Liam had bought the other day for herself and her father, and Omar was brewing coffee.

"Good morning," Liam said. "You don't have another brother, do you? Named Seif?"

Omar shook his head. He wore a loose white shirt over jeans, and it was the first time Liam had seen him out of his dark business suit. "I have no brother beyond Farid. I have never even heard this name before."

"I think he's behind the sabotage at your brother's olive groves."

Omar brought his coffee to the table, and Liam showed him the records Richard had sent. "How did you get this?" Omar asked.

"A source," Liam said. "How about your middle name. Is it Seif?"

"You believe I would open a false bank account under another name and use it to pay someone to sabotage my brother's business?"

"The olive groves were your inheritance," Aidan said. "And now your gay brother is living in the home where you grew up. How does that make you feel?"

"My brother has made his own choices," Omar said. "I cannot control him. But I am glad that the land is still in our family. When my brother and I are no longer on earth, the groves will pass to my daughter."

Leila looked up from her bread. "Uncle Farid's land will be mine?"

"That is the arrangement I made with him and his partner."

"So you don't have any incentive to destroy the groves." Aidan opened the bag of bread. Liam could see all that was left was a chocolate croissant and a brioche. He handed the brioche to Liam and kept the croissant for himself.

"Of course not. I would never harm my brother. And I wouldn't do anything to hurt the land my father tended for so many years, and his father before him. The land that my daughter will inherit."

Liam held the brioche in one hand and tapped the computer with the other. "Then who is this man who has the same last name as you?"

Omar looked at the screen and cocked his head in thought. "Our last name is not uncommon, but our immediate family is not large."

"Could he be a cousin?" Aidan asked. "Farid said your father had a twin brother."

"Yes, and like Farid and me, they were very different, and they often argued." He sat back in his chair. "When we were children, our mother often told us that we must be like two halves of the same coin and never forsake each other, even if we should grow up to be different men."

He sighed. "I believe I have forgotten our mother's advice. I must take steps to repair my relationship with Farid. I do not want us to end up as my father and his brother did, estranged from each other."

"Farid said he didn't know what happened to your uncle. Do you?"

"My father loved the land, and nothing made him happier than working out among the olive trees. But Esam was restless and had no patience for agriculture. He loved to go out and hunt—when they were young, you could still catch wild pigs and goats, and even antelope and gazelle."

Leila handed him a slice of buttered bread, and he took a bite. "Esam was the elder by a few minutes, so according to our tradition he should have inherited the land when my grandfather died. But he was away, and by the time he returned, my father had already married my mother and taken over the groves."

"Your tradition," Aidan said. "Is that from the Koran?"

Omar shook his head. "It is just the way it has always been done in our family. The land goes to the eldest son."

Leila piped up. "According to the Koran, when a man dies and his only survivors are two sons, they should share the inheritance equally."

Omar smiled at his daughter. "Yes, my darling, that is correct. I don't know what my father gave to Esam, if anything. My family was a poor one, and all we had were the olive groves and the materials necessary to grow and harvest the crop. All I know is that when Esam returned after my grandfather's death, he and my father argued, and Esam left."

"Left? For where?" Aidan asked.

Omar shook his head. "I don't know. As far as I know, my father never spoke to Esam again. I would not be surprised if this man Seif is my uncle Esam's son."

"We can check that easily enough." Aidan took the laptop back and sent an e-mail to their hacker pal Richard. If anyone could find records, he could.

Omar finished his bread, then asked, "The man whose bank account you found—this Ayham Samaha. Who is he?"

"He was born on the land next to yours," Liam said. "Do you remember him as a boy? Your brother does."

"I don't. My brother and I kept to ourselves as boys. And the family next door sold their land to my father when we were very young."

"You grew up on the farm where Uncle Farid lives?" Leila asked.

"Of course, my darling. I've told you that in the past."

"It's very nice. Can we live out there when we return to Tunisia?"

Omar patted his daughter's shoulder. "I don't know where we will live when we return. I may need to be in the capital to work."

Leila frowned.

"But would you like to visit your uncle again?"

"I don't care about him or the other man," Leila said. "But I like being out in the olive groves. They smell nice."

Liam shared a glance with Aidan. He would be very glad when they didn't have to look after Leila. "We thought Samaha was sabotaging the farm and the groves because he was angry that his father had been cheated out of the land's true value," Liam said.

"My father was an honest man. He never would have cheated his neighbor. It goes against everything he believed, everything in the Koran."

"No one said that your father did cheat Samaha's father—but Samaha felt that way. James thought he could solve the problem by giving Samaha a substantial payoff to make things right."

"A very American approach," Omar said.

"My feelings exactly." Liam brushed a few brioche crumbs from the table into his hand and then emptied them into the garbage.

The laptop pinged with a new message. "Here we go," Aidan said. "Richard must have hacked into some government database. Seif Mansoor was born in Tebourba, the son of Esam and Jumana Mansoor. He is an only child. Jumana died three years ago, and Esam last March."

"Around the same time my father did," Omar said thoughtfully. "They were born together and died together."

"My guess is that when his father died, Esam decided his father had been cheated out of his inheritance and went out for revenge," Aidan said.

Liam looked at him. Aidan's imagination was acting up again. "We don't know that, Aidan," he said.

"No, I believe Aidan is speaking the truth. And if my cousin is seeking revenge against our family, I believe it is possible that he is behind the threats against me as well."

22 – Patience in Adversity

"You don't think you're being threatened by political rivals?" Aidan asked.

"I thought that was the case," Omar said. "But it never made sense. I couldn't see any of the other political groups having the motivation or the capital to launch attacks against me. And honestly, my group is only one of many that wish for a new government in Tunisia. I believe the American expression is that the Muslim Leadership is only a little fish."

Liam said, "We ought to call Farid and James and tell them to be careful. Right now, they think that Ayham Samaha was the problem, and he's been taken care of."

"I will call my brother."

Aidan couldn't follow most of the rapid Arabic, but he caught a few names and the words for *uncle* and *cousin*. Toward the end of the conversation, though, Omar's speech slowed, and Aidan could make out that Omar planned to go to Tebourba when he returned to Tunisia. "I would like to meet James," he said. "To thank him for what he has done, and make sure he is taking good care of you, younger brother."

That was nice, Aidan thought. He was glad that the twins seemed to be coming together again.

Omar handed the phone to Aidan. "My brother would like to speak to you," he said in English.

"Farid? It's Aidan. Omar told you what we found?"

"Yes. I am very surprised. I do not even remember meeting this cousin. For him to have such a grudge against Omar and me is very odd."

"It's very human. We're going to do some research on this cousin, and then we can talk to you, James, and Omar about a plan." He ended the call, and then Omar and Leila went into the living room to read the Koran together.

Aidan and Liam remained in the kitchen with the laptop. Aidan sent Richard his payment, along with a request to find out anything else he could on Seif Mansoor.

When he finished that, he got busy searching online for anything he could find on Omar and Farid's cousin, while Liam used his phone to send a couple of e-mails to people he knew.

Aidan quickly discovered that Seif was thirty-five, never married, with no children. He had a degree in engineering from ENSET, the École Supérieure des Science et Techniques de Tunis, had worked for a large firm in the capital for a dozen years, then started his own consulting firm. He had worked on the airport and on several other large projects. He appeared to own several patents for machinery used in oil drilling, but the descriptions were so dense Aidan couldn't understand any more than that.

"Look at this," he said to Liam, pointing at the screen. "His specialty is hydraulics. He'd have the knowledge to create the bomb that was thrown at Omar, right?"

"Yeah, but that bomb was thrown in Marseille," Liam said. "Do we know if Seif has ever even been to France?"

"He hired Ayham Samaha to sabotage the olive groves. He could have hired someone here in Marseille. Like Serhan Rimidi."

A very attractive Tunisian woman named Abra Leon arrived shortly after noon with platters of food she had cooked for Omar and Leila, and Aidan was interested to see the interplay between the two adults. Khadija was dead no more than a week, and it looked to him like this new woman was interested in taking her place. She wanted to eat out on the balcony. Before Liam could object, Omar said that it would not be safe. Instead, she began to lay the food out on the dining room table. She asked if Liam and Aidan would like to sit with them, but they chose to eat in the kitchen instead.

"I've seen it back home," Aidan said in a low voice. "As soon as a man's wife dies, the single women swoop around him with stuffed cabbage and potato kugel."

"I don't think that's what they're eating in there," Liam said.

"It's the same thing."

Only a few minutes later, they heard Leila ask to be excused. When her father agreed, she walked down the hall to her bedroom and closed the door. Aidan couldn't overhear anything they said, but he could tell the woman was flirting—the way she leaned in close to Omar, laughed, touched the top of his hand.

An hour later, Omar stepped into the kitchen. "Abra has invited Leila and me for dinner this evening at her home. You will be able to accompany us there? You don't need to stay with us; she says there are many wonderful restaurants in her neighborhood, and I can phone you when we need our escort home."

"Whatever you need," Liam said.

Abra leaned forward and kissed Omar on each cheek. Then Omar escorted Abra to the front door. As they reached it, his cell rang. "Burhan?" he said. "Have the police released Khadija?"

Aidan noticed the woman frown at Khadija's name, but she recovered herself and stepped out into the hallway, waving to Omar as he turned away.

Aidan closed the door behind her as Omar continued his conversation in Arabic. When he ended the call, he turned to Aidan and Liam. "We will return to Tunis on Monday morning," he said in English. "Khadija's funeral will be held on Tuesday."

Liam called Jean-Luc and let him know, and made arrangements with him to return that night around ten. Leila was in her bedroom reading, while Omar sat in the living room, making calls. Aidan and Liam went back to their bedroom to plan.

"Have you ever been to a Muslim funeral?" Aidan asked.

"Only once. A man who used to come to the Bar Mamounia."

"I wonder if it'll be like a Jewish one. There are so many rituals involved."

"Why don't you do some research, then?" Liam said. "I'm going back to the door, and I'll coordinate our flights with Omar's travel agent."

Aidan did some quick research on Muslim funeral customs. As with Jews, the body would need to be washed, ideally as soon after death as possible. The washers were supposed to be women of

Khadija's family; he hoped that her brother would be able to provide the women to take care of his sister properly.

Her body would be wrapped in a white cotton or linen cloth called a *kafan*. He remembered his grandparents talking about very Orthodox people who had been buried that way, in a wrap called a *tachrichim*. If she had died recently, there might be a viewing of the body—but he doubted that, especially if she had been autopsied.

At the funeral there would be a special prayer, called the *Salat al-Janazah*, and then Khadija would be buried in a cemetery without a casket. Omar would be responsible for lowering her body into the ground and turning her so that she faced Mecca. Then those attending the funeral would pour handfuls of soil into the grave while reciting a prayer.

There was another similarity to Judaism—though Aidan's family left the lowering of the deceased into the ground to the cemetery personnel, he had often shoveled dirt into graves. To him, it was an important and moving part of saying good-bye to the deceased.

A short time later, Liam returned to the bedroom and said, "Omar wants to take Leila out. Let's get ready."

The four of them walked down to the old port together, Liam taking point and Aidan following behind. The streets were busy with tourists and locals enjoying the warm, sunny Saturday, and they retraced the trip Aidan had taken with Leila. She chattered to her father about everything, and for a short time, she looked happy.

"Do you know the origin of this road's name?" Omar asked Aidan, pointing to La Canebière.

Aidan shook his head.

Omar mimed taking a drag from a marijuana cigarette. "From cannabis," he said, laughing. "Though back then they used it for rope for sailors and boats." He looked at Aidan. "Do you teach literature as well as English?"

"Just a bit," Aidan said. "I studied English literature in college."

"Then you must know *The Count of Monte Cristo*, by Alexandre Dumas. It was set here, in the Vieux Port, and out there in the harbor, at the Chateau d'If."

Aidan was surprised that Omar would know such a secular work of literature. "You've read it?"

Omar nodded. "When I was in college. But it had more meaning for me when I read it again last year. I understand more about wrongful imprisonment and exile now."

Aidan looked over to where Liam stood at the water's edge, explaining something about a boat to Leila. "But *The Count of Monte Cristo* is also about revenge," Aidan said.

"Yes, that is true. But the Koran says that an attempt at requiting evil may become an evil itself. Instead, one should be patient in adversity and forgive."

Leila returned to her father's side, and they all walked back in the gathering dusk, streetlights and store neon signs popping on. For a moment, Aidan remembered his old life back in Philadelphia, walking back to Blake's apartment after a day spent teaching, the way he felt like one small person in the midst of a bustling city. That feeling disappeared the day he met Liam. Even when they were apart, Aidan felt part of a couple in a way he'd never experienced with Blake.

Instead of going back to the apartment, they detoured past Abra's, a few blocks away, where Omar and Leila would have dinner. Omar took Leila's hand in front of the building and said, "Thank you very much for accompanying us today."

They agreed that Omar would call when he and Leila were ready to go home, and then Omar and Leila went inside.

"So," Aidan said. "We're on our own for a while."

"I'd kill for a great French meal," Liam said.

That was not exactly the way Aidan had hoped they'd spend their free time, but his stomach grumbled, and he had to admit he could use a good meal too. They walked a block back toward the harbor and stopped at a small bistro advertising bouillabaisse fresh from the sea. The smell wafting out of the doorway when two patrons exited was enough to make the decision for them.

Aidan ordered mussels in white wine as his appetizer, while Liam went for the paté. They both ordered bowls of the bouillabaisse, accompanied by crusty French bread. Liam sat back and sighed with pleasure when they were finished.

"You just can't get French food like this in Tunis," he said.

"There's a lot you can't get in Tunis," Aidan said.

"You're not starting that again, are you? Are you really that unhappy there?"

"I'm not unhappy. I'm happy to be with you. But I am frightened and worried about the future."

"It does look like the Islamist parties will have more power in the new government," Liam admitted. "But that doesn't mean they'll be stoning gay men in the streets of Tunis."

"I know. And I don't expect anything terrible to happen. But don't you think we'd both be more comfortable in a more liberal country? Like France, for example?"

"We can't work in France, for starters," Liam said. "You need a sponsor and a *carte de sejour*, a residence permit."

"Why can't we work the same way we do in Tunis—on our own?"

"Because Faisal helped me get the proper permits in place," Liam said. "Haven't you ever wondered about our legal status there?"

Aidan shrugged. "I figured since we don't take salary, we just take our expenses out of the business income, we were getting around whatever rules there are."

"Well, think again. I have legal residency in Tunisia, thanks to Faisal. Louis takes care of renewing your visa every six months, so that you can stay without trouble and work for Madame Abboud when she needs you. We don't have that connection anywhere else."

Aidan sat back in his chair as Liam motioned for the check. "I was just thinking." He realized he should have considered those legal issues before—but he had been so happy with Liam, so scared of rocking the boat, that he hadn't asked any questions. It was a pattern he'd followed with Blake as well. Shut up and accept the status quo. And look where that had gotten him.

They paid the bill and walked slowly back to Abra's apartment building, circling the block a few times until Omar called to say that he and Leila were ready to leave.

By the time they got back to the apartment, Jean-Luc was waiting in the lobby, and Aidan and Liam left a few minutes later for Club XX, wearing the same clothes they'd worn all day. This time as they approached the club, they saw a man fitting Serhan Rimidi's description at the door.

"We should see if we can get him off the door so we can ask him about Seif Mansoor," Aidan said.

"Hold on, cowboy. He's working. We'll keep an eye on him, and when he takes a break, I'll see if I can buy him a drink. Then I'll start asking questions."

"What will we do until then?"

Liam laughed. "You think we can't find a way to entertain ourselves in a gay bar?"

Aidan put his arm through Liam's. "I bet we can."

23 – Never Enough

Aidan watched as the man in front of them greeted the bouncer in French. "Hey, Serhan," the man said, hugging him, then kissing him on both cheeks. "You are handsome as ever!"

Privately, Aidan didn't think Serhan was all that good-looking. He was big but in a brawny, bulky way, like Benoit. He didn't have Liam's waist or muscle definition. His nose was too big for his face, and his bushy eyebrows met in a unibrow that reminded Aidan of Frida Kahlo.

Serhan didn't ask for their ID, though Liam made a point of showing his passport and smiling. The bouncer didn't seem to notice.

But he did pay attention to Aidan, who smiled at him too and licked his lips, just for good measure. The bouncer looked him up and down so lasciviously that Aidan's dick jumped. Well, he thought, we know who Serhan is going to talk to.

"You weren't supposed to do that," Liam muttered as they walked to the bar.

"What? Establish a connection with the man we want to interview?"

"Don't play innocent. You were flirting with him."

"Duh. Don't worry—I'll save the last dance for you." Aidan smiled at him, then turned to head to the bar—bumping right into the arms of a twenty-something Frenchman with a ball bearing through his lip, another in his nose, and a third in his eyebrow. His ears were studded with gold balls.

"Well, hello," the man said in French. Aidan felt the man's hand travel down his back to his butt. "You are all right?"

"Yes, of course. I'm so clumsy. Please excuse me."

"Only if you allow me to buy you a drink," the man said.

He was almost ten years younger than Aidan—but he had a nice smile and what appeared to be a good body under his designer T-shirt and tight jeans. "My pleasure," Aidan said, hooking his arm in the man's. "My name's Aidan. What's yours?"

They walked to the bar, leaving Liam behind.

"I am Philippe. You are American?"

"Yes. And you–you have other piercings? Besides the ones I can see?"

Philippe leaned forward and whispered in Aidan's ear, "Yes. In very personal places. You would like to see them?"

"Perhaps," Aidan said. "After a drink or two."

Over Philippe's shoulder, Aidan caught sight of Liam glowering. But Aidan ignored him and turned back to the Frenchman. He had the feeling it would be easier to flirt with the bouncer if it appeared he was single, rather than part of a couple.

He and Philippe drank their beers; then Philippe asked Aidan to dance. "Sure, why not?"

Philippe was a great dancer. His body moved in ways Aidan hadn't seen in years, and soon they were sliding their bodies against each other, doing a modified lambada, followed by a French version of the Bump. Then Philippe's cell phone went off.

He backed away, making an apologetic gesture to Aidan. So much for seeing his piercings, Aidan thought. Though of course he knew that was never going to be on the menu, as much fun as it might be. There was flirting—and then there was more.

As he walked back to the bar, he saw Liam stalking toward him—and, from the opposite direction, Serhan Rimidi. He pivoted and walked toward the bouncer, who had just arrived at the bar.

"Let me get that," Aidan said in French, putting his slim hand on Serhan's beefy one. "Please."

The bouncer turned to him and smiled. "I never refuse a drink from a handsome man."

"And I never let a compliment go unrewarded." Aidan leaned over and kissed the bouncer on his stubbled cheek. Then he pulled a twenty-euro note from his wallet and handed it to the bartender. "I'll have what he's having."

Surprisingly, the big bouncer was drinking a cosmopolitan. "So, you have good taste in men and drinks," Serhan said. "Do you taste good too?"

"I do," Aidan said, tipping his glass to Serhan's.

Aidan was feeling a bit tipsy after two beers with Philippe and the cosmo with Serhan. That made him horny, and he couldn't resist flirting with the bouncer, rubbing his leg against the other man's, then letting Serhan rest his hand on Aidan's thigh.

Time to get to business, Aidan thought. Before he went too far overboard. He leaned over to Serhan and took a gamble. "I came here tonight to look for you."

Serhan cocked his head. "Really?"

"We have a mutual acquaintance. Seif Mansoor."

Immediately Serhan backed away. Aidan thought he saw fear in the man's eyes as well as anger. "I don't know who you are or what you want."

And he didn't deny knowing Mansoor either, Aidan thought.

"Come back here," Aidan said, holding out his hand. "You may not know who I am, but you know what I want."

"I have to get back to my post."

He turned and hurried back through the growing crowd to the door.

"What the fuck do you think you're doing?" Liam demanded, shouldering his way up to Aidan.

"Trying to get Serhan to talk to me." Aidan downed the last of his cosmopolitan. "He knows Seif Mansoor's name. Did you see the way he reacted?"

"I see that you're drunk. Come on." He put his hand on Aidan's shoulder and pulled him forward.

"Excuse me," Philippe said from behind him, tapping Liam on the shoulder. "You should not treat men that way."

"It's all right," Aidan said. "He's my boyfriend."

He thought for a minute that Philippe might try to start a fight—but the skinnier, younger man looked at Liam and thought better of the idea. He frowned, then turned and walked away.

"You've got a lot of admirers," Liam said.

"Yes, but I'm going home with you. Come on, let's get out of here before anybody else tries to start a fight."

They both kept their heads down as they walked out the door past Serhan Rimidi. When they were a block away, Liam said, "That was stupid in there, what you did."

"What? I flirted with a couple of guys, and I danced. I got the suspect to talk to me and acknowledge that he knew Seif Mansoor."

"And what exactly do we have? He never said that Seif hired him to bomb the restaurant, did he?"

"No." Aidan crossed his arms in front of him and kept walking.

"So what can we tell Inspector Christophe? That a man in a bar flirted with you and then walked away?"

"Don't be a dick, Liam."

"Seems like you're the dick. Or you're the one who was so desperate for dick."

Aidan turned to him. "You're jealous. Come on, Liam."

"You kissed that guy. The pierced one. On the lips. And you kissed Rimidi on the cheek too."

"So?"

"You're not supposed to do shit like that. You're the one who's always going on about wanting one man only. Me."

Aidan stopped and turned to face his partner, looking up at him. "Listen to this, and listen closely," he said. "Blake was jealous of me, even though he had no reason to be. You have nothing to be jealous about either. I kissed a couple of guys, and I danced. I was establishing my cover in the bar. I had no intention of getting naked with either of those guys, so what I was doing had nothing to do with you. And if you keep harping on it, we're going to have a problem."

"Boy, you get uppity when you miss a couple of days of sex," Liam said. "Last night wasn't enough for you?"

Aidan reached up and grabbed Liam behind the neck and pulled his head down so their mouths met in a ferocious kiss. When they were both short of breath, Aidan pulled back. "No, it wasn't enough for me. I can never get enough of you."

"Well, you'll have to wait till we get back to the apartment. I'm not an exhibitionist."

Aidan looked around. They were on a deserted street a couple of blocks from La Canebière. There was an alley ahead, and he grabbed Liam's hand and pulled him toward it.

"What are you doing?" Liam asked.

He dragged Liam into the shelter of the alley, around the back of a fruit vendor's stall, where they were sheltered by the rolled-down awning. Then he dropped to his knees and put his mouth up against Liam's groin.

"Aidan. Not here."

"Yes, here." Aidan unbuckled Liam's belt and unzipped his pants. He licked the outline of Liam's dick through his jockstrap, and Liam began to harden. Aidan pulled the stiffening dick out of the pouch and began to suck it.

"You're crazy," Liam whispered, but he didn't fight. Aidan felt wild and free, drunk and horny and very much in love. He deep-throated his lover and felt Liam's body shiver. He began bobbing his head up and down rapidly as to the sound of a couple's laughter, then car doors opening.

He felt Liam's pulse quickening, and he sucked harder. He grabbed Liam's balls and squeezed. With a barely suppressed gasp, Liam shot off in Aidan's mouth. He suctioned the last come, then licked Liam's dickhead for good measure.

Liam was leaning back against the wall, still recovering from the powerful orgasm.

Aidan stood up. "Thanks. I needed that."

Then he turned back in the direction of the apartment.

24 – Jumping

Aidan was in the living room, and Liam was exercising on the balcony when Jean-Luc arrived at nine on Sunday morning, bearing fresh bag of French bread and pastries.

Leila and Omar joined them all in the kitchen. "Leila, my love, would you please take your bread to your room so that we may talk?" Omar asked her.

"Whatever you say, Abi." She buttered several slices of French bread and put them on a plate. She found a tray in the kitchen cabinet and added a glass of orange juice, then walked down the hall.

When she was gone, Jean-Luc said, "Please tell me what you learned last night."

Aidan had taken a couple of aspirin the night before, along with a tall glass of water, and he felt better than he had in a while. But there was no reason to go into a detailed explanation of the evening's adventures. "Serhan Rimidi, the bouncer, recognized Seif's name," he said. "But he wouldn't say anything more to us. We think it's time to pass his name to the police."

"I agree. I will call Inspector Christophe." Jean-Luc turned to Omar. "Now, what plans have you made to return to Tunis?"

Omar explained about Khadija's funeral on Tuesday. "My brother-in-law believes that we need to make a spectacle of the funeral, to rally people to our cause."

"And how do you feel about that?" Aidan asked.

"Khadija was my wife and Leila's mother. But she was also a public figure and an important member of the Muslim Leadership. She deserves a ceremony that celebrates all she did and mourns for her loss. She and I often discussed such an event—but always with the idea that it would be my funeral, not hers."

He put his knuckle up to his eye, where Aidan saw a tear appearing. "She was resolute that if I were to be killed, she would use my funeral in this way. I must do the same thing."

"I'm concerned that a big public event would put you at risk," Jean-Luc said.

"I cannot live my life in fear. And that is why I have such excellent bodyguards. Aidan and Liam will protect me."

"Will your brother be invited?" Aidan asked.

Omar nodded. "Of course. We are a family first."

Liam leaned forward. "Aidan and I cannot protect all of you by ourselves, especially if you expect crowds."

"Liam is correct," Jean-Luc said. "This is a big operation."

"Then you must come to Tunis with us and help organize," Omar said. "Liam, do you know other men in Tunis you can trust?"

Liam looked at Jean-Luc. "I do, but Jean-Luc's help would certainly be appreciated."

Jean-Luc shrugged in a classic Gallic gesture. "Then I will come to Tunis." They agreed that Omar would take adjoining rooms at the Hotel Africa for himself, Leila, and Jean-Luc until after the funeral. Aidan and Liam could return to their house, helping with security before and during the funeral.

After Jean-Luc left, Liam called Louis to let him know they were returning. While they spoke, Aidan used his phone to call the Ferme Deux Hommes. "How's Hayam doing?" he asked when James answered. "Sorry to stick you with dog-sitting duties. If we had known we wouldn't be coming back to stay with you, we would have left her with our neighbor."

"She's a sweetheart," James said. "She may not want to go back to the city with you. She's enjoying the olive groves."

"Well, we'll be back tomorrow." He told James about the plans for Khadija's funeral.

"Yes, Omar called Farid. We're going to take a room at the Hotel Africa too. That way, we'll all be together."

"Any more incidents at the farm?"

"Nothing so far." He heard James's fist rap quickly. "Knock on wood. What time does your flight arrive?"

"We're taking the Air France that gets in at eleven."

"I'll arrange for a limo to pick you all up and take you to the hotel. We'll bring Hayam with us."

When Aidan hung up, he logged into his e-mail account. Richard had e-mailed during the night with an extensive report on Seif Mansoor. He lived in a sixth-floor penthouse apartment in Gammarth, a wealthy oceanfront part of Tunis. He was very wealthy but apparently cranky as well; he was in the habit of reporting his neighbors to the police for every minor infraction. He was unmarried and had no children.

Aidan wondered if he was gay, like Farid, or simply so consumed with anger that he couldn't live a normal life.

He traveled a great deal, and Aidan was interested to see that Seif had visited Marseille several times in the last year—during the time that his cousin Omar was living there. Had he visited to recruit Serhan Rimidi? The fact that Rimidi was a bouncer at a gay bar hinted that Seif might be gay himself. Then again, it could be a coincidence.

Liam ended his call and turned back to Aidan, who showed him the report from Richard. "Louis have anything to add?" he asked when Liam had finished reading.

"Not much. Rimidi has a criminal record; so does Pierre Badou, the guy from the bakery. Neither of them has been implicated in any bombings before, though."

"Seif Mansoor probably provided all the materials."

"Aidan. You can't keep jumping to conclusions like that."

"As long as I'm jumping, you think maybe Seif is gay?"

"What makes you think that?"

"Single man in his forties. Lots of money, lives in a beautiful place. Travels a lot. And hired a bouncer at a gay bar to do his dirty work."

"Just add a taste for Barbra Streisand and you've got a great portrait," Liam said drily. "Let's leave the investigating to the police. We need to focus on protection."

"Meaning?"

"Louis checked into the funeral details. The prayers will be held at a mosque on the Avenue Taha Hussein, a few blocks from the El

Jallaz cemetery, where she'll be buried."

Together they looked at the map of the cemetery. "Wait a minute," Aidan said. "ENSET is right there."

"Yeah?"

"I'm pretty sure that's where Seif went to school. That means he knows the neighborhood around the cemetery very well."

"Which means he might try to do something at the funeral," Liam said, nodding.

"Makes sense, right? Blow up the whole family at once."

"We'll have to do some recon over there as soon as we get back to Tunis."

Omar had a large meeting going on in the living room all afternoon, and in between letting people in and out, Liam and Aidan tried to do some planning, but it was hard because they kept getting interrupted, and neither of them knew much about the neighborhood around the cemetery.

Liam called Jean-Luc and told him what they suspected, and he agreed it was a good possibility—but that they would have to be very careful around the hotel as well. Leila wanted a pizza for dinner, so Aidan found a halal pizzeria in the neighborhood and then went there to pick up two pizzas. They all ate together in the kitchen, and Leila looked almost happy.

Liam wasn't happy, though. In their room after dinner, he pored over maps of the area around the cemetery and looked up details of buildings along the way from the mosque there. "Can I help you with anything?" Aidan asked.

Liam shook his head. "Just trying to see all the angles. If we're right and Seif Mansoor is the guy behind Khadija's death, the bombing here in Marseille, and the incidents at the olive groves, then he's a dangerous guy. Add in the fact that he went to school at ENSET and must know the area around the mosque and the cemetery very well, we've got a perfect storm coming."

"Come to bed. We'll look at it all in the morning."

"In the morning, we'll be too busy. And this is what we do, Aidan. We figure out where all the threats can come from and how we can neutralize them. You've gotten so caught up in babysitting that you're missing the larger picture."

"I'm not missing anything, Liam. You're the one who's losing sight of the fact that you need to be well rested and clearheaded for whatever comes our way tomorrow."

"Just leave it, Aidan. I can get by without much sleep. You get your beauty rest."

There were times, Aidan thought, when he'd like to reach over and strangle his partner. But since Liam was a few inches taller than he was and a whole lot more muscular, there was little chance he'd get away with it. So instead he got into bed, rolled onto his side, and tried to ignore the blue light coming from the laptop screen.

25 – Energy Buzz

Monday morning was a blur of preparations for departure. Rain showers came and went with astonishing ferocity, blasting at the sliding glass doors to the balcony with the fury of the mistral.

Abra Leon arrived early to help Omar pack, but because he was busy taking phone calls, Aidan was delegated to help her. He was surprised to see how many suits, shirts, and pairs of dress shoes the man owned. "Comes the revolution, Omar is going to have to give up on designer fashions," he muttered to himself as he helped the woman fold and pack.

Liam was antsy and wanted to get moving, but Leila had lost her favorite shoes (they were eventually found in the bathroom), the van Jean-Luc had arranged to take them to the airport was stuck in traffic, and the concierge appeared at the door to find out when they would all be back.

Through it all, Jean-Luc managed everything with an unflappable Gallic charm. He found Leila's shoes and her missing hairbrush, charmed the concierge, and counterbalanced the sense of coiled power that Liam exuded.

The van slipped and skidded through the crowded, rain-soaked streets of the inner city, then picked up what was to Aidan an uncomfortable speed once they were on the D20 highway. The driver navigated the serpentine access road and then dropped them at the main entrance to Marseille Provence airport—a bland building with tall concrete pilasters framing floor-to-ceiling panels of windows.

Several flights had been either delayed or canceled due to the rain, and the terminal was crowded with European tourists, businessmen, and airport workers in colored pinneys, many of them with rain-soaked hair.

Aidan couldn't help noticing the way Jean-Luc shepherded everyone through the terminal. He was just as focused as Liam but in a different way. Liam provided a presence that discouraged anyone from attempting trouble, while Jean-Luc was almost inconspicuous, lasered on the client and on any potential dangers.

He approached an airport security guard and showed his ID, and the guard opened another lane that allowed the Mansoor party to quickly pass through the metal detectors and approach their gate. They stopped briefly so that Omar could purchase a few newspapers and an orange soda for Leila. Jean-Luc and Liam were both on alert, scanning other travelers, always aware of who was around them. Aidan focused on making sure that Leila was safe and occupied.

She insisted on sitting next to her father on the plane, even though Jean-Luc would have preferred to sit there. He settled for the aisle seat across from Omar. Aidan and Liam were seated in the row behind the Mansoors. The long runway stretched out into the Mediterranean, and Aidan wondered, as they seemed to taxi for too long, what would happen if the plane ran out of tarmac and plunged into the roiling sea.

But at what seemed like the last minute, the plane gained altitude and quickly climbed above the streaking rain and cloud cover to a sky of endless blue. The flight was quick, and Aidan was struck again by how close Tunisia was to France. The country had been occupied by France as a protectorate for over a hundred years, and there were still strong economic and cultural ties between the two.

"I have a Jeep parked at the airport," Liam said to Jean-Luc. "We can take Omar and Leila to the hotel, and you can follow us in a cab."

"James ordered us a limo," Aidan said.

Liam turned to him. "And you didn't think to mention that?"

Aidan shrugged. "I forgot. It's not a big deal."

"It means we'll have to split up. I'll take our bags and get the Jeep. You can go in the limo, and I'll follow you."

"Yes, sir," Aidan said. Liam glared at him, but Aidan turned and looked out the window as the plane began descending.

It was only his second landing at Tunis Carthage International Airport. The first time had been nearly two years before, when he was fleeing his broken relationship with Blake and heading into an uncertain future. He couldn't help thinking how different this second arrival was, now that he was going home with the man he loved.

Although if Liam could be less bossy sometimes, things would certainly be better.

James Gardiner had pulled a few strings and arranged for an airport representative to meet Omar as they deplaned. The young Tunisian woman promised to smooth their way through customs and immigration. "We have different passports," Jean-Luc said to her. "Will we have to go through separate lines?"

She shook her head. "I will take care of everything."

"I could get accustomed to this," Liam whispered to Aidan as they walked through the VIP arrivals area. With speed that was rare in Tunisia, they had their passports stamped and their luggage vetted, and left the protected area for the main terminal. Ahead of them, a man in a black suit held a sign which read MANSOOR.

"Just to be safe, let's call James," Liam said. He got the name of the limo company and the driver and verified it with the man. He made sure they were all settled in the multi-passenger van, then hefted his and Aidan's bags and walked toward the garage. Aidan felt a small pang at seeing him walk away, even though he knew it was foolish, and that they'd meet again at the hotel in a few minutes.

Leila was excited to be back in Tunisia, and she kept chattering and pointing at things. Her father kept one hand on her arm and held his phone in the other.

Aidan felt like the inside of the van was charged with all different types of energy, from Jean-Luc's watchfulness to Leila's chatter to Omar's intensity. He was glad when they pulled up in front of the Hotel Africa and he could climb out.

As the driver began unloading their bags, Liam pulled up behind them. A moment later, Farid emerged from the lobby, and the brothers caught sight of each other.

Farid stepped forward. "Omar."

"Farid." He paused. "You look well."

"Thank you. I am glad you survived the attack in Marseille." He turned and beckoned his partner forward. "This is James. Leila has already met him."

James had Hayam on a leash, and as he walked forward, the little dog spotted her masters and began jumping and yelping. Aidan leaned down and picked her up in his arms, kissing her snout.

Omar shook hands with James. "Thank you for all your help. Leila and I appreciate it very much."

Jean-Luc said, "I can take things from here, Liam. You're probably eager to get home."

"I want to get over to the mosque and the cemetery and check things out," Liam said. "We'll rendezvous later and share information."

James picked up a canvas duffle and handed it to Liam. "This is everything you left at our house. Hayam's food and bowls—and the things you asked me to look after for you."

Aidan knew that meant the guns they hadn't been able to take to France with them. Liam thanked him, and then Aidan, Liam, and Hayam got into the Jeep.

"Not exactly the happy family reunion I was hoping for," Aidan said as Liam pulled out onto the Avenue Habib Bourguiba.

"You knew Omar doesn't approve of Farid's lifestyle."

Aidan cuddled the dog on his lap, stroking Hayam's head as she nestled into his chest. "But I thought maybe he would have changed his mind."

Liam snorted. "Why? Because James has been funding Omar's life in Marseille?"

"Because they're brothers. Twins."

"Spoken like an only child," Liam said.

Aidan looked at his partner. As far as he knew, Liam's sisters didn't disapprove of Liam or his sexual orientation. But Liam was right; as an only child, he could only guess at the complicated relationships between siblings.

Liam snared a parking space just a block from their small house. Aidan hopped out and let Hayam loose to sniff all the messages left her by other dogs while she was away, and began unloading their duffles.

"Can you handle getting things settled?" Liam asked, pulling out his cell phone. "I want to get hold of Faisal and go over to the cemetery."

Aidan was a bit resentful that he was being left out of the planning—but he knew that Faisal would be more help to Liam than he would be.

"Sure. Let me know if you need anything."

"You're the best," Liam said, leaning down to kiss him.

26 – STRATEGIES

Liam took his cell phone out to the courtyard and called Faisal. "We're back from Marseille. I need to talk to you about Khadija Mansoor's funeral tomorrow."

"Good idea. Shall we meet at the mosque where the service will be held?"

Liam drove the Jeep through the teeming streets of Tunis, which had returned to commerce. There were no signs that the city had been the scene of violence only days before. The area around the mosque was busy with scruffy students in T-shirts, business people in suits with cell phones and earpieces, and the occasional fashionable mother trailed by young children.

As he approached the old stone building that housed the mosque, he looked it over carefully. Its entrance was a keyhole arch over a thick wooden door studded with bolts. The door was half open, and beyond it he saw a dark corridor which led to an open courtyard at the center of the building.

As he neared the arch, Faisal stepped out to greet him. He was back to his regular attire, pressed khaki shirt and dark slacks, and the dark circles below his eyes had faded. "You always find yourself in interesting situations, don't you, my friend?" he asked Liam.

"They seem to find me."

Faisal led him through the hallway toward the open courtyard. "As you may know, this building is a *masjid*, a smaller sort of mosque where daily prayers are held—as opposed to the *masjid jami*, where larger groups can gather for Friday prayers, like the Zitouna mosque in the medina."

"If Omar Mansoor wants to make a big ceremony out of the funeral, why not have it there?"

"The appropriate permissions could not be secured," Faisal said. Liam noted the way he said it—in the passive voice, avoiding any subject. He realized he had learned that from Aidan, and almost laughed.

"This open area is for group prayers," Faisal continued as they stepped into the courtyard. "Notice the arcades along the sides to provide shade when necessary."

With the sun beating down and the lack of any breeze, it was quite hot out there in the courtyard, but the arcade looked cool.

Faisal pointed up. "The dome there is over the *Musalla*, the prayer room. For Khadija Mansoor, the funeral prayer will be held out here. There will be room for nearly a hundred people—in orderly lines, of course."

"They're having it outside because of the crowd?" Liam looked around the courtyard. The floor was stone, with rolled prayer rugs lined up along one wall.

"No, the proper place for a funeral prayer is outside the Musalla. People will face this way." He pointed. "That is the *qiblah* wall, and the *mihrab*, that depression in the wall, tells us that is the direction of Mecca."

"What can we do about security here?" Liam looked at the

roofline. It would be easy enough for a sharpshooter with a rifle to appear up there and pick off Omar, Leila, and Farid at will.

"We will have officers stationed at the entrance to the mosque, on the street outside to control traffic, and yes, on the roof as well."

"What about after the funeral service?"

Faisal pointed. "Khadija's body will be carried out of the courtyard there. That door leads to a corridor with a door to the side street. The hearse and the limousine will wait there. While the hearse is being loaded and the family is situated in the limousine, the mourners will exit through the main door and form two lines, one on each side of the street."

"You're closing the street, I assume?"

Faisal nodded. "From here to the cemetery. When the hearse passes, the mourners will follow on foot. I imagine there will be many supporters of the Muslim Leadership, but they will be respectful."

Liam hoped that would be the case. "Can we walk from here to the cemetery?"

"But of course."

It was early afternoon, and the sun was high in the sky. Liam and Faisal stayed close to the buildings in whatever meager shade they could find, but Liam was sweating quickly, despite the cool temperature.

They stopped a block before ENSET—the engineering school where Seif Mansoor had received his degree. "My gut instinct tells me that if Mansoor is planning anything to disrupt Khadija's funeral or attack the rest of his family, he'll do it here, in a familiar area. He went to school here, and he worked a few blocks away for several years after graduating."

"What kind of attack do you anticipate?" Faisal asked. "Another bombing?"

"If Seif Mansoor really is behind these attacks on his cousins, he has the educational and work background to use explosives. He could just as easily hire a sharpshooter, though. Or we could be completely wrong, and someone else altogether could be behind this."

"The family will be protected in the limousine," Faisal said. "A sharpshooter along the route could only harm the crowd."

"And cause general chaos. Keeping the police busy and leaving the Mansoors vulnerable."

"You have a vivid imagination, my friend," Faisal said.

Liam laughed. "That's what I usually tell Aidan. But you know as well as I do, Faisal, that you have to look at all angles."

"Sadly, you are correct. Where do you think the most likely spots are for a shooter to be posted? I can detail officers to those areas."

They identified a few good vantage points, protected building roofs with clear lines of sight to the street. Faisal also planned to stage officers in the parking lots across the Rue Taha Hussein from the engineering school.

Then they crossed the dual carriageway of the M1 to enter the cemetery, which rose before them in crowded lines of rectangular stone monuments. There was little shade, and the sun beat down mercilessly on them. Liam felt the sweat pouring down his back and pooling uncomfortably in his butt crack.

A single man in a sports jacket and a white skullcap stood beside a monument, reciting prayers. Small shrubs were interspersed between tombs but there was little shade beyond the trees around the perimeter.

They walked through the grounds until they found the place where Khadija would be interred, at the foot of the hill, in an area of recently erected monuments.

Liam and Faisal turned around in a complete circle, looking for all vantage points. "I don't see any good places for a sharpshooter," Liam said when he had completed his circuit. "Which means that we're looking at another bomb. Not thrown this time—there isn't any place to hide. So that means it would have to be placed somewhere, on a timer."

"I will have a bomb-sniffing dog check the cemetery just before the procession arrives," Faisal said, making a note.

"Is there anything we're overlooking?"

"I think we have done all we can."

By then they were both hot, sweaty, and tired. Faisal radioed for a police car, which picked them up at the cemetery gates and returned them to the mosque. Liam drove back to the house with the air-conditioning on full blast, but he was still hot and sticky when he got there.

"I'm taking a shower," he announced as he walked in. He stripped his clothes off and tossed them on the furniture. Hayam yipped and danced around his feet.

"Liam! I just cleaned up!" Aidan said.

Liam grabbed a towel from the cabinet and strode out to the shower. He turned on the water and let it stream down over him as he thought about the day. What was Seif Mansoor planning? How could they protect their clients?

He thought through as many permutations as he could while he showered, but he kept coming back to the same problem. They didn't know Mansoor well enough, or comprehend what he was capable of, to plan completely. And Liam recognized that understanding your enemy's strengths and weaknesses was the key to the success—or failure—of any operation.

27 – A Confrontation

Liam finished his shower and dressed, then he and Aidan returned to the clients at the Hotel Africa. They drove there with the air-conditioning blasting in the Jeep, though the sun was lower in the sky and some of the oppressive heat had lifted.

They knocked at the door of Omar's suite first. Jean-Luc opened the door, and behind him, Liam could see Farid and James sitting stiffly on one sofa, Omar facing them. Leila was sitting in a chair in the corner, reading her Koran.

"Things are tense here," Jean-Luc said quietly. "I think it would be best to split the brothers up for a while."

"Good idea," Liam said. "We'll take Farid and James and go to dinner."

"I'll stay here with Omar and Leila. We'll order room service."

They walked into the living room, and immediately Leila jumped up and stalked over to Aidan. "You must tell them. I don't want to go off with some cousin I don't know. I want to go to the cemetery with my mother. But Abi says no."

Aidan said, "What does the Koran say about young women like you going to graveyards?"

"There are differences in the Hadiths," she admitted. "Umm Attiyah says that Allah curses women who visit graves and illuminate them." She clutched the book to her chest. "But the Prophet never specifically said we could not, and he says we are allowed to visit graves to remind us of the life to come."

"If the Prophet isn't clear, then I think you should listen to your father's wishes," Aidan said gently. "How about a compromise? Your father doesn't want you to go to the burial, and I understand that. It's a very sad thing. But I could go with you on Wednesday, if you want and your father agrees."

"I think that would be an excellent idea," Omar said. "Leila can pay her respects to her mother without the great sadness of the burial."

Liam watched Leila, once again impressed at the way his partner maneuvered the difficult shores of a young person's adolescence. "If that is what Abi wants," Leila said, lowering her head.

Omar stood up and walked over to his daughter, taking her into his arms. "You will grow up to be a wonderful Muslim woman, just like your mother."

Liam turned to Farid and James. "I thought it would be a good idea for the four of us to get some dinner," he said, indicating Aidan with a nod. "I'd like to hear how things are going at the groves."

"Yes, that's a good idea," Jean-Luc seconded. "I don't like having all targets in one place for too long."

Liam didn't like using the word target around clients, but no one else seemed to mind. Farid and James stood up. "We'll talk later?" Farid asked his brother.

Omar nodded and then took his daughter's hand. "Let us read the Koran together," he said. "I would like to hear what you think about the funeral rites."

In the elevator, Farid sighed and said, "I love my brother, but he refuses to accept me as I am."

"When did you come out to him?" Aidan asked as they reached the lobby level.

"We did not speak of it for a long time. I assumed that he knew because I did not marry and whenever he saw me, I was with other men. I had several casual relationships but nothing serious until I met James."

They walked in a group across the marble floor. James asked the doorman for a cab and directed the driver to an excellent French restaurant—a place Liam knew Aidan had been wanting to go, but it was so expensive they had been waiting for a special occasion. Liam kept his eyes on the road and the other traffic around them, wary of any attack, but the ride passed without incident, and no one spoke much.

Once they were all seated at a large, round table and had ordered, Farid continued the story he had begun at the hotel. "When I met James, I knew he was the man I wanted to spend the rest of my life with, and I arranged to introduce him to Omar."

"Not a very successful meeting," James said. "Omar got angry and walked out."

"We did not speak again for three months. Then my father became ill, and we had to communicate, though Omar made no mention of James at all."

The waiter delivered them all crocks of onion soup. "I knew my father would leave the vineyards to Omar. He had always said that he would. As he was dying, he exacted a promise from Omar that the land would stay in our family. That is when Omar asked me if I would move to Tebourba and manage the property."

"He wanted Farid to be a tenant on the land where he grew up," James said. "All because his father was so stubborn about Omar being a few minutes older."

"After our father died, James offered to buy out Omar and put the land in my name. At first, Omar refused, but eventually he agreed to grant us both a life interest, with the property to pass to Leila when we die or if we choose to move elsewhere."

Liam looked at Aidan. He wondered if that was when Omar had decided to leave the country.

"After our father's death, Omar returned to Tunis and began working more diligently to develop the Muslim Leadership," Farid said. "Very quickly he was a leader of the opposition. Unfortunately, that led to him being arrested on a regular basis."

"Omar decided it was best that he leave the country," James said, pushing away the empty crock, still striated with melted cheese on the sides.

"He lived very well in France," Liam said. "He must have some very wealthy supporters."

He waited for James to say something about funding Omar's expenses in Marseille—but all James said was, "I assume so."

Liam looked across at Aidan. "I need to wash my hands," he said, standing up.

Aidan took the hint. "I should too. We'll be right back."

"I don't like this," Liam said when they reached the men's room. "James is supporting Omar financially, and Farid doesn't know."

"Is it our business, though?" Aidan stepped up to the sink and began washing his hands.

"What if James forced Omar to go to France? Or bribed him? And what if he's the one behind the attacks on Omar? He could have some strange idea that he needs to get rid of Omar to make Farid happy."

"Wash your hands," Aidan said.

Liam looked down at his hands. They looked clean to him—but it was best to carry through their own charade.

"I think James loves Farid," Aidan said, drying his hands on a paper towel. "But I don't see him as a murderer."

"He's a rich plutocrat, and Americans with money think they can buy whatever they want in the third world."

"You've said that before," Aidan said, opening the men's room door. "But I don't think James is like that."

Liam shook his head and followed his partner back to the table. But by the time they had sat down again and been served their entrées, he was sure that the air needed to be cleared.

"We did some research into Omar once you asked Aidan to escort Leila to Marseille," he said. "We both felt that we had to know everything about him if we were going to protect him. And that includes where his money comes from."

"Liam," Aidan said.

Liam shook his head. "James, do you have something you want

to say?"

"I don't know what you mean." James looked down at his plate.

"Liam, we don't need to go into this right now," Aidan said.

"Sorry, Aidan, but we do. Farid, do you know about a company called Gardiner Holdings, LLC?"

James interrupted. "This really doesn't concern you, Liam."

"Yes, it does. If you're not honest with Farid, how do we know you're being honest with us?"

"What are they talking about, James?" Farid asked.

"I set up a shell company to pay Omar's expenses in France. It's not a big deal. The money was nothing to me."

"You paid my brother to leave Tunisia?"

"No, not at all. But I saw him getting arrested and how much that upset you. I had my attorney contact him and suggest that he might be safer in exile. I offered to take care of his expenses if he wanted to move. He accepted."

He looked up. "I wanted the whole family to go. But Khadija wouldn't. She insisted on staying in Tunis with Leila. And see what happened to her? Did you want that to happen to your brother too?"

Liam watched the two of them closely.

"I only wanted to help you and your family," James said.

"Why didn't you tell me?"

"Omar agreed to the vineyard leasehold as part of the deal. I wanted you to think he was doing it for you—not because I was paying him."

Liam noticed that neither James nor Farid had touched their

meals. The tension between them was evident. "You didn't threaten Omar, did you, James?" he asked.

"Of course not! He's Farid's brother. I would never do anything to hurt him."

"And you don't have any connection to Seif Mansoor?"

James shook his head. "I never knew the man existed until you mentioned his name. I'll open all my financial records to you if you want—you'll see there's no connection between us."

"I think you're very lucky, Farid," Aidan said, looking at the Tunisian man across from him. "To have James care so much about you that he'd look after your brother, even when Omar hasn't been accepting of your relationship."

"I wish you had told me." Farid reached out and took James's hand. "You have always been so good to me, and I love you. But no more secrets, all right?"

"No more," James said, squeezing Farid's hand. Then he looked at Liam and Aidan. "Nor from you, either. If you're going to protect us, you need to know everything. Not that it matters, but I also paid the rent on the apartment where Leila and Khadija lived, and Leila's school fees, and gave Khadija an allowance so she could concentrate on politics too."

He sighed. "Now I wonder if that was a good idea. If I hadn't paid her bills, she wouldn't have been able to agitate so much—and perhaps she'd never have been arrested or killed."

"If we're right," Aidan said, "then Khadija wasn't killed because of her politics, but because she was Omar's wife, and Omar was

Seif's cousin."

"And Seif still wishes to kill my brother and me," Farid said.

28 – Jacob's Ladder

Aidan wasn't happy that Liam had confronted James at dinner, but at least the air was clear between all of them, and they no longer believed James had any ulterior motives for his financial support of Omar.

The rest of dinner was quiet and strained, and they all skipped dessert. James had the restaurant call them a cab, and when they reached the Hotel Africa, he said, "I think Farid and I will be all right on our own. We have some things to talk about. We'll meet you back here tomorrow morning for the funeral."

They all embraced in the hotel's driveway, and then Aidan and Liam walked back to where they had left the Jeep. They drove home in silence, both alert to dangers, but the streets had returned to their normal mix of young revelers and late-night workers.

They parked the Jeep near the little house, and as usual, Hayam rushed right past them when they opened the door and paid her nightly visit to the tree out front. Then she returned to them, her whole body wiggling with delight. Aidan picked her up and kissed her ears, then carried her back into the house.

"I don't think you should have confronted James at dinner, but I'm glad we have that all out in the open," he said as he put the little dog back down on the floor.

"We needed to be sure James wasn't a threat."

"Even though he's paying us? That makes him our real client, right?"

"Clients have been known to do stupid things."

"I've got a couple of stupid things in mind that we could do." Aidan began unbuttoning his shirt, looking at Liam with a grin.

"Come here, you." Liam reached out for Aidan and brought their bodies together. Everything Aidan had worried about dissolved with Liam's embrace. He and his partner were a team, and they would face everything together. He was confident that Liam could protect them no matter what happened, whether it be political upheaval or a crazed cousin intent on mayhem.

They stood in the living room kissing, Aidan's shirt hanging loose and his chest pressing against Liam's. Hayam sniffed around their feet for a moment, then collapsed into a heap next to them.

Liam picked Aidan up, cradling him, and Aidan reached an arm around Liam's neck. Liam carried him into the bedroom and laid him down on the bed. Aidan started to undress, but Liam stopped him. "Let me," he said.

He slid Aidan's shirt off, then sat down beside him and began kissing him again, lightly pinching his nipples. Aidan squirmed with pleasure, his stiff dick pressing against his pants and begging for release. But Liam took his time, kissing and licking his way down Aidan's lightly furred chest, using his tongue to tease Aidan's belly button.

Finally, he unbuckled Aidan's belt and unzipped his pants. Aidan's dick pressed against his boxers, and Liam released it through the slit in the shorts. Then he leaned down and took it in his mouth.

Aidan moaned as Liam sucked him. His partner's close-cropped blondish brown head bounced up and down as Liam suctioned him, then pulled back. He grabbed Aidan's pants by the waist and tugged them down as Aidan lifted his hips off the bed. The boxers came down with them, pooling around his ankles.

Liam stood up and stripped as Aidan kicked off his shoes and pants. He was naked by the time Liam reached over to the bedside table and retrieved a bottle of lube. He squeezed some in his hand and stood facing Aidan, fingering his own ass, his mouth open and his head thrown back.

Aidan shivered with anticipation, knowing what was coming next. When Liam had his hole loosened, he straddled Aidan and lowered himself down on his partner's cock. His impressive quads flexed as he rose up and down, using one hand for balance.

Aidan loved the sensation of penetrating Liam. His partner could be emotionally closed, tight-lipped about security, even evasive sometimes when it came to past loves or his time with the SEALs. But when they were joined like this—Aidan fucking Liam or Liam fucking Aidan—he felt like he became one organism with his handsome, buff partner.

He thrust up as Liam lowered his body, then pulled back as Liam rose. He used all his power to slam his dick into Liam's ass; Liam moaned and upped the tempo. He grabbed his own stiff dick with his free hand and began jerking himself frantically. He shot off onto Aidan's chest as Aidan released a load into Liam's ass.

Both of them were sweating and tired by then, but they cuddled up together and fell asleep almost immediately.

* * *

Aidan woke first the next morning and, after a brief stop in the bathroom, went out to the shower to wash away the dried come from his stomach and groin. Liam joined him there a few minutes later. Aidan was already clean, so he soaped Liam and then helped him rinse, and they went back inside to an empty larder.

They dressed quickly and picked up breakfast on their way to the Hotel Africa. When they arrived at Omar's suite, he and Farid were arguing.

"James is not family. He should not ride in the limousine."

"He's my family," Farid said.

"Then you can go with him. If you want to come with me, he will not be with us."

James stood up. "Enough. Liam, do you have your Jeep here?"

"Yes."

"Then I'll ride with you. Farid can ride with Omar and Leila." He turned to Omar. "Will you have Jean-Luc and Aidan with you?"

"That's fine."

"Hold on," Liam said. "I'd rather ride in the limo with Omar and Leila and Jean-Luc. Aidan can drive James in the Jeep."

There it was again, Aidan thought. Liam's sense that Aidan wasn't qualified to take care of the clients. He was about to protest, but Leila interrupted. "I want Aidan. He's nice to me."

That surprised Aidan. Perhaps all the time they had spent

together had begun to affect her.

"I'll be nice to you," Liam said to her. "In the limo with you."

Leila began to cry, first shedding fat tears that rolled down her round cheeks, then gut-racking sobs. "I know you are sad, my darling," Omar said, putting his arms around her. "But you must be strong today. Can you do that?"

She sniffled and nodded. "If Aidan comes with us."

Omar looked up at them.

"I can manage, Liam," Aidan said.

Liam huffed out a sharp breath. "I'll drive the Jeep."

They left a few minutes later to ride to the mosque. The limo driver, a tall, dark-skinned Tunisian man with a goatee and a bad toupee, was waiting for them in front of the hotel. Aidan took one of the back-facing jump seats, with Leila next to him. Jean-Luc was squeezed awkwardly between Farid and Omar.

The day was overcast and humid, and the unsettled weather contributed to Aidan's feeling of unease. The street outside the mosque was already crowded with supporters of the Muslim Leadership. He was uncomfortable that there were so many people there—it was so easy for someone to hide in the crowd. The limousine pulled up next to a side entrance to the mosque.

Jean-Luc got out first, looking up and then around to make sure there was no imminent danger. Then he stood back as Omar, Farid, and Leila stepped out. Aidan was the last one to step out, and he closed the limo door behind him.

Omar led them into the building, then out to the courtyard,

where Khadija's body, wrapped in a white shroud, lay on a platform. Farid stepped aside, allowing Omar and Leila to approach Khadija's body. Aidan noticed how Leila squeezed her father's hand.

The doors to the mosque opened, and the other mourners began to stream in. Aidan stepped up on his toes to scan the crowd for Liam and James. He spotted them standing next to the wall, under the balcony. It looked like Liam wanted to join them at the front of the mosque, but the crowd was already too thick.

Omar and Leila finished their private good-byes and stepped back to join Farid and Aidan. A heavyset older woman approached and hugged Omar. "This is Khadija's cousin Asya," he said in English to Aidan. "She will take care of Leila during the service."

He knelt down to his daughter's level and spoke softly to her in Arabic. She pushed a tear from her eye and nodded her agreement. Then Asya took Leila's hand and led her to where the women stood, in rows behind the men.

Aidan turned slightly to face the incoming crowd. He didn't like being so vulnerable, and he didn't like being separated from Leila when he was supposed to protect her, but he was afraid to go against religious customs. And with Liam stuck at the back of the mosque, Aidan had to focus on helping Jean-Luc protect Omar and Farid.

Clouds moved back and forth over the sun, shifting the shadows in the courtyard, but at least there was little direct sun. Even so, the press of people around them raised the temperature, and the air was sharp with the smell of so many bodies.

The crowd hushed as the imam stepped out. "Omar has decided

to let the imam conduct the prayers," Farid whispered to Aidan. "But he will speak afterward."

The imam stood between them and Khadija's body, centered at her midsection. He began the prayers in Arabic, and though Aidan couldn't understand most of the language, he saw the Muslims around them following him and moving together. Finally, the crowd supplicated, turning their heads to the left and right. Then Omar stepped forward.

Once again, Aidan couldn't understand what was said, but he could tell from Omar's inflections that he was speaking of his wife, his love for her, and her dedication to Islam and to the country of Tunisia. The clouds shifted once more, and a shaft of light fell on the courtyard, illuminating him and Khadija, the Jacob's ladder once again. Aidan felt his heart wrench as he remembered that a living, breathing woman, a beloved wife and mother, had been ripped from her family.

He could not stop looking around at the arcade, the roof line, and the crowd. He saw Liam doing the same thing. Would someone from the crowd stand up and begin shooting? Was there a suicide bomber among them, some young fanatic who would sacrifice his own life to take down Omar and his organization? Or was Seif Mansoor among them right then, planning revenge for the slights he believed had been committed against his father?

When Omar was finished speaking, a group of men stepped forward, and with Omar, they lifted Khadija's body and moved toward the side doorway. Jean-Luc looked back to where the women had been standing. They had already turned and begun to exit. "I don't see Leila," he said. "I'll go after her and make sure she gets to her cousin's safely. Then I'll meet you at the cemetery." He disappeared before Aidan could offer to go in his place.

The crowd began to disperse down the hallway to the front door, talking among themselves in urgent Arabic. Aidan looked around for Liam and James but wasn't tall enough to spot them through the crowd. He stuck close to Farid, who was a few steps behind his brother and the other men carrying Khadija's body.

Even though he'd never met Khadija, Aidan was filled with sadness at the hole her death had caused in the lives of her husband and daughter. His eyes teared as he watched Omar and the other pallbearers gently load Khadija's body into the hearse. Omar rested his hand on the body for a moment after all the other men had stepped back, and Aidan's heart broke.

Omar turned back to them, his eyes glistening, and Farid stepped up and put his arm around his brother. Together they walked to the limousine. Aidan looked for Liam, to let him know that Leila had gone with Jean-Luc and ask if he preferred to ride in the limo. But the crowd was too dense, and he couldn't see his partner and didn't know where Liam had parked the Jeep. He followed the brothers, then slid into the jump seat facing them, and the driver closed the door behind him.

The hearse circled the block and passed slowly in front of the mosque, followed by the limo. Then the mourners began to follow in their wake.

The limo was much emptier without Jean-Luc and Leila. Aidan looked out the back window for the Jeep, but all he could see was a crowd of people. Not knowing where Liam was made him uncomfortable, and he sweated all the way to the cemetery, even though the driver kept the air-conditioning on high.

They entered the cemetery and followed a serpentine path to a parking area. The three of them got out of the limo, and Omar walked to the hearse. The same men helped him carry Khadija's body up to her grave.

As they did, Aidan's cell phone rang. "Where are you?" Aidan asked, scanning the area around the burial site.

"Back at the mosque. Somebody walked off with the distributor cap from the Jeep's engine."

"Fuck."

"My feelings exactly. Faisal's got somebody bringing a replacement over right now, but I won't be able to get out of here until then. What's going on up there?"

"So far, everything's going according to plan. But I can't wait until this is all over."

"Be careful. Something's going to happen; I can feel it. I just don't know what."

"I have to go, Liam. They're starting the service."

Aidan ended the call and turned back toward the grave. Even though he had never met Khadija, he felt a lump in his throat as he watched Omar lower her body into the grave, turning her carefully so that she would face Mecca.

It reminded him of so many family funerals he had attended when he was young. Though he was an only child, his parents had siblings and cousins, and Aidan was in the middle of a large range of first and second cousins. He had been to all his grandparents' funerals, as well as those of elderly great-aunts and great-uncles. When he was still living in Philadelphia, he had begun going to ceremonies for those of his parents' generation. Then both of his parents had died while he was living with Blake.

He pushed away his memories as he watched Omar shovel the requisite dirt over Khadija, tears streaming down his face. Then each of the mourners stepped forward to perform the ritual as well.

By the time the grave was covered, Aidan was emotionally wrecked and drenched in sweat. He was relieved when Omar turned toward the limo, and Farid followed. He stepped away and dialed Liam's cell.

"Almost out of here," Liam said. "The guy just got here with the new distributor cap."

"All right, I'll see you at the hotel," Aidan said.

The driver had kept the limo running, so the interior was cool, and Aidan sank gratefully into the jump seat. Omar and Farid sat at opposite sides of the backseat, each of them sealed up in his own thoughts and grief.

Aidan closed his eyes as the driver returned down the serpentine path to the main street. This would all be over soon, he thought. They'd get back to the hotel, and James and Farid would go back to Tebourba, and Aidan and Liam would return to their little house. He thought it would be nice to take a few days off—perhaps go back to the island of Djerba, this time just for a vacation.

When Aidan opened his eyes, he looked out the back window of the limo and realized that they were on a highway that looked like the one that led to the airport.

"Omar," he said.

Omar looked up and pushed away a tear from his left eye.

"Are we going the right way?" Aidan asked.

Omar looked out the window. "No, we are not. This highway does not take us back to the hotel." He leaned forward and tapped on the glass window between them and the driver. He slid the window aside and spoke in Arabic.

The driver responded in English. "We aren't going back to the hotel at all. We will have a conversation first, and then I will kill you all." He pulled off his goatee and the bad toupee, and Aidan realized he was looking at Seif Mansoor.

29 – Going for a Ride

Omar reached over and tried to open the back door, but it was locked. "You are not going anywhere, cousins," Seif said. "You might as well sit back and consider how badly your father treated mine. Too bad Uncle Yakub is not still alive to suffer for what he did. You will have to take his place."

Omar and Farid both began talking, but the man ignored them. Aidan pulled his cell phone from his pocket. His index finger shook as he pressed the speed dial button for Liam. On the jump seat, his back was already to Seif, but he turned so that he was talking toward the door opposite the driver's side.

"Seif Mansoor is driving the limo," he whispered as soon as Liam picked up, glad for the aural camouflage provided by the quarreling brothers. "He says he's going to take us some place and kill us."

"Can you see anything outside the limo that tells you where you are?"

Aidan took a deep breath and looked out the back window. "We're on a highway. I think we're on our way to the airport."

"You think." There was a gruffness to Liam's voice that only made Aidan feel more nervous.

"Liam, I'm scared. I'm doing my best here."

"All right. Stay calm. You're a smart guy, and you know how to protect yourself and your clients. I got the new distributor cap, and

James and I are going to try and catch up to you. Hold on."

Through the phone, Aidan heard the screech of tires and the blare of car horns. "I'm heading toward the airport now. As soon as you see a landmark, you let me know."

"There's a big park to our right. I think I can see the lake out there."

"Good. Keep your eye out."

"I don't want to keep talking. I don't want Seif to hear me. He speaks English."

"Keep the line open. If you need to tell me something, pretend you're talking to one of the brothers."

Aidan sat back against his seat as Farid and Omar continued to argue in Arabic with their cousin. He felt even worse because he couldn't tell what they were saying. "Is he telling you where we're going?" he finally whispered to Farid, leaning forward.

"No," Farid said in a low voice. "He is telling us how bad his life was growing up without any money. He believes our father cheated his father."

Suddenly, Omar lunged forward, trying to grab his cousin through the window separating driver from passengers. But he could not reach far enough, and Seif laughed. Omar unloosed a string of Arabic invectives unlike any others Aidan had ever heard—a few he recognized, and many he only marveled at.

"What's going on?" Aidan whispered to Farid as Omar kept yelling and banging on the glass.

"Seif has said that he arranged to have Khadija killed at the women's prison. How little money it cost him—and therefore how little Khadija's life was worth."

Aidan saw the signs for the airport, but they continued past it on the P9 highway, then made a left turn. Omar gave up yelling and sat back in the corner of the limo, his arms crossed over his chest.

Aidan made sure the phone was near his mouth and said, "The heliport? Are we going somewhere on a helicopter?" in a voice loud enough for Liam to hear.

They bypassed the heliport, though, and continued on a deserted road that ran behind the perimeter of the airport. "I guess we're not going on a helicopter if we're driving past the heliport," Aidan said.

"You are a stupid man," Seif said to him in English. "Be quiet."

He stopped at the end of the road, next to a Mercedes sedan, shut off the limo, and turned to face them. "I will speak in English so that your supposed security guard can understand why he will die as well."

Aidan bristled at the word "supposed," but he had to acknowledge that he and Liam hadn't correctly anticipated what Seif would do.

"Uncle Yakub ruined my father's life by cheating him out of his inheritance, and that ruined my life as well."

"Your life wasn't ruined," Aidan said. "You grew up, you went to ENSET, you started your own company, and you made a lot of money. How was your life ruined?"

Farid kicked him, but Aidan ignored him.

"Everything I did was to gain revenge against the man who hurt my father. He deserved his fair share of the property!" Seif pounded the steering wheel. "It is a very old story, back to the very first days of man on earth. The story of Jacob and Esau. They were twins too. Joseph was going to leave everything to his oldest son, but Jacob tricked him."

"But my father did not trick yours." Omar crossed his arms over his chest. "Your father did not want to work the land. He walked away from his inheritance. It wasn't theft; it was abandonment."

"That does not change anything." Seif turned the engine off. "There is a bomb under the dashboard. I am setting the fuse now. You will have some time to consider your fates and beg Allah for forgiveness. By the time you go to your reward, I will be long gone."

He hopped quickly out of the limo and slammed the door shut.

"Liam?" Aidan asked into his phone. "Did you hear that?"

"I'm on my way. I'm on the P9 heading toward the heliport."

"Hurry. We don't know how much time we have—it might only be minutes."

Omar pressed futilely against the door handle. "We are locked in. This bastard will kill us." As the three of them watched, Seif got into the sedan and drove away, leaving a plume of smoke behind him.

"You must disable the bomb, Aidan," Farid said. "Immediately."

Aidan turned around and began smashing at the glass partition to make it big enough to climb through. But the glass was too sturdy. "I can't break it," he said. "Liam, where are you?"

"Turning at the heliport. Can you see the timer on the bomb?"

Aidan twisted around, trying to get as much of his body through the window as he could. "No. I can see the reflection of the light on the carpet, though. It seems like the display is changing."

"Hang on. I see the heliport ahead of me."

"Can we do anything to protect ourselves?" Farid asked. "Get down on the floor?"

"If the bomb is strong enough to blow up the limousine, there's no place we can hide," Aidan said. "Liam, in the glove compartment of the Jeep, I put one of those banger things that lets you knock out a window if your car goes underwater."

"James, did you hear that?" Aidan heard. "Open the glove compartment."

"Oh, no, James is with him?" Farid said.

Out the back window, Aidan saw the Jeep approaching. "Omar, lie down on the floor. Squeeze over so that Farid can get next to you." He directed the brothers down. "If Liam smashes out the window, there's going to be broken glass."

He shifted aside so that Omar and Farid could flip up the jump seats and lie down, side by side. When they were in place, he shifted his body so that he was on top of them. It wouldn't be any protection if the limo blew up, but at least he might be able to shield them from glass fragments.

He lay down on top of them as he heard the Jeep screech to a halt outside. The sour dirt smell of the carpet rose up, mixing with the sweat and fear of the two brothers. He made sure that his face was shielded as much as possible and pulled his shirt collar up over the back of his neck.

"*Ana uibbuk*," Omar said to Farid, the words nearly a mumble as his head rested on the limo floor. "I love you, my brother. If we survive this, I promise you I will accept you as you are."

"I love you too, my brother. You have always been my other half."

Aidan heard the Jeep screech to a halt. "Protect yourselves!" Liam yelled; then he swung the tool into the limo's window. The first swipe cracked the window into spidery strands but didn't penetrate. Aidan could feel the sweat pouring down his back, and he kept trying to count down the seconds on the bomb's timer.

"Trying again!" Liam yelled. This time, he was successful, and the noise was nearly deafening, followed by a rain of glass like pieces of shrapnel. Aidan felt that his back was coated with the stuff, and it shook off as he struggled to get up without trampling on the brothers beneath him.

He managed to shift himself to the limo's backseat, then moved into a squat. He brushed as much of the glass off as he could, then reached down to help Farid get up. As he did, Liam was smashing away the remains of the glass to make a safe opening.

Aidan pushed Farid toward the window, and Liam reached in and grabbed Farid's hands. Aidan lifted Farid's legs and pushed him out. He saw James take over as soon as Farid was mostly out of the window, grabbing him under the arms and pulling him the rest of the way.

By the time Farid was out of the limo, Omar was right behind him, ready to climb out. Liam grabbed him under the arms, and Aidan lifted his legs. Both he and Omar were sweating heavily, and Aidan's hands were slippery.

He saw James take over as Omar was almost free.

"Now you," Liam said. "Fast."

As Aidan pushed himself through the window, he scraped his hands on the shards of glass. Liam pulled him forward. James had taken Farid and Omar and begun running toward the Jeep.

Aidan stumbled. He had scraped his shin on the glass in the window, and he was bleeding from his hands and leg. Liam hooked an arm around his waist and half pulled, half dragged him toward the Jeep.

Omar clambered into the back, extending his hand to his brother, who fell forward. James put his foot up on the back lip, and Omar grasped him, heaving him inside, where the three of them huddled in a big heap.

Aidan got his footing and ran around to the passenger side of the Jeep. The air was full of the sound of planes taking off and landing, the smell of jet fuel and salt water. Liam hoisted himself into the driver's seat and pushed the gearshift forward. "Everybody hang on," he yelled, turning the Jeep in a wide circle and gunning the engine.

The Jeep's canvas flaps provided little relief from the overwhelming roar of a plane taking off just above them. Aidan dug their first aid kit out from under the front seat as Liam rocketed down the road toward the highway. Fighting the whole time against the restraint of the seat belt and the bumps of the road beneath them, he pulled a bandage out of the kit. Then he began wrapping his wrist where it was bleeding.

He risked a glance backward and saw James clutching one side rail, Omar the other, with Farid sandwiched between them. They were only a few hundred feet away when the limousine exploded, sending a hot rain of metal and gasoline into the sky. Aidan felt the heat of the explosion and fire as they sped forward toward the P9.

30 – Interesting Offer

Aidan rolled up his right pant leg as the Jeep rocketed forward. There was blood on his good khaki slacks; that wouldn't come out. He managed to get another bandage applied to his leg wound as Liam merged from the heliport road back onto the highway.

"I had James call Faisal," Liam said once they were far enough away from the airport that they could speak in normal voices. "He put out a bulletin for Seif's car, and he sent officers to the cousin where Leila is. The officers are going to pick up Jean-Luc and Leila and bring them to the hotel."

Then he turned back to where the three men were jammed together in the back of the Jeep. "Are you all right back there? Anyone hurt?"

"I'm getting close to my brother-in-law," Omar said. "We are all fine, but I am worried about my Leila."

Liam's cell rang, and Aidan answered. "Faisal, it's Aidan. Is Leila all right?"

He listened, then turned back to Omar. "She's already at the hotel with Jean-Luc and a police officer."

"Allah be praised," Omar said.

Aidan turned back to the phone. "Did you get Seif Mansoor?"

"We have not spotted the car yet," Faisal said. "But we are watching."

Aidan ended the call and leaned back against the seat, all the adrenaline draining away. His arm felt like he had rubbed it in broken glass, and his leg throbbed with a dull ache. His mouth was dry, and his pulse was still racing.

Liam slowed the Jeep to a more sedate pace as they turned off the Trans-African highway and navigated the local streets to the Hotel Africa. He jumped out as soon as they pulled up and hurried around to the back of the Jeep to help Omar, Farid, and James get out. The bellhops stood uncertainly by the main doors, waiting, Aidan assumed, to see what this crazy Jeepload of men meant to do.

Aidan took an extra minute to climb out of the passenger seat. He felt tired and drained. They left the Jeep with the valet and rode up to the suite James and Farid had rented. Leila rushed for her father, and he pulled her into his arms and stumbled toward the sofa. Farid laid a steadying hand on his arm.

Liam helped Aidan to a chair and knelt next to him to look at the bandage on his leg. James went for the minibar, retrieving a couple of small bottles of Jack Daniels and a can of Coca-Cola. "Not my favorite drink," he said. "But I think we can all use a boost."

Leila demanded, "What is going on? Jean-Luc would not tell me anything."

"We had a little scare, that's all," Omar said, wrapping her in his arms. "But everything will be all right now."

"Hope this doesn't offend you," James said to Omar as he handed glasses to Aidan, Liam, and Farid.

"I am in no position to be offended by anything. But I will just have a glass of soda water, if you please."

"Coming right up."

Aidan sipped at the Jack and Coke and felt some strength returning. When he could stand easily, Liam led him to the bathroom, where he examined Aidan thoroughly and replaced the bandages. "You'll live," he said, standing up.

"Good to know." Aidan smiled weakly, and Liam leaned forward and kissed him on the lips, then wrapped him in a hug.

"Don't know what I would do if you didn't," Liam murmured in his ear. Then he stepped back and smiled.

They rejoined the others in the living room. Omar and Leila were in one corner, reading Leila's Koran. James and Farid sat next to each other on the couch, sipping their drinks as if they'd just come in from the pool instead of surviving a kidnapping and an exploding limousine. Jean-Luc was on his cell phone, and when he finished, Liam called him over.

"If you can manage things here for a while, I want to take Aidan home. I'll call you if I hear anything from Faisal about Seif Mansoor."

Jean-Luc stuck out his hand. "You both performed admirably today."

He shook first with Aidan, then Liam. "All in a day's work," Aidan said, though the catch in his voice belied his exhaustion.

Liam redeemed the Jeep from the valet and drove them home. Aidan slumped against the door and closed his eyes, and was surprised to discover, when he opened them again, that they were already parked in front of their house.

"Long day," Liam said as he got out. "How do you feel?"

"Tired."

"Then let's get you to bed." Liam opened the door to the house and let Hayam out, and as soon as she had finished her business, he led Aidan gently to the bedroom. "Take a couple of these," he said, shaking some pills out into Aidan's hand. "Then lie down."

Aidan was asleep almost immediately and slept through the night. When he woke, the pain in his arm and leg had been reduced to a dull throb, he desperately had to pee, and he was starving.

When he was finished in the bathroom, he went out to the kitchen, where he found Liam making them cappuccinos and toasting cinnamon bread. "How long have you been up?" Aidan asked, helping himself to a piece of toast. He slathered it with butter.

"Long enough to go out and get us breakfast."

"Any word from Faisal?"

"He started looking into Seif yesterday as soon as I called him. Got a search warrant and went into his apartment. He had a safe, which was open and empty. Some clothes missing too. And they found that he owns a speedboat, which he kept docked at the marina in Monastir."

"And?"

"And they found his car there. The boat's gone."

"Any idea where?"

Liam shook his head. "Not yet. But there have been a lot of boats leaving for the island of Lampedusa, which is the closest part of Italy—Faisal says there are thousands of refugees trying to get out of Africa that way, boats sinking and people dying. It's chaos over there at the port and in the refugee center. But he's reached out to the police over there."

"What do we do?" Aidan asked.

"I'll look at those bandages on your arm and leg and see what's going on."

"I meant about Seif Mansoor."

"There's nothing we can do, Aidan. As far as we know, he left the country, which removes the threat to our clients. Right now, he's thinking that Omar and Farid are dead, and he might as well enjoy a little holiday."

Aidan grumbled, but he let Liam take the bandages off and inspect the wounds. "Already starting to heal," he said. "Let's get you in the shower, and then I'll wrap them up again to keep things clean."

Aidan had to admit that he liked being pampered by Liam; it was so often the other way around. It was nice to lie back in bed, have Liam bring him breakfast, and make sure he was comfortable. Shortly before noon, James called. He and Farid were going back to Tebourba, and Omar and Leila were going back to the apartment off the Rue Mongi Slim. Leila would return to school, and Omar had located a young woman, a distant cousin, who would look after her in the afternoons, prepare their meals, and keep the apartment clean.

Both brothers got on the phone to thank them for all their help, and James said that he'd expect a bill from them that would cover everything they'd done. "Happy to oblige," Aidan said.

He hung up and turned to Liam. "If I'm going to be stuck in bed today, I could use some company."

Liam grinned at him. "Oh, you could, could you?"

Aidan patted the bed next to him, and immediately, Hayam jumped up. "I believe that invitation was for me, not for you," Liam said, lifting her up and putting her back down on the floor. Then he lay down next to Aidan, who rested his head on Liam's chest.

They were just getting comfortable when they heard someone knock, and Hayam went flying out of the bedroom, barking up a storm.

"That had better not be Abdullah," Aidan grumbled.

Liam stood up. "Sounded like the front door. Abdullah would come through the courtyard."

Aidan heard a murmur of voices and couldn't stand the suspense. He pulled on a T-shirt and a pair of cargo shorts and walked out to the living room, where he found Liam pouring a glass of Vieux Magon for Jean-Luc Derain.

"I thought you'd be on your way back to Marseille by now," Aidan said.

"I have a flight later this afternoon. But I wanted to talk to you both first."

Liam brought out a third wineglass for Aidan and poured, and they sat on the couch, facing the Frenchman.

"Have the two of you ever considered leaving Tunisia?" Jean-Luc asked.

Aidan picked up his glass. "What do you mean?"

"I was very impressed with the way you work together. I would love to hire you both if you wanted to move to France."

"To Marseille?"

"I handle the whole southern region, and you could pick wherever you want. Marseille, Cannes, Nice, Cap d'Antibes. Not Monaco; it's a sovereign principality, not a part of France. But almost anywhere else. I need men who are smart and resourceful, and your knowledge of Arabic would be very useful as well."

"You could get us the residency permits?" Aidan asked, remembering his conversation with Liam about how they were able to live in Tunis.

Jean-Luc nodded. "I have many contacts from my days as a flic."

Hayam yipped, and Aidan reached over to the counter for a treat for her. "What about Hayam? Can we bring a dog into France?"

"Aidan…" Liam began.

"Not a problem, as long as she has her vaccinations," Jean-Luc said.

"The more important questions are about what kind of work you'd have us do," Liam said.

"What you do here. We have many clients with security needs. For example, during the Festival du Film in Cannes, we work with existing teams to cushion movie stars and executives from overzealous fans. There are wealthy expatriates and high-profile celebrities who have homes on the Côte d'Azur and need protection when they visit."

Jean-Luc sat back on the sofa. "Agence de Securité handles all the billing and other paperwork. We offer a benefit package that includes health and life insurance."

Liam folded his arms over his chest. "I'm not interested in a corporate situation. I like having the flexibility to pick who I work for."

Aidan glared at him. This seemed like the perfect opportunity to get out of Tunisia, to eliminate the precariousness of their financial situation, living from job to job and never knowing when the next assignment would appear. They had been fortunate to have snared a few high-profile assignments that gave them some financial cushion, but who was to say that would continue?

"Can you put something in writing?" Aidan asked. Liam swiveled his head, but Aidan ignored him. "Then Liam and I can have something to consider."

"I will e-mail you a full package when I return to the office." He drained the last of his wine. "And now I must head to the airport."

"We can drive you," Aidan said.

"That is very kind, but I have a driver waiting outside." They all stood and shook hands. "Once again, I would like to say it has been a pleasure to work with you."

They walked him to the front door, and when Aidan opened it, he saw the cab idling outside. They watched Jean-Luc get in and the cab drive away.

"What do you think?" Aidan asked as they went back to the bedroom.

"It's an interesting offer. I'm hesitant about getting into a corporate situation, but I recognize there's a lot more stability there." He hesitated. "And I've been thinking about the things you said, about our future. The truth is that we don't know what's going to happen politically in Tunisia."

Aidan got back into bed and leaned against the pillows. "I felt like I could learn a lot from Jean-Luc. He has a different kind of energy from you, a different style. What do you think about that?"

"I think you're more interested in living on the Riviera." Liam lay down next to him, and Aidan leaned forward so Liam could wrap his arm around Aidan's shoulders.

"I'm happy wherever you are, sweetheart. You know that. But I'm not sneering at a life in the south of France."

"We'll see what the offer looks like." Liam leaned down and kissed Aidan's cheek. "And now, I really am ready for a vacation."

Acknowledgements

Zoë Sharp's terrific books about Charlie Fox inspired me to write a bodyguard book of my own. As always, I owe a debt of gratitude to all the baristas at Starbucks who kept me fueled with caffeine as I wrote, plotted, edited, and groaned in frustration.

Thanks to all the fans, bloggers, and reviewers who have supported my writing, both in mystery and in romance. For more information, visit my website at **http://www.mahubooks.com**.

Dedication

To Marc: You might think I'm crazy, but all I want is you.

About the Author

Neil lives in South Florida with his husband and two rambunctious golden retrievers. He is a four-time finalist for the Lambda Literary Award in Best Gay Mystery and Best Gay Romance.

www.ingramcontent.com/pod-product-compliance
Lightning Source LLC
LaVergne TN
LVHW011946060526
838201LV00061B/4225